Tribute

A Showcase

A 2021 Anthology of Short Stories
by the Springfield Writers Group.

Edited by Jan-Andrew Henderson

A Black Hart Publication

UK. Australia.

Tribute
Published by Black Hart 2021
Edited by Jan-Andrew Henderson.
Cover Artwork by Pamela Jeffs.
Illustrations by Caitlyn McPherson.
Copyright © 2021 The Springfield Writers Group.

Black Hart Publishing
6 Redgum Close, Bellbowrie, Qld, Australia 4070.
www.greenlightliteraryrescueservice.com

The rights of the authors to be identified as the authors of these works has been ascertained in accordance with the Copyrights, Designs and Patents Act 1988.

Book Layout © 2019 BookDesignTemplates.com.

A Catalogue-in-Publications entry for this title is available from the National Library of Australia.

Tribute
ISBN 978-1-63625-846-1
ISBN 978-1-63625-847-8 (eBook)

This book is a tribute to the author Aiki Flinthart (1973-2021).

She ran the Springfield Writers Group and worked tirelessly to turn it from a motley bunch of individuals into a creativity machine

Like everything else Aiki attempted, she succeeded brilliantly.

The 2021 anthology is a thank you, a promise to keep writing and a last goodbye.

Mission accomplished, Aiki.

CONTENTS

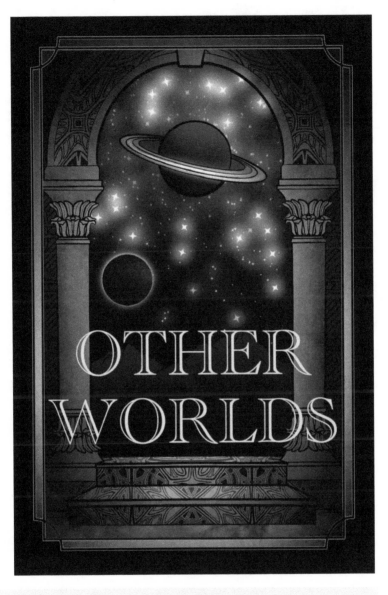

Science is my territory, but science fiction is the landscape of my dreams.

Freeman John Dyson

Honey And a Hanging

A i k i   F l i n t h a r t

Being human wasn't so difficult. It mostly consisted of talking crap, eating, sleeping, and resisting the urge to kill annoying people.

Clare O'Malley crouched and dabbed a gloved fingertip into a puddle of golden liquid, shimmering in Viking III's midmorning fires-of-hell daylight.

Not being human - or rather, not being human while seeming human - that was an art. An art her target was extremely good at. He'd need to be in the tiny, xenophobic, shit-hole colony of Viking III.

She studied the street. Her heads-up display darkened to filter out the white sunlight, glaring off crumbling, white sandstone buildings; potholed, white concrete roads, white sidewalk; and broken, white frigging trees, for feck's sake.

Where would Gredek be hiding? And what as?

So far, the Benwerian had passed himself off as a Yasti (rodent), a Kronck (insectoid) and even an Aquanorian - complete with wobbly tentacles on his face. In reality, apart from gold blood and a third eye, Benwerians looked basically human.

Was that why Captain Vorik and the Hegemon Alliance wanted Gredek so badly? As far as every database showed, there were no shapeshifter species in existence.

What would the Hegemon do with the skill? That was none of her business.

Bounty-hunting, that *was* her business. This week, anyway. An ability like shapeshifting could be very handy in her line of work.

9

Clare's helmet beeped and she gave a triumphant cry. The viro suit's sensor had come back positive for Benwerian blood. It also signalled some sort of indecipherable medical jargon, which she ignored. The sensors were old and quirky and usually bearers of bad news.

Gredek was here. Assuming there were still colonists on this dust-bowl, finding him would require being smart and careful. Well, smart, at least. Careful was overrated.

What fun. They were nearly the end of their hide and seek game, with a hundred thousand Hegemon credit reward as the prize. She mentally kissed her fingers to the working girl on Pinnea II, suggested she stop in the Epsilon Eight Hegemon waystation for cheap fuel. And to Captain Vorik of the Hegemon Grey Guards, for finding her in Epsilon's bar and hiring her to hunt down Gredek.

Normally Clare didn't work for the Grey Guards, even when she wasn't on their wanted list. But the hundred thousand would go a long way toward much-needed repairs for the *De Lune*. And the pardon Vorik offered would get the authorities off her back.

She laughed softly. Mac would be happy. He worried when the *De Lune* was shot at every time it flew into Hegemon-controlled space.

The smell of sweat trapped in her viro suit wafted into her helmet and Clare squinted up. At two white dwarf suns. Did this planet ever have a night phase? Dialling up the coolant did no good - the crapped out old suit was barely coping. The helmet and neck connection had hardened in the heat and the suit's skin crackled ominously. She sorely needed a new one.

Best get this over with fast. She surveyed the bleak, glaringly white street ahead. Why had Gredek come to such a marginal world? Maybe Mac had found something useful in the Hegemon's planetary database.

"You there, Mac?"

She edged as close as possible to the nearest scrap of shade - cast by the brittle, leafless branches of a skeletal tree. She looked closer and saw it was a sculpture made of metal and painted to look like peeling bark and dead wood. These colonists were certainly... unusual.

"I am cool and relaxed," Mac replied over the comms, "Sipping Moktian iced tea and lounging in the temperature-controlled interior of the *De Lune*."

He added a slurping sound.

"Enjoying yourself out there?"

Clare bared her teeth - a wasted gesture since the visuals were switched off. She needed every ounce of power in this fecked up viro suit to combat the heat. Even then, sweat trickled down her back and into her butt-crack. Revolting.

"It's delightful. Balmy. Tourist trade should be booming."

"Liar," he replied. "You'll be glad to know we evaded the Grey Guards troopship that left Runcorn Five just after us."

"You were being paranoid. Admit it."

"Fine. I'll give you that one." The offsider gave an easy laugh. "Any luck finding Gredek? If you're wondering why he chose this place, I have no idea. Masochistic?"

"What does that make me for following him?"

"There's no safe answer to that."

"Database have any clue what he might want."

"Not much that I can see. Sand? What's the settlement like?"

"Got a hundred-year-old *Trespassers Will Be Shot* kinda vibe. Unmanned, dusty stunners mounted on every roof. No windows. Buildings are giant bricks. Falling apart, half of them. Place looks like a dried-out beach sandcastle that's about to be stomped on."

"Just a typical job, then. Any plan for finding our fugitive?"

She turned in a circle. Where would a wounded, desperate Benwerian go, if he were trying to hide? He couldn't leave the planet. He'd abandoned his stolen cargo ship and its antique nuclear engine was dead in the water. Or Sand.

Couldn't leave town, either. Beyond the single street lay vast wastelands of white sand, followed by more white sand. Clare maxed out the binocular setting on her visor. In the distance was a butte, made of white sandstone. What a surprise. Whichever Hegemon Alliance stamp-licker thought settling Viking III was a good idea deserved to be strangled by the colonists.

She returned to checking out the weathered buildings.

Nobody in sight. No noises.

If there were humans alive, could she find Gredek before they realised he wasn't one of them and messed things up? Her target wasn't going to blend in well this time, if the splashes of gold glistening on the street were any indication.

Then again... surely no-one was stupid enough to leave a trail that obvious?

Next question was: which building to try?

"Mac, look for body heat signatures, would you?" Sweat dripped into her eye and she blinked rapidly to salve the salty sting.

"Everything out there will glow like an angler-fish lure in the flip-void. Not going to be easy."

"Do I sound like I care?" she snapped. "My feet are swimming in boot-swamps. I'm pretty sure my toe fungus loves the heat so much, it's about to turn sentient and take over the galaxy."

"There's an image I didn't need in my head,"

"The tree I'm trying to hide behind is so dead it's fake. If you don't find our target soon, I'll end up as jerky and you'll be stuck, too."

"Always with the over-dramatics, O'Malley," He laughed. "I could just take the *De Lune*, flip across the galaxy, and leave your withered corpse behind."

"Not without the nav computer unlock code." Clare gave an evil chuckle.

"Got it already. Hacked your computer a week after you broke me out of prison and I unwisely agreed to partner with you in this life of crime."

"And adventure," she retorted. "Don't forget adventure."

"Your version of adventure usually involves me being shot at. Point is, you die, I fly."

"Point is, I knew you'd hacked my computer, so there's backup security. You need my prints as well."

"Have those, too. Sedated you two weeks after we met. Also a retina scan and DNA sample, just in case."

"That's thinking ahead, if somewhat creepy," Clare said, admiringly. "Though I'm disappointed you don't trust me."

"Only as much as you don't trust me."

"Touché. But you'd still be screwed." She fingered the thruster regulator she'd pocketed before leaving the ship.

"What did you do? Leave a window open?"

Was that a hint of irritation? He was hard to annoy, which is why it was fun to try.

"Find my runaway Benwerian and I'll tell you."

"Tell me and I'll find your Benwerian."

"For feck's sake, Iain Angus MacDiarmid. Fun as this banter is, just do as you're told before I activate the ship's self-destruct." More sweat dripped into her eyes. Her toes squidged stickily in the dusty.

"I disarmed your remote access to that last Tuesday."

OK. he'd won this round. Clare began to recite a long list of ways she intended to torture him when she got back.

"Hold that thought." Mac's easy-going tone sharpened. "I can't distinguish our sneaky friend, but there's a gathering of heat signatures in the biggest building on your street. Right at the end. Can you see it? How'd they get in there, though? It was empty a minute ago."

"Do a geophysical survey."

"Well, well," Mac replied, "feck me."

"You're not my type, as I keep reminding you."

"I'm everyone's type."

"You wish. Find water down there?"

"Rivers of it," he said. "How d'you know?"

"If I'd been dumped on this hothouse, I'd dig tunnels. And I'd only stay long enough to do that, if I knew there was water. Also explains why the buildings up here are in ruins."

She stamped a foot and a puff of powder rose.

"There's probably a whole complex underground, after a hundred years of living here. If you can call it living. The only reason they'd come up to the surface is…"

"If someone arrived who's unwelcome in their nice, cool, watery subway system."

"Mmmmm." Clare licked sweat off her upper lip. "The question is: me or Gredek?"

"Only one way to find out. Shall I join you?"

"Depends on how murdery you're feeling. You tend to be a bit trigger happy and Gredek's worth nothing if he's dead."

"You wound me."

"And you wound everyone else. Or slay 'em."

"For a pirate, thief, and bounty-hunter, you have a weird reluctance to kill."

Clare let that one ride. Everyone had their limits. Hers was killing people who weren't doing anything horrible. Mac heaved an over-the-top sigh.

"I'll curb my desire to wipe out every idiot who crosses my path. Give me a minute to lock up and put the cat out."

"Cat?" Clare started. "Since when do we have a cat?"

There was a groan.

"It's a figure of speech. We don't have a cat."

"Maybe we should. I like them."

"Of course you do. Look, if you want help, you'll have to shut up long enough for me to close the ship."

Clare cut the connection. Mac would catch up. She followed golden droplets up the street toward the largest building. This time, a huge, arched window broke the blank face of one wall. It appeared to be stained glass, but the image was impossible to interpret with two suns glaring off the surface. Must make for a delightful hotbox inside.

A rusted-steel door stood beneath the window. Nope. Going in entrance was for newbs and idiots. She was neither. She subvocced a request to her visor.

"Locate back entrance."

The heads up display flickered and she could almost hear the inbuilt processor complaining. A line-drawing of the building appeared, overlain on the real thing. Undoubtedly an old plan, since the shape and size didn't fit reality.

"Stupid machine," she muttered. "Mac? Why we didn't we print out a new viro suit for me? One with an updated database and better coolant system?"

"You used up the last of the graphene-dycerium to print a blanket." The sound of an air lock whooshing open almost obscured his reply.

"The blanket was for that old lady on Beckerman IV, remember?" She rounded the corner of the building and rolled her eyes. Yet another blank wall.

"Yes. The one who drugged you and stole your shoes."

"I got the info she had on Gredek and I needed new boots, anyway." Clare studied her dusty footwear. "These have a grav-mag, knives, and teeny thrusters built in."

"Which you've never practised with."

"When I get time, I'll use them to fly all over the place. You watch."

"I will. With great amusement."

"Is that a hint of condescension I hear?" Clare screwed up her nose. "You're not taking me seriously."

"One of the few things you like about me."

Sliding around the western corner of the building, Claire halted.

A side door. The ceramic handle turned stiffly under her hand. Sand flaked off the lock, but it finally opened and she slipped inside, one hand resting on her stunner.

Cooler and darker. Two favourable points. As was a large painted screen, covered in stylised murals of a spaceship and stars. It blocked off her view of the interior but stopped anyone inside seeing her.

Good chance to catch her breath. She sighed and leaned against a bare wall. Her suit chirruped happily and praised her for the decrease in external temperature. The visor adjusted for lower-light conditions.

The sound of raised voices echoed across the high ceiling, too muddled to understand. Impossible to tell if they were speaking Standard or some other language. Clare crept up to one end of the mural-painted wall and peered around.

Well, well, well.

"You seeing this, Mac?" She tapping for dual-vision and sent the display to his helmet. The door she'd entered was on a narrow mezzanine walkway that ran around all four walls. Four sets of stairs led down a stepped series of terraces into shadows below. In the corners of each sandstone path stood statues of unrecognisably strange beasts. Things with too many arms, tentacles, teeth and heads. Perhaps some mythological monsters of this culture. The place had the feel of a temple.

On the lowest level, a crowd of maybe two hundred milled about.

"Town meeting?" Mac asked.

"With two men holding another prisoner? Lots of pointing fingers, waving hands, and shoutiness? Looks more like a lynching."

"You'd know, I suppose. Having been on the receiving end of a few."

"Hey!" she said. "I resemble that comment."

"See our target?" Mac chuckled.

Clare inspected the crowd. They were bathed in multicoloured light, streaming through the giant stained-glass window. Always the same on these backwater colony planets. Some great tableau glorifying their ancestors, who came to this godforsaken place as idealists intent on creating the perfect world.

This one showed the white-sand planet, extending what looked like golden tentacles enfolding the newly landed colonists. Maybe some sort of welcome-to-your-new-home kind of thing?

She shook herself and refocussed, zooming her visor onto the man being held captive. Caught a glimpse of his face before the visor packed it in and became nothing more than a window. A low battery error flashed. Great. Now she needed to save power for returning to the ship.

She slipped along the mezzanine and down the stairs, sticking to the shadows, trying to inch closer and get a clear visual. No point in arresting the wrong man... Benwerian. Hell, it might not even be Gredek. She'd have to get him back to the *De Lune* and test his DNA to be sure.

She made it to the bottom and peeked around the corner. Feck! They were hauling the man onto a stage – and it wasn't so he could do a party piece. On the stage stood an old fashioned gallows, rope, trapdoor and all.

Clare swallowed and scratched at the stiff neck seal of her viro suit.

"Mac?" she whispered.

"Ya."

"Where the feck are you? I've got this totally under control, of course, but it might be nice to have backup."

"Stopped at Gredek's ship to check his log. Wanna know something interesting?"

"More interesting than the fact that they're about to hang him? At least, I think it's him."

"Potentially," Mac said conspiratorially. "He's been here before."

"Seriously? I can understand landing here by accident. But why the feck would anyone come back?"

"Hang tight. I'm heading your way. Should be there in, maybe, ten minutes."

That wouldn't be quick enough. The rope was already around the prisoner's neck. Clare surveyed the room and its seething mob of angry people. They were all taller than her, muscular, with mushroom coloured skin and short-sleeved cloth outfits.

There was no way to get close to Gredek without being seen and she certainly didn't blend in. At least ten people had guns, mostly old stunners. A couple looked like projectile weapons of a type she'd only seen in museums, on those mind-numbing childhood occasions when her parents had wanted to play happy family.

What to do? Clare tapped a finger to her lips. Best wade right in.

Mac would call it a terrible plan, but he was overcautious and thought all her schemes were terrible.

She ran full-tilt down the terrace stairs and drove into the crowd. The first dozen or so stumbled out of her way, helped by a shoulder, hip, or straight-arm, as needed. Shouts went up. Hands reached out, scrabbling at her suit. Luckily it was impenetrable and slippery.

She drove her elbow into a liver. The man yelled, clutched at his companions and pulled them down too. That opened a path to the stage. Clare leapt onto the raised platform, breathing hard.

Almost there.

A shot rang out. Something whizzed past her ear and ricocheted off the far wall, chunks of sandstone spraying into the dusty air. There was another shot and a statue's head fell off.

Bit extreme, shooting at her already. She didn't bother looking around, but this needed to be over quickly. And her way, not theirs.

She checked her suit's power levels. Eighteen percent. Cutting it close.

The prisoner on stage stared at her, open-mouthed. A shock of dark hair fell over his pale forehead, so she couldn't tell if he had a third eye. That was assuming he hadn't taken human form. No time to check, either. His two guards reached for their stunners.

Still sprinting, Clare tackled hopefully-Gredek around the waist.

"Thrusters at max!" she hollered. Her new grav-mag boots burst to life with a roar.

The extra weight slowed her lift-off but she aimed for the great glass window. Hopefully-Gredek struggled and shouted in her arms. The thrusters lifted them like a pair of wobbly, skeet-shooting targets.

Nearly there.

Power levels down to ten percent. Eight. Seven. Rainbows of light half-blinded her. More projectiles screamed past her head. Glass shattered and fell in sharp shards.

Wow, these colonists were terrible shots.

The boot-thrusters coughed and cut out.

Clare swore. Perhaps aiming for the window had been a bad idea, as the floor was now a long way down. Hopefully-Gredek gave a high-pitched shriek and buried his head in her armpit.

The viro suit hardened to absorb the shock of hitting the ground and the helmet protected her head. Gredek's suffocating weight on top of her still hurt, though.

Groaning, she shoved him off and struggled to her feet. The open ends of gun barrels pointed at her head.

"Feck it," she muttered. "Mac?"

No answer.

Hands grabbed her arms and hauled her to the stage, hopefully-Gredek stumbling along beside her. Her disruptor and stunner vanished somewhere. Arms waved. People argued. It was an old version of Standard, so Clare only understood a word or two. She did catch the words human and Benwerian. Promising.

The stink of sweat rose in her suit as the air filtering systems stopped. There were manual filters but they didn't work well unless she flapped her arms like a demented chicken. She'd have to take off the helmet in fifteen minutes or suffocate.

Feckity, feck, feck. Where was Mac? What else could go wrong?

Movement in the crowd caught her eye and she gargled a small scream.

Monsters. There were monsters everywhere. Not the Hegemon's normal array of alien species, but honest-to-deity-of-your-choice creatures.

Things that had been people now sported more arms, teeth, fangs, and even heads than a Festovian carnival. Weirdly, no two were the same, but they all advanced on her, wearing their nastiest scowly-faces. She was by no means a speciesist, but there were wayyy too many teeth, claws, and poison-tipped stingers for comfort.

Some captors changed shape again, reverting to human form. They grinned at her. Not the happy kind of smile that promised alcohol and general silliness. More the type that anticipated the slurping of blood and eating of liver.

Hopefully-Gredek gave her a sideways look.

"Whoever the feck you are," he muttered. "Don't take off your helmet, if you ever want to leave this planet."

Cord went around their necks, but he looked amazingly unfazed for someone about to die.

"You're amazingly unfazed for someone about to die," Clare said.

"It's not a hanging for me," he replied. "You're bait and I'm being cured."

"What? Like bacon?"

"Not quite." Hopefully-Gredek shrugged. "Thanks for following me here. I almost lost you a couple of times."

"What the..."

Trapdoors dropped and the cord tightened around Clare's neck. She swore and kicked her feet a few times, partly to entertain the monstrous audience. After all, the suit's neck seal was protecting her against strangulation. What did hopefully-Gredek mean by bait? Was he saying he'd led her here for a reason? And the nonsense about being cured?

He certainly didn't look cured. His head angled awkwardly and the lock of hair slipped to one side. Three eyes. Confirmation of Benwerianismness. Wait, was that a word?

Her heart sank. He had stopped twitching and his face was an unpleasant shade of shit brown. Feck it. The bounty fell to nothing if he was dead and it would be hard to discover the secret to his shape-shifting ability as well. How irritating.

The crowd were leaning forward, multiple eyes trained on a point just over their heads.

Something honey-gold and glistening oozed out of Gredek's nose. If he was bleeding, then his blood had the ability to defy gravity. The twining trickle of gold crawled over his face and up the cord.

A huge cheer erupted from the audience. Various members shifted into even weirder shapes.

The honey-coloured... thing inched along the beam separating ex-Gredek's hanging rope from her own. It reached hers and started down. Towards her head.

The eager crowd hurrahed, flailed, and clapped.

This had gone about far enough. She couldn't take her helmet off and slip free of the noose. The outfit wasn't in perfect condition, but it might keep that... goo out. Although, if her fall had caused any cracks or holes...

Crap!

No point in counting on Mac. He'd probably found something in Gredek's ship to replace the thruster regulator and taken off. That would be the smart thing to do.

The golden stuff oozed closer. She sagged, pretending to be dead. The crowd cheered. Fecking sadists clearly weren't aware of the last century's advances in viro suit technology. Pity the boot-thrusters had run out of juice.

The crowd began stomping and chanting, arms and tentacles swaying like they were at a music concert. That sludge must be getting close. The screaming and chanting reached fever pitch.

Clare hesitated. What if it was the secret to shape-changing? She couldn't leave it behind. Then self-preservation kicked in. She liked her body and brain the way they were, not hijacked by gold snot. Time to ditch her local fan club. They really should have tied her hands.

A quick snatch at her ankle and one knife came free from her boots. A single slash with the monomolecular-edged blade parted the cord around her neck. She dropped to the stage and rolled.

Chaos erupted. Yelling. Sprays of stunner fire. People screamed, collapsed, ran in circles, pushing and trampling over each other.

Mac must have arrived, after all.

Clare scrabbled across the stage. Gredek's body hung limply, his eyes blank. Feck. No bounty and no information, either.

More people fell. Bullets pocked the sandstone walls. If the shooters were aiming at Mac, they really were terrible. He was in the other direction, half-hidden behind the mezzanine floor screen, stunner in hand. She flicked him a quick salute and leapt off the stage, knife ready. He cleared a path. Anyone who reached for her crumpled in an unconscious heap.

A blobby tentacular being pointed Clare's own disruptor at her. She slashed off the limb and snatched her weapon. Another tentacle stretched out. She turned the disruptor on and the creature dissolved in a messy puddle of reddish goo. A ropy gold worm wriggled out and headed in her direction. Clare ran for the stairs, trying not to remember that the thing she'd killed might have been human.

Stunner fire brushed her leg and she stumbled. One limb numb, she hopped onward. Behind her, screams faded.

Clare put a foot on the bottom stair riser. Stars sparkled in her vision. Each breath felt thick and empty. Running. Low. On. Oxygen. She dragged herself up a few more steps. Should she take the helmet off and risk any local infections?

Not far away, several more golden parasites snaked in her direction.

Something smacked into her back and the visor lit up. Her viro suit resumed its background humming. The exhaust fans and coolant control whirred. Clare sucked a deep breath of newly oxygenated air. And another. Stale suit air had never tasted so fine.

"You good to go?" Mac's deep voice rumbled in her comms. "New battery working ok?"

He towered over her, lean in his close-fitting viro suit, disruptor in hand.

"Done quite a bit of killing," he said. "My apologies."

"You came for me?"

"You thought I wouldn't?" He handed her a weapon.

"It had crossed my mind."

"Is he dead?" She pointed to a body hanging off Mac's arm. It looked like a child.

"No." He aimed his weapon past her and shot one of the gold parasites. It squeaked and melted into the sandstone floor. "Thought we could take him to the ship and question him, since you seem to have let our target die."

Struggling to her feet, Clare steadied herself on the wall.

"Let's just question him now." She fired off a shot, as the assailants retreated. "I sorely need a few things cleared up."

Mac shrugged his broad shoulders and set his burden down. He injected a stimulant into the boy's arm, while Clare kept shooting and watching for returning colonists. Tingling in her leg indicated the stunner was wearing off.

No more parasites appeared. Nor did any people. Or monsters. The youngster groaned, sitting up, hand pressed to his head. She tapped the translator system in her comms to life and crouched before him.

"Hey, kid," she said, pleasantly. "What was all that about?"

She jerked a thumb over her shoulder at the wreckage of the room behind.

"We just came to pick up a bounty. There was no need to try and hang me. Bit rude."

A stray tentacle emerged from his elbow. She slapped it aside and pointed her disruptor at his chest.

"Look, I really don't like killing... people. Name?"

"I...I don't like being killed," he gulped, the Adam's apple in his skinny throat jumping.

"Name then."

"Duck."

She dropped lower, glancing around. The boy shook his head.

"It's my name. Duck."

Mac stifled a laugh.

"So, Duck," Clare said, "Answer truthfully and I won't kill you."

The boy nodded vigorously, words burbling from his lips so fast they were almost incomprehensible. Clare held up a hand to stem the flow.

"So, basically, you colonists all have this... worm thing."

"The Golden Ones." He sounded guilty.

"Whatever." Clare rolled her eyes. "It's up your nose?"

"It's everywhere in us."

"And it allows you to change your DNA at will and shift into any shape?"

"Except it only works with humans." His head bobbed. "We tried with Gredek but his body was killing the Golden one. And we don't have enough humans here for all the newborn Golden Ones that hatched this year."

A small smile trembled on his lips.

"That's why Gredek was sent out, in return for removing his Golden One."

"Holy feck!" Mac's whisper sifted through her shock. "Gredek was a fecking lure."

Clare smacked her head, barely feeling it through the suit.

"Gredek was probably Captain Vorik, and the old lady on Beckerman IV, and the working girl on Pinnea III, who all so helpfully pointed us in his direction."

Mac reached for the kid but Clare shoved his hand aside. There was still more to know.

"Why'd you kill Gredek, if he was helping you?"

"We didn't mean to." Duck shrank away from Mac. "The only way to get a Golden One to change hosts is to stop the blood flow to the brain. Just for a few seconds."

He glared at Mac.

"When this guy started shooting, though, everyone got a bit distracted.

"He was shooting because I didn't fancy being goldenized."

"Being a host wouldn't do you any harm," Duck objected. "Plus you'd get to morph into any creature you want."

"We'll pass" Mac snorted.

"For what it's worth, I didn't think forcing people to accept Golden ones was fair, either." the boy said miserably. "But I'm only a kid and nobody listens to me."

Clare exchanged looks with her crewmate.

"But only me and Mac came. Surely that isn't enough new hosts?"

Duck's eyes widened. He looked past her and pointed.

"There's a lot more than you two."

Clare and Mac whirled. The boy used their distraction to scurry up the stairs. Mac took a step to follow but Clare pulled him back.

"Let the boy go. I believe him."

"Thanks Lady!" Duck yelled. "I owe you one."

The iron door burst open and Grey Guards poured into the building, in their usual, gung-ho, rule-following fashion. All serious and shooty.

"Let's get the hell out of here," Mac urged. "Look."

He pointed. Dozens of honey-coloured blobs squirmed their way towards the approaching Guards.

"Gredek played us," Clare muttered. "All of us. He tipped the Grey Guards off and put them on our track. Gah! I'm an idiot."

"Time to go, idiot." Mac tugged on her arm. "Our disruptors are almost out of charge."

Clare wrenched free and handed him the thruster regulator.

"Go, if you want to. I can't leave these poor suckers to be infected."

Mac stared at the tarnished part and stuffed it into his pocket. Clare shot another parasite before it reached his boot.

Mac sighed. He grabbed her again and swung her around. His eyes narrowed and he shook his head.

"Clare O'Malley, your bizarrely misplaced sense of ethics will get you killed. Today, we run, even if I have to carry you."

He nodded at the Grey Guards.

"Besides, it's too late."

He was right. Most of the guards lay on the temple floor, twitching, gargling and sprouting tentacles from random places. Clearly the parasites could get through even the best viro suits.

"Let's go, then."

She ran up the stairs to the back entrance and out into the blasting heat.

They hurried through the deserted street and past the Grey Guards' troopship, parked near the *De Lune*. They hadn't even left personnel to secure the vessel. Clare pursed her lips. Overconfident, feckless, stupid...

She stomped into her ship and closed the door behind.

Mac replaced the thruster regulator and the *De Lune* took off. Clare sat in the captain's chair and glowered.

Once out of the atmosphere, she stared moodily at the planet spinning below. No bounty and no pardon, either. Now a bunch of infected Grey Guards would be let loose on the galaxy and she'd probably get the blame.

This day had so not gone to plan.

Beside her, Mac's fingers flew over the *De Lune's* control panels. Three torpedoes burst forth from the rear bays and sped toward the settlement.

"What the feck did you just do?"

"What needed to be done," Mac replied, grimly. His eyes were on the weapons trace.

"You can't!" She reached for the self-destruct settings.

Too late. Three red and gold flowers bloomed and merged into one huge mushroom cloud.

She shuddered and glanced at her offsider.

"I'm not sure whether to shake your hand for a job well done or push you out the airlock as a psychopathic murderer."

"Someone had to do it and you're too soft. That parasite cannot be allowed off the planet. And it certainly can't be handed over to the Hegemon to study. It would be weaponised within a year."

His jaw tightened

"Do you really want to be chased down by Grey Guards that can alter their species as easily as they change clothes?"

"Maybe? I do like a challenge."

"Liar," Mac said. "So now what?"

He stared out the window at the rotating planet. Streaks of dust and smoke streamed out like a banner away from the settlement.

"Blowing up the colony may not get rid of the parasite entirely," Clare said.

She punched a few buttons and several small drones burst forth from the *De Lune*.

"What were those?"

"Quarantine biohazard satellites. Should keep all but the utter idiots away."

"You do know how many utter idiots there are in this galaxy?"

"But these are terribly official-sounding. Complete with gruesome death threats." Clare tapped the transmit button and the satellites began their looped message. Mac pulled up the specs.

"They're Hegemon. Where did you get them?"

Claire smiled smugly. Mac groaned and rubbed a hand over his face.

"You stole them, didn't you? From Epsilon Eight. From the fecking Hegemon way station where we picked up this job."

"Stole is such a judgemental word." She pouted. "They were lonely. They wanted a home and someone to love them."

"No wonder they were so keen to chase us down." He paused and tilted his head, as awareness dawned.

"No. You knew! You knew Gredek was Vorik and those others. You knew this whole thing was a setup." He slumped back in the chair. "Why?"

"Vorik is a by the book stickler. When found me in that bar and offered me the money and a pardon, I figured out straight away he had to be Gredek."

"How?"

"As if the Hegemon would ever offer a bounty that high for anything. Plus Vorik would never set foot in a bar."

"So you knew it was a trap, but you went anyway?

"I like surprises." Care frowned. "Didn't want all those Grey Guards killed, though. Wasn't expecting Gredek to lead them here as well. Didn't know about all those worms, either."

"So we're still on the wanted list and broke to boot." As the *De Lune's* engines warmed up, Mac eyed her. "You're awfully cheerful for someone who didn't earn a hundred thousand credits and who is now officially on another Hegemon blacklist."

He sat back in his chair. Clare hit Go on the flip drive course she'd mapped out.

Once they'd entered the dark emptiness of the flip void, something clattered in the ship's galley. Mac rose, disruptor drawn. Clare stood beside him, one hand on his arm.

There was a long silence as they both stared at the galley entrance.

A small, fluffy white kitten emerged, mewling pathetically. It sat on its haunches, head tilted to one side and blinked golden eyes at them.

"Ah," Clare said. "We appear to have a stowaway."

Mac's finger tightened on the trigger but she pushed his weapon aside.

"He won't harm us. He owes me. And it will certainly be handy to have a shapeshifter tucked away somewhere, in case we ever need it."

She punched a new set of co-ordinates into the nav computer.

"Let's take this little fellow to visit an old university friend of mine. Prof Beckteron in the xenobiology department."

"Let me guess," Mac glared. "The cat's name is Duck?"

Clare smiled.

Editor's note: This was the last story we could find that Aiki was writing before she died. She would probably have polished it up more, if she had time, but it's still damned good.

Revelations

Pamela Jeffs

I love the smell of raw steel and the feel of metal shavings crunching beneath my feet. It's an unusual trade for a woman, being a blacksmith, but my hands are broad and built to wield hammers and pull files. They are hard hands, but clever. Their skill enabled me to buy my freedom and a smithy of my own after a full sixteen years of slavery.

I run my file down the almost-smooth cheek of the figurehead I've been commissioned to make. She will replace the one damaged on Althea's Run, a space galleon captained by the Governor's pirate-hunter, Captain Bayard. The work is cathartic, pulling Althea's beautiful face from the metal. I have made her eyes wide-set, framed by a tumble of curls over one shoulder. She is exactly what I imagine a daughter of mine would look like.

If only I could have children.

I curl my fist around the file, knuckles paling to white. There will never be daughters for me. My legacy is destined to be my art and a heart full of parental hate.

The doorbell over the workshop entry rings out. The small chiming sound is delicate; not like the mountain of flesh that follows it.

A man, built like a cliff, bursts through the door. His steel-grey hair and sun-weathered skin mark him as a sailor type. A green bottle hangs from his hand. He runs through the workshop but trips, his boot catching the edge of a pile of lumber stacked by the forge. He falls, landing face down on the ash-strewn floor, and is still.

My stool scrapes the flagstones as I push it back. Metal shavings tumble off my leather apron, a glittering curtain swept away by the breeze blowing through the open door. I stride over to the man. With my boot I roll him over.

A brand glares at me from his upturned wrist. Irrefutable proof this man is a criminal. And not only that. He's a thrice-damned pirate, like my parents, Jon and Liza Lester.

"Did you abandon your child on the streets of New Providence as well?" I mutter. "Get up and get out."

The man seems dazed. His mouth moves but the words are mumbled. Perhaps the fall concussed him.

His hand twitches and the green glass bottle rattles against the flagstones. I kneel down to pry it free. The man flinches, his grip tightening.

His eyes blink open. Sea green. A colour that almost matches my own. His gaze locks onto mine and he pushes the bottle into my hand.

"Please," he says, his words suddenly clear. "Take it. Hide it,"

And I do. The vessel is barely concealed in my apron pocket when two mechanical guardsmen burst through the door.

Their copper limbs gleam in the sun filtering through the doorway. The governor's brand imprinted into each of their chest plates glows with the light of the power gems fitted behind them. The guards' expressionless faces scan the room.

"There," states one, his voice a series of mechanical clicks.

"Take him," says the next, sounding identical to the first.

The pirate scrabbles to his feet and swings at the lead android. He misses. The guards, their strength inhuman, grapple with the man and throw him to the ground again. He lands with a heavy thud. The guards show no compassion as they clasp iron cuffs to his wrists and ankles. I almost feel sorry for the pirate. Seeing him bound like that reminds me of an aged draft horse being led to the slaughterhouse.

The man struggles. I respect his determination but the guardsmen give him no quarter. They twist the pirate's arms backwards and he cries out before he is subdued once more.

His gaze, still defiant, meets mine.

"I'm sorry, Pandora."

A shiver crawls down my spine. I have no idea how this man knows my name. Nothing about him is familiar to me. I stand silent, uncertain, as the guards drag him out the door and down Industry Street, towards the jail.

A third guardsman, Sheriff Clockman, enters the workshop. His mechanical eyes swivel strangely as he takes in the lay of my smithy. The quiet hum of his motors fills the silence. Then he speaks.

"The pirate knows you?"

"So it would seem," I reply. "But I assure you, I've never seen him before."

"Did the pirate say anything else to you?"

It was Clockman's cold hand that dragged me to the Slave Guild, all those years ago. His precise hand that sterilized me, so I could never have children. For that reason alone, I lie to him.

"Nothing."

"Did he give you anything?"

"No." The bottle suddenly feels heavy in my apron.

The hypnotic spin of the Sheriff's irises slows.

He may be suspicious but he can't prove anything. I ask a question of my own.

"Who was that man?"

Clockman's gaze flickers to the broken door and then back to me. He seems to hesitate, metal limbs rigid as he considers me. The moment passes.

"Bold Jon Lester," he says. "He and his pirate crew were apprehended attempting to steal Althea's Run."

Clockman's casual mention of my father's name astonishes me. My vision wavers and I swallow hard, fighting to keep my expression neutral. This skill, hard learned as a slave, serves me well now.

"Jon Lester?"

"Yes," Clockman's voice is cold. "He is scheduled to be terminated at sunset."

Terminated. He means hung by the neck until dead.

I have no intention of letting Jon Lester die. He is the only one who can give me an answer to the question I've spent a lifetime asking.

Why was I abandoned?

Finished with his questions, Clockman bows and turns to leave. As he does, my mind is already working on a plan to free my father.

It'll need to be sunset before I go for Bold Jon. In the meantime, I inspect the bottle. The glass is worn, almost opaque with a motley collection of scratches. The neck is corked and sealed with red wax. I pull a thin, flexible file from my toolbox and guide it in along the edge of the seal. The sharpened tip slides easily through the stopper. Wax crackles and falls, scattering across my scarred timber worktable.

I tip the bottle over and a small roll of paper slithers free. I ease it open and lean in towards the lamplight. The document is fragile, the paper worn to translucence. Across the surface crawls a tangle of faint brown lines, outlining a jagged coast, an unnamed reef, a lagoon protected by cliffs. But it is the bold, blood-coloured 'X' in the top left-hand corner of the map that grabs my attention.

Treasure.

Thoughts crowd my mind.

Is this why Bold Jon and his crew were going for a ship? What treasure would a man like him hunt? Gold? Power gems?

A more personal question comes to mind.

Did he come to New Providence looking for me, or was it by chance he fell into my workshop?

I glance out the window. The sun huddles low over the industrial quarter buildings. It's almost time. Time to get answers.

Time to save Jon Lester.

With trembling fingers, I re-roll the map and carefully slip it into my sleeve. Anxiety sours my stomach. I am unable to decide if I relish or fear the encounter to come.

The streets to the gallows are filled with food vendors setting up for the evening. The greasy, thick scents of fried fish and grilled flatbread waft towards me on the light wind blowing in from the docks. Any other time I would be tempted to stop, eat and socialize. This evening my focus is elsewhere.

There is already a raucous crowd gathered in the hanging ring. Old matrons wearing salt-stiff skirts, burly sailors, their palms knotted with calluses, and loud-mouthed drunkards. All stand about, shouting, muttering or cussing, anticipation running high as they await the executioner.

The gallows stand central to the courtyard. The wooden structure towers above the people, the noose swaying gently in the breeze. Such a primitive way to kill in a world filled with technology, but it's a method that appeals to the people, and a way to control them. The guards encourage the spectacle, as a warning for humans thinking of causing trouble.

I slide further down the street, hugging the line of buildings. At the far end are the jail cells and twelve men can be counted behind the bars. Jon Lester's crew, no doubt. They are a motley bunch, both young and old. Many sport injuries, black eyes, and arms nursed in makeshift slings. It looks like they gave the guardsmen a good fight. What kind of man is Jon Lester that so many would follow him to their deaths?

A good man? A decent one?

No.

My stomach knots on the bitter taste of old hate. Bold Jon is the man that left me as a seven-year-old child, to fend for myself on wicked streets.

Skirting the outer edges of the crowd, I make my way towards the jail. I pass the baker's son, his face red from hollering, and the fishmonger's wife.

"Kill them bastard pirates," she screams, a skillet brandished in her small hand.

When did this town become so full of hate?

The jail barracks are relatively new. Painted, timber plank walls stand stout but, while clean last summer, they are now weathered and stained with gull droppings. I work my way around to the back of the building, cursing as my boots slosh in a puddle of mud - one that reeks of rotting fish guts and cat piss. I continue past the first cell and on towards the next - the cubicle with a weak point.

It's a flaw I learnt about last New Year's Eve. The night when warm ale sloshed over my knuckles as the builder's daughter, drunker than was wise, toasted me, declared me her friend, and shared her own father's secret.

I feel around the bottom edge of the third plank from the ground. A solid pull and the timber comes away. The girl was right... her father had saved gold by using silicone to fix the logs at the back of the barracks, not concealed screws as they were like at the front. I shake my head. Everyone, even the tradesmen, is a pirate in this town.

I hear the click of a key in a lock and the clang of steel as a cell door opens. Time is running out. I reach in and pull again. Another plank tumbles free. I shuffle back, letting it fall to the ground. A small, dirty face peers from the hole.

It's a boy, no more than ten, with startling blue eyes.

"Thanks for the bust out, Ma'am!"

He is small enough to slither through the gap. Once free, his gap-toothed grin is full of mischief. He winks at me.

"Ponch is the name." His smile widens. "Let's get the others."

With the first plank free, the rest are easy to lever away. Men, one by one, crawl free. But none of them are Bold Jon. Out the front, there is the sudden snap of falling timber, a short, sharp cry and the creak of a rope pulled taut. A surge of adrenaline rushes through me. Was it Jon? Am I too late? Then I hear the mutters from the men behind me.

"Fare thee well, Tom."

Not Jon but a crew member. Then the men are moving again. No chance to pause for grief.

"Cap'n is in the next cell," whispers Ponch, his eyes wide with fear.

"Then it's one more cell and we're out of here." I smile to reassure him.

With the help of three men, five more planks are pried loose, to give Bold Jon his freedom. He rolls out of the opening with a grunt and a groan, landing on all fours.

"Thank ye lads," he whispers. "Although hanging might have been better than this headache old Clockman gave me."

I hang back as his crew gather around, helping him to his feet. Hate for the man boils in my chest. How dare Bold Jon sound so reasonable? How dare his men love him so?

But there is no time for conversation. A scuff of boots sounds out from around the corner. I glance back to see Clockman with six guardsmen, a blaster held in his cold, rigid fist. His eyes fall on me. Their irises stop circling for a moment then resume, spinning faster.

"Recognized your father then, did you?"

The Sheriff's head tilts and he shoots.

The sudden crack of laser-fire is followed by the sickening stench of burnt flesh. The man next to me slumps sideways, his linen shirt stained with blood.

A pause - heartbeats long. Then chaos erupts.

As the condemned men flee, a small hand slips into mine. Ponch. Bold Jon stands next to him.

"Time to leg it, lass," he says.

We run through the back streets. My boots pound the mouldy cobblestones; the stink of human excrement surrounding me. My breath comes sharp and heavy and my mind races. If caught, no doubt I'll swing with these damned pirates.

The smell of salt grows stronger and a cool breeze fans my face. We round the corner of a warehouse and are met with the glittering lights of the docks.

Ships of all sizes rock quietly against their mooring ropes. Space freighters, galleons and low, sleek zoomers hover over the water, their solar sails fanning like sea eagle wings against the night. The forged metal figureheads appear almost alive, in the flickering glow of the power gems that line the hulls. On any other night, it would have seemed magical.

Tonight it's different. Tonight I am led by the pirate Bold Jon.

"This way," he whispers, leading me towards the farthest pontoon.

Ponch bounces at my side, all signs of fear replaced with wild glee. He grins wide.

"Just wait, you're gonna love her!"

"Love who?" I whisper.

"You'll see."

Bold Jon is silent, as he weaves from shadow to shadow. He moves with confidence, showing no sign of fear. Despite myself, I begin to see him, not as a devil, but as a man more capable than most.

The outline of a ship materializes ahead, sleek and elegant. No figurehead graces her bow. No lights illuminate her solar sails. She rests in complete darkness. Ponch squeezes my hand.

"*Althea's Run*," he whispers. "Was I right? Do you love her?"

The lines of the vessel solidify as we move closer. Ponch is right. Captain Bayard's ship is a work of art. Her smooth, metal lines are a testament to the designer. Her polished hull hovers just above the waves, like a dancer floating in air. Ornate rails line the slightly scooped edges of her bow. The crystal-faced, faceted gems fitted to the hull, while not powered, still catch and reflect the dock lights like a thousand eyes. Even without her figurehead, still sitting back in my shop, *Althea's Run* is stunning.

Bold Jon escorts us out of the gloom and towards the ship's gangplank. I am surprised at the lack of sentries but do not question it, as I am led aboard. I stumble over a partly coiled power lead but check myself.

My father stops and turns to me. His rugged face is lit by orange lambency, for the full moon has just cracked the horizon. The touch of his large-palmed hand against my cheek is soft. His eyes glitter. A part of me wants to pull away but another part longs for my father's embrace. Bold Jon's voice is a whisper.

"I'm sorry, Pandora. Ye were in my thoughts always."

The question that has burned in me for so long flows out like molten steel.

"Why did you leave me, then?"

My father glances at the docks. They are still empty. He looks back.

"Clockman accused yer mother of stealing power gems in the market. I defended her, and so he arrested us both for piracy. Captain Bayard took us away." His jaw clenches and releases. "Then left us on an outer rim island wit' no way to return. A freighter found us only last year."

He runs the back of his hand under his nose. His pirate brand is bared briefly with the movement.

"I've been looking for yer ever since."

There is sincerity in his tone. And despite the years of hatred, I find myself daring to believe him. Daring to forgive him.

Damn him.

"Where is my mother?" I ask.

"Do ye have the map?" Bold Jon lowers his hand.

The map? I reach into my sleeve and pull it out.

"Good lass. Now you'll need to take it and sail for the island. Yer mother is waiting for ye at the spot marked 'X'."

"My mother?"

"Aye," he says sadly. "She's buried there."

My breath hitches as the memory of the blonde haired, blue-eyed woman I once called ma fills my mind.

"She's dead?"

"Died of a broken heart, love." Bold Jon looks down at the deck. His fingers worry the edge of his tattered shirt. "Never got over losing ye."

Lost in my thoughts, I barely register the shadows of the men creeping up the gangplank. Bold Jon's crew. They have found their way to the ship.

The sound of clanking footsteps draws my attention back to the present and I glance over the rail. Pounding their way down the length of the dock is a contingent of guardsmen, their blasters drawn. At their head races Clockman.

Bold Jon's large fingers pull my chin around, so I face him once more. His eyes are filled with fierce fire.

"Yer mother was my treasure. As she lay dying, I promised I would find ye and bring ye to her grave." He points to the ship's wheel. "Use the map. Take my men and this ship. Go to her."

The anger and the pain I have held against him for years bleeds away. All I can do is nod as he pulls me into a rough embrace. I breathe in the salty scent, as the heat of his tears touches my neck. Then he steps away.

"One last thing," he says. "Look after yer brother. He's a good lad."

Brother?

Bold Jon kneels down before Ponch and ruffles the boy's hair.

"It's time, Boyo," he whispers. "I gotta go. Now, be sure an' help your sister."

Then he is on his feet and, quick as a hammer strike, he is gone. His boots thud on the gangplank and a mighty roar echoes out, as he barrels down the dock towards Clockman.

I am about to run to his aid, when I feel a tug on my sleeve. It's Ponch. My brother.

"Don't break Da's promise to Mama," he pleads.

I look down at the docks. My father, surrounded by guards, is outlined in lamplight. He fights fiercely, not for his life, but for his children and the promise he made to his dying wife. In that moment, I know I'll do as he asks. I'll become what I once despised. A pirate. A criminal. And all because I see that Bold Jon is a good man. A man worth honouring.

I turn to the waiting crew. They stand uneasy, one eye on the shore, awaiting my order. No need to delay them longer.

"Heave the ropes, lads," I command. "Set course for Jon's island."

The crew move quietly, but quickly. Mooring ropes are slipped from ties, and beneath my feet the ship's engines whir to life.

Then *Althea's Run* floats soundlessly into the night sky. I stand at the ship's rail, holding my brother's hand. The solar sails above us creak, as they catch the wind and we are pulled away. As the docks shrink, I watch Bold Jon Lester.

Keep watching until he drops.

My broad hand clenches and the map in it gives, its paper creasing to fit my palm.

"Fare thee well," I whisper, my voice cracking as the fallen figure of my father diminishes in the distance.

Smoke and Dreams

Monica Schultz

The cage should be empty for cleaning before I'm sent in. But today is not the first time I've felt the predatory gaze of a dragon.

I wipe the smears from the thick glass window and use its reflection to scan my surroundings. Dense foliage gives this enclosure the illusion of an endless rainforest, suitable for a colony of Green Tree Dragons. Yet, with half a dozen juveniles crammed into the compact space, the reality is a breeding ground any free dragon would shudder to call home.

I pause as a shadow shifts over a moss-covered branch, revealing yellow, slitted eyes. The young beast's tongue flickers out of its mouth, tasting the air. My heart thunders, urging me to run, but I know they enjoy the chase. Without taking my eyes off the dragon, I repeatedly jab the emergency alert on my wristband, until a responding buzz tingles up my arm. Message received. Yet it would only take a minute for a Green Tree Dragon to wrap its enormous tail around my waist and crush the life from me.

I have to distract it.

I take deep breaths and relax my subconscious. The creature's mind bounces between thoughts, as it records each minute shift in its surroundings. Only one notion remains in focus. Food.

I shudder, but refuse to severe my weak connection.

"Hello," I say.

The dragon registers my voice and tucks the sound away, joining other useless noise, like crickets chirping. The branch groans under the weight, as it unravels its tail from the trunk.

Please, Táo, hurry.

"You don't want to eat me," I urge, "I'm a friend."

I focus mentally on the word friend, adding memories of laughter shared with Táo, to make my intentions clear. Yet the dragon slips through my grasp, its muscles tense. My stomach plummets. The cool glass presses against my back, sealing off any hope of escape.

I whimper.

The branch cracks, and it falls with a thud, a bright red dart sticking from its limp rump. Relief washes over me, as I slump against the window.

Táo bounds over rocks and fallen debris, tranquiliser gun slung across her back.

"Chieko!" she calls, "are you ok?"

She crouches before me, cheeks flushed from running. Even with her brow creased from worry, she is beautiful. If I hadn't grown up with her in the orphanage, I would never believe someone so lovely could work in our trade.

I tilt my head back and take deep breaths to steady my racing heart.

"I'm ok. Just shaken."

"We should go, before the sedative wears off." Táo clasps my trembling hand and gently squeezes.

I peer over her shoulder at the slumped dragon. The webbed barbs along its spine twitch and its snout presses into the mud at an odd angle. After losing its meal, the creature will be murderous when it wakes.

My shoulders sink. I must have been insane to think a dragon would listen to me, let alone be coerced into helping my escape. Swallowing the lump in my throat, I return Táo's squeeze and stand.

"Thank you." I offer her a weak smile.

She leads me out of the enclosure, the door seals shut behind us and we link arms, like we used to when we were little.

"Don't mention it," she says, "We'll get you a glass of water and report this to Master Jeong."

"He won't care," I scoff. "He's not paid enough."

"Maybe. But, at least, the incident will be recorded. You never know, it could help Ki-Yoon's case. His family deserves to know how sloppy things are getting here."

I bite my tongue to save Táo from my cynicism. Master Jeong would never admit fault. Ki-Yoon died young, but the dragon trade purposefully hires those who are disposable. Countless citizens are killed every year in Dromore. Doing jobs only the desperate will take in order to feed their children. Even if it leaves those children orphans.

Our footsteps echo in the empty corridor as we pass other spotless display enclosures. The Race begins on the President's birthday and the press will need clear shots of the future dragon generations to build up excitement.

An overhead speaker crackles with static and a disconnected voice booms through the building.

All citizens report to the nearest common room.

Táo and I freeze and I glance at my wristband. The screen flashes with a new message but I close the alert without reading it. I've been through the drill before.

"I didn't realise the time," I say, as the announcement repeats itself.

Doors slide open and other workers file into the corridor. Táo and I join the steady flow of bodies towards the common room. We shuffle together, filling every spare inch of space, like cattle ready for slaughter. The rank breath of a co-worker blows against the back of my neck, but at least Táo is nearby. Her pointy elbow digs into my hip, reminding me to focus on the choosing.

Chairman Yang's projection hovers above a stack of dirty dishes, yet to be cleared from lunch. His arms gesture grandly, as he reminds us what an honour it is to serve our city through racing. According to Yang, the Race ensures peace for all citizens, by indulging the primal urge for violence the lower classes crave. I scowl at the floor and grit my teeth. Resist the impulse to scream that he's wrong.

Nobody dares speak.

Eventually, Chairman Yang returns to the script on his wristband and the projection expands to allow each chosen citizen to be displayed.

"Citizen code 7-3-B-4-F-G," he reads.

The ID photo of a young man with slicked black hair appears. Murmurs ripple through the crowd, concealing Táo's whispered words.

"Rich family. He should be able to afford a crossbow and a sword."

I take in the healthy glow of his skin and nod in agreement.

"Citizen code 9-I-4-5-6-T."

A photo of a middle-aged man with bags under his narrow eyes replaces the last. I grimace at his sunken cheeks, evidence that he could never afford the equipment he needs. I shake my head at Táo, cutting off any comment. This man could've easily been one of our fathers, if they weren't already dead.

"Citizen code 8-5-J-C-3-E."

A young girl with limp black hair and hooded eyes stares at me from the projection. My jaw drops. Her nose is wide and jaw square, just like mine, but surely that isn't *me*. My wristband flashes with a new message.

You've been chosen! The screen reads, as if I've won a prize.

Táo clings to my arm. Tears drip from her chin and her mouth moves, but I can't hear over the blood pounding in my ears.

The crowd parts as two peace officers appear, batons swinging from their belts. I press my lips into a thin line and try to shake Táo off. Her fingers claws at my arm and her pleading stare tears my heart to shreds. I push her away without meeting her eye. A co-worker has the good sense to hold her back before a peace officer intervenes.

They'll take care of her, I assure myself.

"Chieko!" Táo calls after me.

I stiffen at the desperation in my friend's voice but don't turn back. I am the pillar of our friendship, her shoulder to cry on. I can't let Táo see me crumble.

Head held high; I follow the peace officers.

I wipe pork grease from my chin with the back of one sleeve. The assortment of fried gyozas sits heavy in my stomach, after a lifetime of rice and cold soup. I slide the empty tray back through the slot in the door. Meals are the only indicator of time in this cell. Without a window or Wi-Fi connection, I can only guess that this is now the third day.

I pace the twelve steps that make up the length of the room to help my stomach digest. The cell is a luxury compared to our sleeping brackets in the compound. Every inch of compact space flaunts the lifestyle that is possible for those victorious in the Race. I pause before a mirror embedded in the wall. The surface shines, revealing blemishes and scars from each failed attempt to speak to feral cats outside the orphanage. I wince at the thought and become even more convinced my plan will fail.

With a groan of frustration, I sink to the concrete floor, denying myself the comfort of the foam mattress. Since there are no visible cameras in the room, I can only assume the mirror acts as a window for eager Race viewers. Hunching my shoulders, I carefully pull out the only personal belonging I bothered to fetch from my sleeping bracket. The coin purse is lighter than I would prefer, but contributing five yuan to Ki-Yoon's funeral felt necessary. I count the remaining money until my fingers stop trembling.

Click.

The door bolt slides open and the seal pops. I scoop my coins back into their purse and secure it under my shirt.

"Citizen 8-5-J-C-3-E, it's time to meet your dragon." The peace officer's voice is muffled by a riot helmet.

My eyes sweep the room, searching for something to delay the moment. There is nothing, just slate grey furniture built into the walls and one pocket of light shining behind the officer. I force my feet to walk towards it, each step like trekking through muck.

"There is time, if you've changed your mind, to visit the contestant shop," he says. "A simple chest plate can make a world of a difference."

"No thank you." I push my shoulders back. "I'll need every fen to survive outside Dromore."

"Suit yourself."

Staff hurry down corridors and dart out of sight, as the officer leads me through the compound. Growls thunder and shake the walls, the sound humming through my veins. I peek around corners, but the dragons are nowhere in sight.

"How come I couldn't hear them from my room?" I ask.

The officer chuckles at my wide eyes.

"When they arrived this morning, they were still full from breakfast."

With each step the cacophony of snarls and roars grow louder. My defiance slowly fades, until my legs are trembling so violently, the officer almost has to drag me. His gloved fingers crush my wrist, only releasing me to jab a code into an enormous iron door. It opens, revealing a dozen cages lit with fluorescent lights.

My heart crawls into my throat as I stare at the ferocious creatures. The juveniles I worked with are nothing compared to their adult counterparts. An emerald dragon, legs thick as ancient oaks, wears glittering chain mail that clinks against its scales with every breath. The armoured young man sitting astride it ignores me but the beast's black eyes track our movement as we pass the cage.

The next enclosure houses a wyvern much larger than the last dragon. Topaz scales ripple over lean muscle, as its neck twists back to preen tail feathers. On impulse, I roll my shoulders and open my thoughts to it. The wyvern's head whips around to face me, rage rolling off its mind like steam. I jump away and dart behind the peace officer.

"Best not to make eye contact," he advises.

I gulp and recoil my tendril of thought.

"Don't worry. Yours is a little less feisty."

We stop in front of the last cage. The dragon's golden scales have lost their lustre, but it appears every bit as brutal as the wyvern. It paces the cage on skeletal legs; shackles scraping against the floor with each step. A black collar circles the creature's throat and a saddle rests between its wings.

The peace officer unlocks the cage and shoves me towards a waiting attendant. The helper's uniform is no flashier than my shapeless jumpsuit, but she glares at my sweat stained clothes in disgust.

"Any experience with dragons?"

"Only cleaning their cages."

The attendant harrumphs. She yanks the leather rein that connects to the dragon's horns and leads it closer. It snaps jagged teeth and hisses. Hot spit splatters my face.

"Enough!" The attendant snaps. She clicks a button on her belt, and the dragon shudders, before dropping to a crouch. The creature's gaze locks onto the belt and a low growl rumbles through its throat - but it remains on the floor.

"Don't worry about her," the woman says. "She knows to finish the race if she wants her next meal."

I chew the inside of my cheek and watch the dragon from the corner of my eye. After a few beats, the attendant shrugs and kicks a stool into place.

"Step up on this," she instructs. "Put your left leg in the closest stirrup then swing your right over her back."

I mount, receiving a few scrapes from grasping at the dragon's neck spikes. As soon as I am upright, the attendant straps me in place. With each yank, my legs press tighter against the dragon's ribs, until pins prick at my feet.

"Are you sure that's necessary?"

"Trust me." The attendant hands over the reins. "You'll be thankful once you're in the air. You'll definitely not win if you fall off, eh?"

"I'm not trying to win," I blurt out. "Just survive."

"You won't do either." The woman fusses over my saddle a moment longer, before looking me dead in the eye. "But, this way, you won't humiliate your family by breaking your neck the moment the race begins."

I open my mouth to protest but the attendant quickly steps out of the cage.

Good luck, she mouths.

I wrap the reins around my fists until my knuckles are white.

Focus on the plan, I scold myself. Everyone knows the arena is open air. I just have to convince the dragon to flee from the course. But I am bound as tightly to my own mind as I am to this creature.

Focus. I fixate on the sweat trickling down my spine and the air wheezing out of my tight lungs.

Thud.

My attention snaps back to the present. The dragon growls, the sound vibrating through my legs. The roof splits open, flooding the cage with natural light and the clamour of an expectant crowd. I squint against the sunlight and gulp down lungfuls of fresh air.

The platform rises.

Spectators fill the arena to the brim, their cheers and heckles creating a constant wave of noise. Drones hover like flies buzzing around each dragon shackled to the platforms. A double-sided jumbotron displays the live stream, captured by multiple drones, for all guests wealthy enough to attend the Race in person. I catch my pale, nervous face on the screen before my mount swats away the drone.

"Thanks," I mutter.

Though each dragon probably detests the drones for their unnatural whirring, it reminds me to keep my expression blank. Táo is watching, along with every other citizen of Dromore, at one of the mandatory viewing centres. She shouldn't have to worry about me.

I concentrate on the red light and crouch over my steed. My stomach swirls as I extend a tendril of thought towards her.

"I have a plan," I say.

The dragon recoils at the sound of my voice. The crowd counts down from ten. I speak louder, forcing confidence into my words.

"When the shackles release, don't join the race. Instead, fly out of here. Let's leave Dromore for good."

A horn blares and the dragons leap into the sky. My back spasms in pain, as I am jolted backwards. I yank on the reins, fighting the wind that whips at my clothes and stings my eyes. Curling inwards, I hunch over my mount's neck spikes and wait for the wave of nausea to pass.

"This isn't the plan!" I scream.

She beats her wings harder, propelling us into the fray. A shadow looms overhead and I glance up. A scarlet lung dragon blocks out the sun with its serpentine body. Blood from its last victim drips from the creature's maw and splatters over me. The rider perches at the base of the beast's skull, grinning triumphantly.

I dive as far forward as the straps will let me and thump my dragon's neck, to get her attention. A shuriken, flung by my opponent, grazes the back of my hand. I shriek and press it against my chest. The lung dragon swoops closer and another star lodges in the back of the saddle. Realisation clicks into place.

"They're aiming for your wings!"

My warning comes too late. Another throwing star tears through the membrane and we swerve, colliding with a drone. My mount roars, smoke pouring from her nostrils and her mind slams into my own, merging the two. Rage cascades over us and our blood boils at the thought of being forced to fight our own kind. I blink back the torrent of her thoughts.

"You hate this too," I mumble.

She snarls at the sound of my voice, and I sense her aching ribs, bruised under the pressure of my legs. I grit my teeth, grab the shuriken from my saddle and force it under the strap, until the leather breaks.

"My name is Chieko," I say. "Let's get out of here."

She understands. I can feel it.

I cut through the next strap, blood coats my fingers and making them slick. Pain shoots up my arm, but I don't stop.

I hate this race. I'm hungry. They make me work hard for nothing. They don't care if I die.

Finally! Our thoughts are as one.

She tucks in her wings and dives, veering away from the course we have been instructed to take. I scream as she flies in an erratic pattern, leaving the rest of the pack behind. The wind wrenches at my free leg and I am almost catapulted off.

My dragon slows. She twists her neck and stares at me from the corner of her violet eye.

"Where I am from, they call me Zahira."

I catch my breath at the musical chime of her voice.

"There is a better future out there," I urge. "If we work together."

We hang mid-air. The remaining dragons are colourful jewels sparkling in the distance, as they hurtle towards the finish line. Zahira smacks away approaching drones with an expert flick of her tail. Spectators hurl insults, but distance mutes their words.

"I know a place that's safe for dragons and where the people smile more," Zahira says. "But I need your help."

"Anything!" I plead. "Just make it fast."

"Use the shuriken to release my collar. I can't fly past the boundary with it on."

The distance between my saddle and the collar stretches like an eternity. Stars dance in the corners of my vision.

"Can't you get your head any closer?" I ask.

"Not if you want to stay airborne."

"Great." I slip the shuriken under the last of the saddle straps to free my other leg. My heart gallops. I tuck my feet underneath me and lean forward until my navel presses against the first neck barb.

"They're coming," Zahira warns.

I glance behind us. An army of drones, crackling with electricity, blacken the sky. The authorities have guessed what we are up to. My limbs freeze.

"I can't do this."

"Bit late, now. You don't have a choice."

I spot the twisted body of a contestant far beneath us and square my shoulders. Biting down on the shuriken, I use my hands to inch up Zahira's neck. Hands shaking, I hack through the collar. Zahira's lips pull back, revealing teeth longer than my fingers.

"Hold on tight."

Her wings sweep through the air in massive strokes. I drop the shuriken and hook my arms around her neck. Hell, I hook my legs around as well. Her scales scrape my skin raw and I sway with every gust of wind. We pitch sideways and Zahira's wings brush against sky scrapers, as we weave through the city. A drone explodes as it crashes into a billboard. Another four follow, only a few meters away.

"They're still following us," I warn.

My wristband buzzes, the electric pulse dancing up my arm. I scan the message.

Return to the track or risk forfeit. A chill spreads through my veins.

"Zahira, they're tracking my every movement."

The dragon plummets, talons scraping the ground as she bounds off the pavement, sending the rest of the drones careening to their doom.

"I've got a plan too," she says.

Zahira winds through several side streets, wings clipping the windows of the buildings. Breathing heavily, she drops to her hind legs in an alley. Stray dogs yelp and scurry for cover.

"Get off," she commands.

I leap down, fighting a wave of dizziness. Zahira stalks towards me and I cringe. Smoke puffs from her nostrils.

"Chieko, child of a thousand blessings, trust me," she says, "Trust me the way your parents did, when they gave you a name with the hope for a better future."

I bite my bottom lip. Pain radiates from every inch of my body. Blood drips from Zahira's wounded wing.

I nod and close my eyes.

Her teeth sink into my wrist and I scream in agony, my arm spasming. She spits out my wristband, crushed, yet still flashing. I slump forwards, but Zahira catches me with a paw.

"Are you all right?"

"I will be. Thank you, my friend."

Zahira studies me for a moment before lying flat on the ground.

"Climb back aboard, Chieko. We have a long flight ahead of us."

There are all kinds of love in this world
but never the same love twice.

F. Scott Fitzgerald

Waking Up

Sue Stubbs

"She should be coming out of it pretty soon."

The nurse buzzed around the room and dimmed the lights. She tucked the sheets a little tighter, creating a cocoon around me, pointed a thermometer at my forehead and wrote notes on a chart.

Beige tinted light trickled through the crack in my eyelids. Too afraid to move anything but my head, I turned, wincing at the sound of hair scraping against starched cotton. I squinted, searching the breadth of my view, hopeful someone, anyone, would be there. Tightness wrapped my chest and the constant force of downward pressure created a dull throbbing ache, threatening worse to come.

"Hey, you're awake."

Ally, with her beautiful smiling face was standing over me.

"Would you like some water, Claire?" The nurse brought a cup and straw to my mouth, supporting my head. "The doctor says the operation went fine. They think they got everything, though we'll have to wait for pathology results to know for sure. Are you in pain?"

"Not... too bad... yet". My voice sounded raspy.

"Buzz me when you start to feel it. Better to have some meds and get on top of things from the start." She winked at Ally. "Alright, I'll leave you two for a bit. Going to see who my next victim is."

She chuckled as she left the room.

Ally leaned in and held me in the longest, gentlest hug, careful not to disturb my bandaged chest. I smiled at her but it may have been

55

lopsided. I didn't feel quite in control of my body. The nurse returned, mid hug.

"You two are sweet. Look really great together. It's nice to see partners who care for each other. Not like some of the poor women we see here. Going through it all alone because their lazy bum of a husband can't be bothered to visit."

Ally carefully released me and straightened up.

"Oh, we're not…"

The nurse kept going, attaching a blood pressure cuff.

"She's been here the whole time you know," she said to me. "I told her to go get coffee and come back later, but she wouldn't budge. You're lucky."

I opened my mouth but nothing came out.

"You're okay now, love," the nurse gave a reassuring pat on my arm. "We'll have physio round in the afternoon to get you up and about. Until then, just rest."

I smiled my thanks and she bustled out of the room again.

Ally sank back into the chair, out of my view. The bleep of machines filled the awkward silence.

She continued to visit me every day until I went home. But our conversations from that point on were safe and polite.

Two weeks after my mastectomy, I still struggled to find a position that let me sleep. A flat chest had shifted my centre of gravity and left me feeling exposed and vulnerable. Kenny growled, soft and low beside me, stretching his legs, then flipping onto his back. I lay straight as an arrow on the remaining quarter inch of vacant mattress. I stretched too, gingerly testing the healing progress of my stitches. Better than yesterday. A little itchy, even. A good sign.

I peeled back the cotton sheet and pulled myself upright, careful not to disturb my wounds. Kenny eyed me from his upside down perspective as I shuffled toward the mirror. Third day since the bandages had come off and still no redness. The anxious knot in my stomach relaxed a little. I resisted the urge to scratch.

"Looks good, boy."

He sat up on the bed, ears to attention, waiting for the magic word.

"Sorry Kenny." I ruffled his golden ears. "No w-a-l-k today. Still too sore."

He tilted his head and hazelnut eyes looked earnestly into mine. I couldn't resist scratching his belly. He grumbled again, still hopeful.

"Maybe later. Maybe we'll ask Ally to come over, hey?"

Ally was all he needed to hear. He jumped off the bed and trotted to the front door, whining and circling, pleading his case.

"Later. I promise." Later meant no, in Kenny's vocabulary. "It's only 4.30am. I can't call her now."

Kenny flopped on the lounge room floor, dramatically sighing his disappointment.

"We'll have to do something to thank Ally and her folks for looking after you while I was in hospital. Although I didn't hear them complaining. I think you were spoiled rotten by Emma and Peter."

He pled guilty with a single thump of his tail.

"I'm sure they'll have you stay over anytime. Perhaps Ally will find somewhere of her own and we can visit her. That'd be nice wouldn't it? I hope she stays in town."

Getting dressed was a ballet of slow, considered movements. I opened the back door to let in cool autumn air. My favourite time of year. Eventually, I felt brave enough to extend my corridor walk to the garden. Frequent stops to catch my breath gave me the chance to admire Ally's work. She came over every day, pulled a few weeds and walked Kenny. The pair had become firm friends and his tail lifted up high and proud whenever they went on a walk.

Lost in thought, I stooped to sniff a flower and received a vicious, blinding reminder the operation to remove my cancer was not that long ago. Kenny trotted out the back door to investigate my painful yelp and nudged my hand with his wet nose.

"I'm okay Kenny. But I think I should sit down for a bit." My breath was ragged as I slowly turned towards the safety of the back porch.

He was happy to take over my garden inspections and pounced on plants to chase out any skinks that were hiding. I passed the comfy reclining chairs and opted for an upright cane seat at the table. Pain rippled across the ribbon of stitching on my chest. Kenny returned, defeated, and settled next to the porch steps.

"What are we going to do Kenny?"

His ears pricked at the sound of his name. Not sure if he was in trouble, he gathered up long legs, sauntered over and slid his head onto my lap.

"Those bills inside aren't going to pay themselves."

Still uncertain, his tail started a slow side-to-side wag. Not his usual helicopter rotation when he saw his lead and my hat being collected.

"It's alright." My fingers scrunched his skin up and down in a mini massage and his face relaxed. He plopped his rump down and pressed his head a little heavier onto my lap.

"Looks like I'll have to find a job sooner than we thought. Peter said he'd see if there was free-lance writing work at the local paper but I think he was just trying to make me feel better."

Kenny's eyebrows rolled left to right.

"Don't look at me like that. I can't teach in this state. Don't even know if I'll be able to play the piano once I'm healed."

The jangle of the doorbell sent Kenny skittling through the doorway frantically searching for traction. I heard Ally talking to him. A smile curled my lips and excitement bubbled up from my suddenly nervous belly.

"God, Kenny, you scared the bejeezus outta me."

"Come in," I cried. "I'm out the back. Kenny! Settle down!"

Ally's perfume floated into the room and tickled my nose. Light musk with earthy floral undertones. I could soak in a cloud of it all day.

"Have you been a good boy?" She ruffled his ears as he slid his body against her legs. She had to brace herself in a wide stance, to take the force of his adoration.

"Yes, I'm excited to see you but first let me say hello to your mum."

"Kenny! Stop jumping around." I put on my stern voice, which he completely ignored. "Sorry Ally. Tell him to get on his bed."

"It's okay." She sat down next to me. Kenny was happy to lie between our chairs, confident an excursion was in his near future. My fingers knotted themselves with nerves.

"You know I adore taking Kenny for walks." We both flinched and looked in his direction but thankfully he was dozing and hadn't heard the magic word. "But I actually came to see how you were going."

I lamely smiled, hoping it was engaging enough for her to go on.

"How are your stitches?"

Oh, God, she expected conversation.

"Yeah, they're good."

Nicely done, you moron. Say something else.

"They're starting to get itchy."

Great. What a scintillating reply.

"That's good," she said. "No redness or swelling?"

"None. I'm really relieved."

"I bet you are."

"Did you want to look at it?"

What the hell! Who asks their unspoken love to look at their sunken bony chest, marred with puckered stitching serving as a jagged, lifelong reminder of the removal of their breasts?

"Yeah, I would actually. If that's okay?"

"There's nothing left to see, anyway."

Even I didn't know if my laugh was nervous or sad but Ally's face lifted into a small smile. Encouraged, I fumbled the buttons and folded one side of my shirt over to expose the carnage.

She leaned forward looking intently at my stitches.

"Heck of a boob job isn't it? I'm thinking of asking for a refund."

"Claire!" She erupted into a fit of giggles. "Stop it!"

I loved that I could make her laugh, at least. Ally reached out and carefully stroked the line of stitching.

"Do you have feeling there?"

"It's starting to come back."

"And the pathology results?"

"As good as can be expected. I had my check-up the other day and the doctor said he was satisfied there was no spread. I have to go on a special tablet that does something to my hormones, so the cancer won't grow back anywhere else. That's the theory, anyway."

"Good news at last." Ally's face relaxed. "Will there be any chemo?"

"No, they got it all and it hasn't spread to my lymph glands." I patted my hair. "My luxurious locks are safe."

"I'm so pleased". Ally leaned in and wrapped me in an awkward hug, which I didn't resist. Besides, my arms couldn't lift any higher, so they hung around her hips. Warmth spread through me, I hoped we could stay like this a while longer.

"So, what are your plans?" Ally pulled away and sat back down.

"I've been looking at my budget and I think I can save quite a few dollars, now that I won't be buying all those sexy bras I love."

That got her laughing again.

"Seriously though, I have to bring in some money. The bills are mounting and my savings are disappearing fast. I'm not really sure what I could do, though." My hands waved around my chest to emphasise my self-pity. "I mean, who would employ me?"

"Didn't dad say he could get you some freelance work?"

"Yeah, but it's not regular and I don't know there's much around. I think he was just trying to boost my spirits."

"What about teaching?"

"I'm not sure about that. I seem to have lost my confidence, along with a lot of my motor skills."

A warm flush of embarrassment reddened my cheeks.

"Aw, You'd be great," she replied with all the enthusiasm she could muster. "It wouldn't take much to get you set up and Dad could use his contacts at the paper to put an advertisement in. Mum and I would definitely put the word around school."

"Sounds like you've been thinking about this more than me," I said sheepishly.

"The town needs a music teacher and you'd have regular students bringing in steady income." She smiled excitedly, hoping for a matching response. "I know you can do it."

"I just don't know if I'm..." My voice trailed off. I looked down at my fingers, too ashamed to return her gaze.

"If you're what? What's holding you back?"

"I don't think I'm good enough." I needed to come clean. "I have a diploma but not an official *degree*." I made air quotation marks.

"So?" She refused to be deterred. It was one of the things I loved about her. "You'd probably make a better teacher than a lot of those who do. All you really need is the ability to connect and have a sense of what works with the kids. You've got that in spades."

She was beaming again and I couldn't help but smile back. Maybe she was right. Maybe I *could* do it.

"I suppose. I might check if anyone is interested."

"Of course they'll be interested. The parents of a few kids in my classes have been moaning about trying to find a decent music teacher. Now I can tell them."

"You're always so sure of things," I said admiringly.

"What do you need to get started?"

"An injection of confidence and a new body?"

"Get your thinking cap on, then," she giggled. "Cause I'm spreading the good news. Your phone is gonna start ringing off the hook."

"Okay, okay." I held up my hand in defeat. "Looks like we've got something to keep us busy now, hey Kenny?"

He jumped up at the sound of his name and wound around our legs, whining.

"Shall we go for a walk?" The upward inflection of Ally's voice hyped Kenny into overdrive and he spun his way to the back door. Ally detoured into the kitchen and retrieved a notebook from the junk drawer.

"Here you go. Get planning and I'll see you in a little bit."

Turns out Ally was right, as usual. Once I was sufficiently recovered, I had a string of eager students filing through my front door and my faithful upright piano was soon joined by a modern keyboard. Between lesson planning and sending out invoices, I didn't have much time to feel sorry for myself. Although, during the nights when sleep refused to come, I found myself pondering the same old question.

Could Ally and I be more than friends?

Ally had left a messed up marriage and landed back in her parent's house. Luckily, her mum, Emma, taught at the local school, so Ally scored a locum teaching job. Her Dad let it be known he was very happy his daughter was no longer married to 'that asshole.'

He and Emma would be happy if Ally settled here. I would be happy if she settled here too. But it was quite a leap to go from friends to lovers, when you'd known each other since school.

Still, I could dream. And I did.

Was I imagining the lingering touches of her hand against mine, the ones that made my stomach zing? Or the carefully guarded looks while she thought I wasn't paying attention? Or was it a pipe dream? It took both of us by surprise when the nurse assumed we were together, but Ally was quick to deny it. We hadn't talked about that moment since and I hadn't dared bring it up.

Until today.

Ally came over for her usual cup of tea, after school finished and before my afternoon piano lessons began. She looked on edge, hovering on the doorstep before finally striding in, as if she was about to make an announcement. She put the kettle on and fussed about searching for cups and biscuits, like it was the first time she'd been in my kitchen. Finally she sat at the table and gestured for me to join her.

"Are you alright?" I asked.

"I need to talk with you," she replied nervously. "About what was said at the hospital."

She wouldn't look at me.

"What do you mean?"

Yet I knew exactly what she meant and my stomach churned.

She took a deep breath and continued, throwing out words as if they were hot rocks she couldn't get from her mouth quickly enough.

"Am I the only one that remembers what the nurse said?" She laced and unlacing her fingers. "About how good we looked together?"

"Of course I remember," I blurted out. "Haven't stopped thinking about it since."

"Oh." Ally flicked a quick glance up at me. "I tried to tell her we weren't, you know?"

"Together?"

"Yeah, that."

My heart slipped out of my chest and landed in a steaming mound of I-told-you-not-to-get-your-hopes-up. Come on, you idiot. This is your chance to say something, save the day and win her over.

"You didn't ever think what it might be like?" I kept going, losing poise with every word. "You know, like, if it ever was, or could be, a thing?"

"I don't know" She shrugged and dropped her head. But not before I saw her blush.

She *did* think about us. I scooped my heart out of its pool of self-pity, wiped off the doubt and hoped it would shine.

"Because it probably would be quite nice." I stole a quick glance at her and kept going. "We've always got on pretty well and…"

Ally was staring at me, which I took as a positive. Or perhaps she thought I was nuts. Too late to back down now.

"You're beautiful, inside and out," I plunged ahead. "I would like it. Being with you."

I was lightheaded with joy at finally admitting my feelings and nauseous to the point I might need to run to the bathroom, for fear she would laugh at me. Or worse, get angry.

For a few moments, all we heard were the cries of laughter and friendly jibes as neighbourhood kids dragged their school bags up the street. Even Kenny was asleep at our feet, oblivious to the widening chasm of regret threatening to suck me in.

"I like you too, Claire."

My heart jumped.

"But things have been complicated. Jason is coming back into town…"

"So, you're going to go running back to him." I couldn't help my disappointed outburst. "Of all the stupid things to do."

Her eyes narrowed to angry slits.

"How dare you judge me like that?" She spoke quietly and deliberately. "You have no idea what's happening in my life. If you weren't so damn self-absorbed you might notice I have a few problems too."

"Last time I checked you still had both your breasts." I sounded like a petulant child. "Which I'm sure Jason will appreciate, just fine."

"I can't believe I open up about my life and you act like an ass about it. You've made your thoughts about my ability to run my life, very clear." Ally scraped the chair back and stomped towards the back door. "Your first student is here."

An afternoon of encouraging little hands to play music left little time to think. Truthfully, I didn't want to dwell on the mess I'd made of our conversation, and our friendship.

I didn't see Ally for days after our disagreement. Didn't know what I'd say if I did. I felt humiliated and bitter. Lashing out like a juvenile throwing a tantrum. But to be fair, what the hell was she doing hooking up with Jason again? He was bad news and everybody knew it. Ally was an emotional and financial wreck when she left him. He'd gambled their savings and, despite denying it, Ally was pretty sure he'd had an affair. Why would she go back?

A brooding storm cloud hovered above me as I walked through town. When I saw Emma, it was too late to dart into the nearest shop before she spotted me.

"Haven't seen you for a few days, Claire. Got time for a cuppa?" She linked her arm through mine and took my weak smile and lack of resistance as a yes.

"How are you? Music lessons keeping you busy?"

Emma obviously knew about my falling out with Ally. As mother and daughter, they were very close. But she was smart enough, in the ways of being a mum, to not broach the subject head on. She once said children, particularly adult children, were like deer in the headlights. You approach them indirectly so they didn't get frightened and run away. Emma was an expert at this parenting technique and I had acted like a child, so fair enough.

Our coffee was hot and we sipped in silence, peaceful in our thoughts for a minute.

"You look like you needed that." Emma gave me an encouraging smile.

"I did. Thanks for the invite. I've been a bit of a hermit recently."

I smiled sheepishly at her, hoping she would take this as an acknowledgement of my momentous stuff up with her daughter. I wondered what her view on it was. She had always been very generous to me, cheering me on from the side lines, when none of my family had bothered. But this was different. Emma would protect her child at all costs. I began to panic, wondering what she thought of the possibility of her daughter being with another woman.

"I haven't seen Ally about." I finally broached the subject. "Is she okay?"

"She's out of town for a few days with Jason."

I could feel a sulk settle on my face and instantly regretted my lack of self-control.

"You didn't let me finish." Emma shook her head. "Apparently it's a bad habit of yours."

"Sorry."

"I love you Claire," She raised an eyebrow. "But you're going to have to grow up a bit if you want to stand a chance with my daughter."

I gaped at her.

"I'm not silly. I've seen the way you look at her. It was adorable at first but now it's just frustrating."

My perplexed look made her chuckle.

"You remind me of Kenny when you tilt your head. But I'm hoping you've got more brains."

"Sometimes it doesn't seem like I do." I sat upright, hoping to give a more mature impression. But I'm pretty sure I looked even more like Kenny, when you asked him if he'd been a good boy.

"I need to apologise to Ally." I agreed. "I said some pretty disrespectful things. I'm not sure she'll want to see me again."

"She was upset and angry but don't write yourself off just yet. I think an apology would go a long way to getting your friendship back on track."

Emma looked at me intently and spoke a little softer.

"Claire, I say this with all respect. Isn't it about time you started to foster some self-belief? I know growing up was tough and your parents tried their best, but they didn't exactly teach you to be proud and to make something of yourself."

"No, not really."

Emma's straightforward way of presenting things started me thinking. Why exactly was I wallowing? I didn't have to forever be the daughter, left by her siblings to care for her ageing parents. There was no reason to continue living like a timid mouse, after they'd passed away. This was my life and I only had one shot at it.

"I know you've had a rough trot with the cancer, but you got through it. You're strong, Claire. I'm not asking you to forget it and get on with things. I'm asking you to look ahead. To see the happiness you could have. I know you'll always worry about the cancer coming back but don't let it consume you. Yeah?"

"You're the only person who seems to understand," I said. "Once you've had cancer, you're always looking over your shoulder."

I blinked hard, forcing the stinging tears down.

"It's okay to be afraid." Emma reached over, covering my hand with hers. "Just don't let it control you."

"Thank you" was all I could manage.

"Now let's get a plan of action going, because I can tell you this. I'm sick of Ally moping about the house like a wet rag."

"I thought she was back with Jason?"

"She *was*. To meet the solicitor and sign a property settlement to finalise her divorce, you daft thing."

My jaw dropped.

"She should be back this afternoon. It's been a long dragged out process but now she's considering buying a house and settling down here."

Emma squeezed my hand.

"I want my daughter to find someone who loves her, respects her and makes her happy," she said. "It doesn't matter to me if it's a man or a woman. I voted yes for the gay marriage bill for goodness sake. So if you want to be with Ally, you have my blessing."

"I don't know what to say."

"Whatever it is, say it to Ally." She pulled me into an embrace. "I swear to God if you mess this up, Claire, there'll be hell to pay."

"Emma, thank you. Thank you so much." I hoped she could hear me from within the jumble of jumpers and scarves, as she hugged the breath out of me. "I know I haven't always been the easiest person to get along with and I've been so preoccupied with my issues."

I mentally kicked myself.

"It must have been so tough for Ally. Listening to me and my problems, while dealing with the mess left by Jason. I hardly ever asked her how she was going."

"Why do you think she visited you every day?" Emma's face scrunched into a look of mild frustration. "Why do you think she looked at your stitches? Do you know she gets queasy at the sight of blood? That day she came home white as a sheet. Had to have a cup of tea with sugar and a lie down."

Emma laughed at the memory.

"She loves you."

Bubbles fizzed through my body and I thought I was about to faint. We both settled back into our chairs, smiling at each other. The Cheshire cat had nothing on us.

"Emma, may I call in to your place this evening?" I said formally. "I'd like to invite your daughter out on a date."

"Why wait until tonight?" Ally's voice came from behind me.

How to Slide on Rainbows

Sam Brown

Lacey stormed out of her house, silencing the blah blah blah with a slam. Couldn't they leave her alone, just for a while? Today, of all days? She marched to the old abandoned roller rink without planning it. She'd discovered a way to get in a few weeks ago and the acoustics were perfect. When she got there, her fury had faded to fire.

She threw her school bag over the fence, wriggled through the gap at the bottom and made her way to the fire exit, hidden behind an overgrown bush. Wiggled her ID card into the space between the lock and the door. She was always faintly surprised when the lock popped open. She half-expected the trick to fail someday, or for some boring adult to appear and turn her away. Good omen.

Lacey closed the door, made her way down the corridor to the rink and began to sing.

You don't have to feel like a waste of space

The sound shattered the silence and made her whole body smile. She dumped the schoolbag and kicked off her shoes. The wooden floor of the rink was smooth as glass; polished to perfection by thousands of hours of skating, in days gone by. In socked feet, she could glide across its surface like a dancer.

You're original, cannot be replaced

It was fun, skating madly around the oval, acting out the lyrics. She saw the music as cascades of colour in her mind.

Baby, you're a firework
Come on, let your colours burst

69

Make 'em go, Oh, oh, oh
You're gonna leave "em all in awe, awe, awe.

Bitter memories of the fight at home left her, as she chased the ascending notes. Her body followed, lissom and lithe as her voice. It was like sliding on rainbows. Why couldn't life be uncomplicated like this? Making a joyous noise, without a care what anyone thought?

As her sparkling vocals faded into the rafters, Lacey checked her phone.

Shit! She would miss the school bus if she didn't hurry. Not on the day the Grammy Academy auditions were announced! She skidded to her abandoned things. Mrs Malone would rip her a new one. Lacey pictured the old battle-axe: arms folded, eyes glowering. She moaned and sprinted back to the fire exit, throwing her bag back over the fence.

Racing to the bus stop, Lacey breathed a sigh of relief. The vehicle had been held up by some harried mother, struggling with a twin stroller. Good omen!

She smiled at the woman and lifted the other end into the bus, swiping her Transit card on the way.

"Excuse us, excuse us," she warbled, forcing reluctant commuters to make way and shrugging off the woman's thanks. She was so relieved not to be late, she smiled all the way to school.

Lacey's smiled faded as she approached the Home Room. Cherry West and her crew were gathered at the bottom of the stairs, near the piano cells. Could she go a different way? Too late. Cherry had seen her and her pouty lips curved into a predatory smile.

"Lacey."

It was more summons than greeting. Cherry considered herself queen of the senior class and most pupils went along with it. Some of the teachers too. Cherry's gaggle of loyal supporters turned to stare as Lacey reluctantly walked over.

"Like, Oh. My. God. Isn't today the worst?" Cherry fluttered, demanding she be the focus of attention. Obediently, her crew turned back. She was standing on the first step, forcing them to look up at her.

Entirely unnecessary, Lacey thought: she was like a sexy ginger giraffe, taller than almost everyone else.

"Ohmygod, Cherry," Ryan soothed. "You don't have to worry."

"No. You don't have to worry," Lacey echoed.

It was true. Everyone had expected Cherry West to go on to the Grammy Music Academy since the start of grade 7.

Lacey met Cherry's eyes. They were cold and hard. The ridiculous lips pouted, and Cherry stretched out her slender hand towards Lacey's middle.

"How's your tum-tum? Butterflies?"

The fake sincerity made Lacey want to punch her. Cherry's crew snickered.

She batted her hand away and pushed through the group, her face burning and, yes, her stomach churning.

Lacey sang before she spoke, her mother told people. That was how she remembered it too. Mum and Dad, singing with her, all the time. When Lacey was seven, they went to a Grammy Academy concert in a park. That was when she decided she wanted to perform and nobody doubted she could... until the first time she sang for a real audience. As she waited, watching the other performers, Lacey became gripped with certainty she would go down like a lead balloon. Instead, she had puked over the side of the stage and cried so much she couldn't go on.

It was always like that. Sometimes she got on stage and froze. Sometimes the effort to not throw up made it impossible to sing. She was fine in front of people she knew and trusted, but to get into the Academy she would have to audition properly, maybe even to an industry audience. The thought made her physically weak.

The bell rang and pupils obediently fell into place. Lacey submerged her anxiety under the banal routine of a typical Thursday morning: Homeroom, English, Business Principles. But it got harder as the minutes ticked closer to noon. She'd waited for this day for so long. What if her dream died here? Oh God. She popped open the mints in her pencil case and shook out a Valium tablet she'd hidden. There was always a risk it would knock her out but she couldn't cope otherwise.

Oh God, what if she didn't get in? Oh God, what if she did get in? What if she was offered a sponsorship and had to audition in front of even more strangers? She forced herself stop the panicky thoughts and breathe slowly out, then in. What was the teacher talking about? She glanced at her classmates, bored and unconcerned. She popped the tablet under her tongue.

Assembly time. Discord and disorder, like an orchestra tuning, one that magically settled into harmony once the senior teachers took their seats on the stage, and Ms Praeter strode up to the lectern. When she mentioned the auditions, Lacey didn't so much hear the words as feel a ripple of energy running through the room. Students craned to see where she and Cherry were sitting. The Girls Most Likely. Solitaire, on Lacey's right, nudged her.

"You got this," her friend whispered. Lacey merely grimaced.

"As you know admission to the Grammy Music Academy of is reserved for a very few, highly talented students from across the world. The yearly audition process is extremely selective and only the most promising are invited to apply for sponsorships. It is a matter of pride for this school that, in the past twenty years, we have produced a number of students who have attended the Academy, and even one who was awarded a sponsorship, now better known as the international recording artist Linda Millarre.

Ms Praeter paused for the whoops and applause.

Industry sponsorships pretty much guaranteed stardom. Better yet, all expenses were paid. You didn't have to tie to a label until later, but were pretty much guaranteed a contract. You had to be invited to apply, and then to audition in front of a panel of music industry executives, some live in the room with you, some watching via satellite.

It was Lacey's nightmare.

"As you know, this year, two senior students were put forward to the Academy. Never before has this school prepared two in one year." Ms

Praeter beamed with pride. "Today we find out the result. I am immensely proud of both young women for their hard work."

She waved an envelope aloft, lifted glasses that hung from a chain around her neck and peered through them. It seemed like an age until she spoke again. Civilizations rose and fell. Lacey stopped breathing.

"Oh my. The Grammy Music Academy has invited both students to audition for places. For the first time in the history of this school." She paused for dramatic effect. "Cherry West and Lacey Lumbly!"

At the Ch in Cherry, the queen's entourage erupted in squeals of delight, and the rest of the school followed with applause and cheers. Lacey's name was almost drowned out and, if it wasn't for Solitaire dragging her to her feet in a bear hug, she might have believed she imagined it.

I did it I got an audition. I got an audition, and I might get sponsorship.

It was outlandish. Unreal. But she was being jostled by her classmates' congratulations and there was Ms Praeter smiling down at her.

I did it, Mum. I can audition for a sponsorship.

But, despite the joy, her stomach was doing somersaults.

The afternoon was a blur of congratulations. Everyone seemed thrilled that Cherry would have competition. After school, a whole gang wanted to take her to the juice bar at the mall. Lacey let herself be swept up in their excitement: she didn't want to go home, anyway. At the school gates she passed. Cherry and ever-faithful Ryan, were climbing into a shiny Porsche SUV.

"Congratulations, Lacey." Cherry paused.

"Congratulations to you as well."

Cherry fake smiled, as she folded long limbs into the car.

"I'm just so grateful I don't have to worry about stage-fright."

Lacey pretended not to hear.

So many people turned up at the juice bar to celebrate Lacey's acceptance, she was amazed. Even Derek, though Lacey had been sure he fancied Cherry, like everyone else. But she couldn't catch the mood.

Her supporters' voices were drowned out by the memory of that cow's bitchiness.

I'm just so grateful I don't have to worry about stage-fright

She made her excuses and left. There were messages on her phone. Dad. Deanna. Congratulations. The school must have told them. She texted back.

My friends are celebrating with me. home by dinner XO

Instead she went back to the roller rink. She felt close to her mum there, not that they'd ever been to the place together. But mum loved the roller skating movie Xanadu; they had watched it on many rainy afternoons. When Lacey sang Olivia Newton-John's songs she could close her eyes and pretend her mum was singing along.

An everlasting world and you're here with me, eternally.

The day had left confused feelings crawling under her skin.

If only I had a magical muse to make me a success she wished, as she finally left.

She had barely opened the front door before Stevie rocketed over and clung to her like a limpet.

"I knew you would do it!" the eight-year-old screamed into Lacey's belly. It was impossible not to grin. Dad stood in the kitchen doorway, tea towel in his hands, pride lighting up his face. Lacey's grin grew. When Deanna stepped into view beside him, Lacey didn't even mind. At home with her family she could allow herself to celebrate.

"I did it!"

"I am so proud of you kiddo," Dad growled into her ear. He lifted her off her feet, like he'd done since she was a baby, and tickled her.

"I cooked your favourite, and Deanna picked up a cake from that bakery you like."

Stevie stuck a hand between them, holding up a card.

"I made this last week, that's how sure I was you'd get in."

"It's really just an audition." Lacey opened the card and laughed out loud at Stevie's hand drawn cartoon of her winning the Grammys. "I like my boots."

"Just nothing," Dad scoffed. "You've worked hard to get here. Your dream is within your reach! Be proud!"

He pushed her toward the dining room, dressed formally for the occasion with a Christmas tablecloth and folded paper napkins. A metallic ribbon spelling congratulations hung from the light fittings and helium stars floated above her chair. The best night for a long time.

She tried to hold on to that belief once she was alone in her room.

"Did it, Mum," she whispered.

But it was Cherry's voice that hissed back.

There's only room for one for one of us. You're going to fail.

It was hard to argue. Cherry had everything. The face. The name. The ridiculously long legs. The family connections. Lacey Lumbly had none of those things.

Next day, she took the route to the rink on purpose. She didn't want to see Charry and term was almost over. Nobody seemed to notice when she didn't turn up until lunch time. Being at school was stifling. People were all over her. There were only a few, like Derek, who she didn't mind.

As the days passed, she began to skip school altogether. Kept her skates at the abandoned rink. She tried to teach herself tricks by watching YouTube videos. She was getting quite good and going backwards was fun. She rehearsed for the auditions in solitude, relishing the sound of her voice in the rink. She pretended to herself this would be a good excuse, when she inevitably got found out.

"Skipping school is not OK, Lacey!" Deanna's voice was cut off by the slam of the front door. Lacey smirked as she marched down the street: some consolation, at least.

"This is not over!" This time Deanna followed her outside. The cheerful Indian woman at number 25 stopped piling kids into the car and stopped to look.

"Take a picture why don't you?" Lacey snarled. The woman looked taken aback. Something else to fume about: bloody interfering Deanna making a scene and upsetting the neighbours. Though she knew, deep down, she was just as much to blame.

Deanna's voice echoed in her head. Lacey tried to drown it out with Megan Thee Stallion, tinny from her phone, not loud enough to over-power the knowledge that Dad was going to be pissed. Or, worse: disappointed. The playlist shuffled to an angry anthem. Lacey focused on walking as fast as she could, channelling her anger and fear into screaming lyrics. It felt great. Resting afterwards, her phone pinged.

Where are you Lacey?

Dad. Shit.

Rehearsing with Solitaire XO

She knew he wouldn't believe her. The Daughter Who Cried Wolf. She watched the dots that indicated typing go back and forth. It took a long time but the message that eventually arrived was brief.

Be home when I get there.

She missed her mum so much sometimes she couldn't breathe. Why did her dad have to marry Deanna?

Her phone beeped again. It was Derek.

At the juice bar can you come?

Be home when I get there.

She couldn't face her father. She replied to Derek instead.

Sure XO.

Dad came to the mall, face like thunder and demanded she leave with him. She didn't argue. By the time they were alone in the car his anger was gone. Instead, he looked lost. Grey with grief like in the long, long months before Deanna. It hurt to watch.

"Dad," she croaked with a burning throat.

"You skipped your private coaching?" He blinked at her and shook his head. The air in the car was noxious with nervous sweat.

She had to look away. She couldn't explain that her body just carried her away from school. Couldn't say she was afraid to face Cherry or her teachers, and the certain knowledge she would fail. She pressed back tears.

"Don't you want to audition?" His voice was incredulous. "Going to Grammy Music Academy has been your dream since you were seven years old. Have you changed your mind?"

She shook her head.

"I know you get nerves, kiddo. That's why it's important to practise." His voice was softer now, and the energy in the car changed. Lacey looked at him and found the courage to speak.

"What if I fail?"

"I know it's a lot of pressure on you." His eyes were kind. "You can't just skip out though. It's disrespectful to your teachers and scares the hell out of me."

He fake punched her arm and smiled to lighten the mood. She rewarded the effort.

"I didn't mean to alarm you."

She willed him understand how scared she was. Scared of Cherry. Scared of not being good enough. Everyone knows she'll get in; she knows she'll get in. There's not room for both of us and she knows I'll blow it. *I* know I'll blow it.

Her father gave her a sad half smile and turned his attention to the car.

The next morning Lacey's voice was ragged. She guessed excessive crying did that. Dad dropped her at school, so she couldn't skip and Mrs Malone kept her back after Homeroom.

"What's going on with you, Lacey? Ms Praeter is asking and I don't know what to say."

The teacher sat opposite Lacey, looking her in the eye. Up close her skin was soft and her eyes were searching, not unkind.

"We can't both get in," Lacey croaked.

"Lacey, your voice! The trial audition is tomorrow!"

"I think I caught a cold," Lacey said quietly. "Probably won't be able to perform."

Mrs Malone's eyes turned hard, and her lips pinched. She stood and pulled out her phone.

"I am sorry, Headmaster, but Lacey Lumbly's ill."

Lacy heard stern mumbling from the other end of the phone.

"Yes, her trial audition is tomorrow, in front of school alums and board members: people with industry connections. Important people to the school.

"Her lips almost disappeared.

"Oh, I will, yes, thank you Head."

She put the phone in her trouser pocket and clucked at Lacey.

"Come with me and let's get you to the nurse."

Dad collected her from school, watched her like a hawk at home, and delivered her to the audition the next day. It was good to have an excuse not to talk.

"You've got this," he said as he left. Ms Praeter shepherded her to the Green Room to dress.

"You have every bit as good a chance as Cherry West," she cajoled. "Knock 'em dead."

A sceptical voice in Lacey's head whispered that her father and teacher were just being polite. She tried to ignore it.

All the skating meant her clothes were looser and the outfit carefully chosen for the audition now sat awkwardly. Lacey glared at her reflection in the Green Room mirror.

Everything is against you, the image wailed. Tears glinted in her eyes and both hands shook when she applied her make up. Her stomach cramped.

Not today. She breathed out, and in. Not today.

When the cramp passed, she took an anti-nausea wafer from its packet and slipped it under her tongue. Then a Valium tablet.

Ms Praeter escort her to the wings and they watched the end of Cherry's performance. Under the stage lighting, in a sequined sheath that made her look like a model, her red hair a fiery halo, she seemed every bit the star she believed she herself to be. Sounded like one, too.

Lacey's knees went weak. The dread certainty she was not good enough gripped her once more. As Cherry left the stage, she paused beside Lacey, towering over her on stiletto heels.

"May the best singer win," she murmured. "That's probably me."

Lacey's mouth was too dry to form a response. She reached for a water bottle and found she was clinging to one. As she chugged the drink, Ms Praeter stepped out to introduce her. Lacey fumbled the bottle, splashing water on her crotch. She looked around for a towel but Ms Praeter was calling her name. She stumbled inelegantly out onto the stage.

She blinked at the lights. Smile, smile. Her mouth was dry again. She licked inside her lips. Sing. Sing. Sing for your supper!

I know how to do this, she thought. Her hand brushed the wet patch on her crotch. Cold familiar dread. The music started. Counting in; 3, 2, 1.

"My mouth is dry again. Can I start over?" Lacey heard herself slur. Counting in again, she knew what was happening but tried to resist. She managed a few shaky bars, but her head was swimming. At the end of the first chorus, everything went black.

"My sincerest apologies." Ms Praeter stepped up to the microphone. "Lacy told us she was ill and we should never have persuaded her to go ahead."

An ambulance was called, and they took her in for observation. Dad was at the hospital with Stevie, worried.

"It's my fault," Lacey apologized. "I took a Valium. I knew there was a risk this might happen."

"The fact a girl your age felt she had to take Valium…" Her father shook his head. "Maybe this industry isn't for you. I don't want you to become Amy Winehouse."

"Yeah, Lacey. You have to be around to play with me!" Stevie added.

She was too weak to reply. She'd heard the arguments before. Talked about it with her counsellor. She felt most like herself when she was singing. Stopping wasn't an option. But how could she overcome this crippling stage fright?

The doctors gave her two days off school. Ms Praeter said the Academy was willing to give her another chance, but she had to decide whether to audition again or not, by the time she came back to school.

As soon as she could escape, Lacey went to the rink. She sang *Xanadu* softly as she laced up her skates. Maybe she didn't need the Academy? Maybe she could just be happy teaching singing or something.

She thought of the movie the song came from.

Where's my muse to show me what to do?

"Where's my Kira?" she asked the rink. The sound made her laugh. She often imagined she was Olivia Newton-John, in her flowy skirts while she was skating. Even though Cherry looked more the part.

Ugh! She pushed the thought aside. Refused to let her rival into this happy place. The rhythm of her skates on the rink put music in her mind and her voice responded.

Come take my hand
You should know me
I've always been in your mind
You know I will be kind
I'll be guiding you

Mum had loved the movie. They put it on every rainy day. After she died, Lacey didn't watch it again. Then she saw the rink from the bus and it drew her like a magnet. It didn't take a psychologist to figure out the connection.

From where I stand
You are home free
The planets align so rare
There's promise in the air
And I'm guiding you

As she glided across the wood, Lacey remembered the first time they watched *Xanadu*.

"I love Olivia Newton John," she'd said. "But who's the old guy dancing with her?"

"That's Gene Kelly," Mum had replied. "He used to get beaten up the other kids because he took dancing lessons. When he grew up and moved to Hollywood, critics said his athletic dance style would never catch on. Instead, everyone started copying it. When he began choreographing his own moves, he was told it would be a disaster. Instead, it made him one of the world's biggest movie stars. When he started to bring ballet into his routines, he was told it would sink his career. Instead he popularized ballet. When musicals started to fade, people said his career was over. Instead, he became an oscar-winning director.

"Wow!" Lacey breathed. "I didn't know."

"Olivia Newton John is beautiful and she can certainly sing," her mum smiled. "But that 'old guy?' Now he was a true original

A fundamental truth stopped Lacey in her tracks.

"Fuck Cherry." she laughed at the sound. "FUCK CHERRY WEST."

So what if she had all the legs? So what if she looked like a model? Cherry might resemble people's idea of a star, right now. But true stars are unique.

You're original. She smiled and shifted her weight, pressing the skates into action again.

A million lights are dancing and there you are, a shooting star.

She made a star of her body, leaning backward, hands high, drifting in a slow arc. Then she sang, because singing was who she was.

On the day of the audition, her throat was still sore. Her new costume hadn't arrived, yet she didn't care. She would sing in her street clothes.

Lacey faced the audience, half-hidden behind the lights. Her mind was alert, her heart full. She felt the music rather than heard it, closed her eyes and swam in a kaleidoscope of sound. She was at the rink, skating on rainbows. She imagined her mother in the audience.

Her muse.

She sang from her heart. Sang for her mum. Sang for herself.

At the end, she thanked her audience, though her words were almost drowned out by the rapturous applause. Even Deanna was clapping.

"Ladies and Gentlemen, I'm Lacey Lumbly."

She winked at her father, beaming from the front row.

"And there's never been anything like me."

New Places

Carrie Molachino

"Where is everybody, Mummy?" Maggie yawns. "Is the meeting still on?"

"I'm not sure love." I check the time on my phone again.

A burst of laughter drifts through venetian-clad windows. I crane my neck to see into the playground, where the other mothers stand chatting. Maybe I should have called to them before and reminded them of the meeting. Told them about the chocolate and champagne.

But shyness still plagues me in this new place.

I swivel back to the staffroom table, where I've decorated an arrangement of dark chocolates with raisins and rosemary sprigs. It's an explosion of colour, a children's fantasy come true.

"Can we go home, then?"

"We'll wait another few minutes, just in case."

Dark smudges under Maggie's eyes remind me of her sleepless nights. Settling into the new school. In the new place.

"Would you like to read some books?" I hand her a satchel and gesture to a bean bag in the corner.

Her eyes bulge with excitement as she peeks in, and the sight of her knock-knees and French braids almost makes me want to cry. How is it possible to love another human being so much?

I flick through my paperwork and re-read the notes. It might have been a mistake to hold the meeting on a Friday afternoon but every other day is a workday for me. With a heavy sigh, I slump over the table and rest my chin on one hand. Pinned to the noticeboard, a multi-coloured

83

banner says *Choose Positivity*, hemmed in by an anti-bullying poster and an advertisement for the teacher's union.

Movement outside catches my attention. A man with a long scraggy beard is crossing the assembly area. I've seen him wandering around the school occasionally, keeping to himself.

Surely he's not planning to come to this meeting? Surely, he'll make a left turn towards the carpark.

He keeps walking in my direction. A burst of claustrophobia grips me, and I have the sudden urge to run.

Please don't come in. Please don't come in.

He steps into the doorway.

"Is this the meeting for the chocolate fundraiser?" The kneecaps of his jeans are worn to threads and I'm mesmerised by the hair there. That is, until my eyeballs are assaulted by the fluorescent-green of his joggers.

I nod, and he gazes at me with piercingly blue eyes.

"Mind if we join?"

A girl screeches past him, wearing a superhero cape, her auburn hair spilling out of a lopsided piggy-tail.

"Sure." I should probably say something more welcoming, but words stick in my throat.

"Hello Maggie!" The superhero looks overjoyed to see my daughter.

Over in the corner, my daughter's eyes are filled with horror. The superhero flies up and stands so close to me, one of her shoes sits top of mine. She looks up and smiles so exuberantly it seems like her face might break in two.

"We're getting a new puppy!"

"Hey now." Blue-eyes gives me a wink. "I said we'd look into it."

Surely such an important decision needs to be handled with great responsibility. I give the bearded man a judgemental frown but my disapproval goes unnoticed. Instead, he dazzles me with a smile. His teeth are quite lovely, all straight and white and sparkly.

"I'm Dale."

"Sally," I say breathlessly.

He reaches over the little girl, still standing on one of my toes. I hesitate for a second before shaking his hand. His grip is strong but gentle, and when my eyes meet his, it's like staring into the depths of the ocean on a sunny day.

I remove my foot from under the tiny superhero's. She pirouettes to the right, then swan-dives away.

"This is my daughter, Courtney." Dale tilts his head in the girl's direction. She is now standing on a table and I point, so he can tell her to get down.

"She's always doing that," he grins. "Thinks she can fly."

My lips purse at his lack of discipline.

"You expecting many to show up?" He looks around.

"I was hoping for more than two." I glance through the blinds, where another burst of laughter erupts from the self-assured women.

"They're not a bad bunch," he says. "They'll do their bit when it comes to the fete. Great cause by the way. To raise emergency funds for families in need?"

I nod, still lost for words.

"It's good of you to take this on." Dale studies me intently. "Especially as you're so new here. Maggie only started in the middle of term?"

He waits for me to answer.

"I think communities should help those doing it tough." I re-position a stray rosemary sprig. "Plus I have a selfish reason. I'm using it as an excuse to get to know people."

Dale's eyes flick towards the empty chairs and I blush.

"It's nice to meet someone so compassionate," he says eventually. "Seems a rare trait these days."

A tugging at my skirt alerts me to Maggie's presence.

"Mummy." Her bottom lip wobbles. "I don't like Courtney."

"Sweetheart," My cheeks heat even more. "That's not a very nice thing to say."

Dale watches me with a half-smile and a twinkle in his eyes.

"Sometimes people have different... styles and... personalities," I continue. "We should learn to accept that and try to get along."

"She put a spider in my hair."

Wait-a-minute, this is the kid that put a spider in my little girl's hair on her first day!

"That was a horrible thing to do." I glare at Dale, my jaw clenching as I remember Maggie's chest heaving with sobs. Now I've witnessed the father's lackadaisical approach, it explains a lot.

Courtney leaps off the table, her superhero cape flying. Down on the carpet, she does a rolling somersault then crawls, commando-style under, another table. My shoulders sag. She's just an innocent child, poor little thing. It's not her fault she's starved of parental guidance.

"I hope it wasn't a real spider." Dale smiles angelically. "She had this fake one she carried around for months. I had to confiscate it in the end. Broke her little heart."

He clutches his chest dramatically. Courtney cartwheels over to Maggie and yanks her blonde braid affectionately, making me flinch.

Still Dale does nothing to stop her.

I let out a huff. I need to get Maggie far away from this spider-wielding supervillain.

"We should get started on the meeting." I sit down and glance at my notes, trying to keep the girls in my peripheral vision. "I've calculated we'll need about a hundred and fifty boxes for a school this size..."

Nerves cause my voice to squeak. I'd imagined a table full of mothers when I rehearsed this spiel, not some sparkly toothed, laissez-faire boho. I choose to ignore his mischievous, half-smile.

"We'll need to confirm the timeline and get some dates in the calendar." I slide ordering forms, tally sheets and templates across the table. "We'll give each classroom a list of instructions and an outline of dates. Does that all sound okay?"

"Perfect."

I blush, despite myself. I seem to be pathetically pleased by his enthusiasm. I must be starved of affection.

"This looks amazing." He scans the table.

If it weren't for the shaggy beard, he'd be really rather cute. His casual but positive attitude is growing on me and I'm struggling not to like the guy.

"I'm impressed," he says. "Shame there aren't more people here to enjoy this."

I'm suddenly self-conscious about all the effort I've gone to. Trying too hard is a character-flaw. Or so I've been told, many times.

"At least it means more for us, eh?" When he grins again, I soften a little more. "And you've brought excellent refreshments."

His eyes slide to the champagne bottle, sitting in a cooler bag.

"This is the best fundraising meeting I've ever been to."

"I don't think..."

But he's already leaning across the table. He pops the cork and pours the bubbly into two plastic champagne flutes, filling them to the brim. I take the glass that he hands to me, and a spark of electricity zaps where his fingers brush mine.

"To the Chocolate Fundraising Committee of 2021!"

"Cheers." I glance around guiltily.

"Come try some chocolate, girls." He waves an arm at them and my eyes are drawn to the well-defined muscles under his sleeves.

The girls cheer and move over to the table. Wait-a-minute... when did they become best friends?

Maggie climbs delicately onto a chair, while Courtney bounces onto the one next to her, like she's leaping a skyscraper.

"The children's section is this end." My voice is still a bit squeaky.

Maggie's eyes light up as she surveys the table. She picks out three chocolates, arranges them neatly on her plate and takes a dainty nibble of one. Next to her, Courtney stuffs the pieces into her mouth in one go. She laughs and a bit of chocolate spit goes flying.

"This one's got a kick." Dale eyes me over the top of his glass and my stomach does a somersault. I wonder what his face is like under that mass of hair. I take a bite of rosemary-infused chocolate.

"Oh, wow, this is really good."

"You need to try the rum and raisin." I realise his voice is melodic and polished, at odds with his dishevelled appearance. Down at the children's end, the girls squeal with laughter. Their faces and hands are smeared with melted chocolate and smudges cover their uniforms. Maggie is happy. I'll worry about the stains later.

"Excuse me." A high-pitched, nasal voice drifts in from the doorway, where a stern-looking woman is hovering.

"Are you here for the fundraiser meeting?" I belatedly notice Dale giving me a warning headshake.

"In a way, yes." The woman floats in.

"Please, sit down." At least there'll be a third person to share the workload with.

"I'm not staying. I just wanted to let you know that I'll be making an official complaint." She surveys the table with revulsion. "I thought I should let you know. Out of courtesy."

I frown, trying to process her words.

"We have enough obesity problems, without encouraging children to eat unnaturally sweet, artificially processed foods." Her lips curl.

"Um..."

"You don't have to respond." She holds up a hand. "Although I wouldn't count on getting P&C funds to order the chocolate." She narrows her eyes at my empty champagne flute, and the girls' smeared faces.

"But it was approved at the last meeting," I object.

"By who?"

"Everyone?"

"I'll be checking the minutes to confirm that." Her lips tighten, as she walks out.

I glance over at Dale and give a nervous chuckle. He stifles a laugh of his own. The girls join in, not really knowing what they're giggling about but not needing much excuse.

Yet worry starts to niggle.

"Do you think she'll cause a problem?"

"Like you said, it was a unanimous vote. I say we make a decision before the end of today and place the orders on Monday morning. Donna's well known around here for giving the tuckshop grief." He shrugs. "She means well, though."

It's the second time he's used this phrase. Does he not have a nasty bone in his body?

"I won't be able to get to it on Monday. My job…"

"I'll take care of it." He waves a hand, casually. "My hours are flexible and I often work from home."

I let out a breath. It's nice knowing I'm not alone.

"Thank you. That's… well. Thank you."

"I think you should come to my place," he says.

"What?"

"It's only a block away. We can sample more chocolates there and make decisions without being interrupted."

My heart starts to hammer. I don't know this unshaven man. Would it be crazy to go to his house?

"There's no jealous wife or girlfriend to worry about, in case you're wondering."

I look out at the playground, empty now except for a black crow pecking at an abandoned lunch box. I glance at my daughter, smiling as she licks the face off a chocolate bear.

"Let's do it."

We pack the tablecloth, plates and cups into my car and walk to Dale's house. He carries my laptop bag, chocolates and champagne, like they weigh nothing.

I study his physique from behind. I'd expected him to be wiry, but though his waist is narrow, the shoulders are broad and muscular. His longish hair is held together with a band, like a character on the cover of a cheesy romance. I can't seem to match the body with the hair.

The girls tumble along the grassy footpath chattering continuously. Then they burst into song.

"We're going on a bear hunt."

"We're gonna catch a big one."

"I'm not scared."

"What a beauuuutiful day!"

When they reach the end of the tune, Dale puts down the bag, bares his teeth in an angry snarl and throws his hands up. "Raaaaaaaagh!"

The girls scream and roll about in hysterics. When was the last time I saw Maggie so relaxed?

Dale slows at a recently renovated house, backing onto the river. The front lawn is a little dug-up and a couple of paint cans sit on a piece of scaffolding near the fence. Still, this place must be worth a fortune.

"Don't worry, I'm not breaking and entering. It's mine."

I manage a weak laugh. The old me would never have been intimidated by someone because of their financial situation.

I miss old-me.

Maggie rips her shoes off at the door, but Courtney runs in with hers still on.

"Come and look at my superhero cave, Maggie!"

I go to follow but stop in my tracks.

It's a disaster zone.

A cubby house made of blankets spans one half of the living room. A tricycle, a baby doll pram, a skipping rope, and a half-built Lego castle litters the rest of the floor. It reminds me of a war-torn battlefield. My ex-husband would have had a fit. A wave of dizziness sweeps over me and the strength goes from my legs.

"Are you okay?"

"Yep. Just..."

"Here, sit down." Dale guides me to the table and pulls out a chair. "I realize the place is a bit of a mess."

He stares at me, blue eyes filled with concern.

"Sorry about that. Probably just low blood pressure." It's too embarrassing to admit that his messy house almost caused me to have a panic attack. "Happens sometimes. Nothing to worry about."

The sight of his kind face defuses the tension and I feel weirdly okay. In fact, I feel more than okay.

Because this is a home. The mess is only made up of toys and I realize Courtney is one of the happiest children I've ever met.

"I'll get you some water." Dale looks unconvinced. "Maybe you haven't eaten enough? Could I fetch you some crackers and cheese?"

He moves to the kitchen. Through the doorway I see it is sparklingly clean.

"Please don't go to any trouble. I'm perfectly fine."

Except for my fingers, which are itching to tidy up. I clasp them in my lap.

"No trouble." Dale brings over a board laden with cheese, a box of crackers and two glasses of water. He puts them down on the coffee table and I catch a whiff of his deodorant. Or maybe it's the soap he uses. Whatever the smell, it's intoxicating.

"Really. I'm okay."

His concern is so endearing, I'm compelled to explain.

"My ex-husband had a bad temper and was OCD about mess. I just had a minor... flashback."

I try to sound flippant, but my voice wobbles.

"I'm so sorry." He looks appalled. "Is that why you moved here? To get away from him?"

"It's not like we're on the run, or have to keep our identities secret." I try to make light of the situation. "I'm not frightened or anything. I'm mainly just wary of myself. Of being weak enough to get lured back."

"You still see him?"

"I've got full custody, so no."

"That's pretty intense."

"I'm alright now, thanks to a few hundred psychology sessions." I smile but, for once, he doesn't see the funny side.

"So things are definitely okay?"

"Fully recovered and one hundred percent stable." I realise I'm describing my mental health, when he was probably just wondering if I was physically all right.

We sit in silence, sipping our water. I look beyond the mess - which I'm miraculously able to ignore now - out to the river behind his house. The setting sun twinkles lazily on the surface, its reflection broken by ripples. At the other side, a mass of giant gum trees cast shadows over the choppy water. How luxurious it must be to have such privacy and tranquillity in your own backyard.

I think of the dingy rental property I share with Maggie. The stained carpet, torn fly screens, taps that drip, pipes that creak in the night and the noisy neighbours we share a fence with. Still, I'd rather be poor than feeling on edge all the time.

"I guess we should get back to business," Dale says.

"Of course." I'd almost forgotten why I was here.

He unpacks the contents of my bag and carefully arranges the chocolates on the table. I realize he's trying to replicate the set-up I had at school. It's such a sweet gesture my eyes well with tears.

I feel a genuine affinity for this kind and caring man, with his laissez-faire style. The way he values fun over rules and routines.

"I wish I could be more like you." The words tumble out before I realise what's happening. "I have this strict routine, and every day I write a list with tick-boxes. I iron on Sundays, have a menu plan for the week and vacuum each evening. I don't even know why - it's not like the place looks any better for it. And I always put toys back in the cupboard."

I glance at his living room.

"Always."

"Now you're just bragging," Dale laughs. Then he seems to give my confession real thought. "Maybe you were running on adrenaline for so long, you still have a lot of it in your system. You haven't quite realised it's okay to finally let your guard down."

"That makes sense." For the first time, I blame myself less for my predicament. "Thank you."

When was the last time I had a conversation like this with another adult? I pick up a piece of the rum and raisin chocolate and slip it into my mouth. He pours more champagne.

"I think we should order half the adults-only boxes and half the children's variety packs. It's an easy decision, really."

He hands me a glass.

"Then we can spend the rest of the evening relaxing and enjoying ourselves."

As I sip, my eyes settle upon a photo on the sideboard. A younger, chubbier version of Courtney sits on a park bench with two glamorous adults, arms wrapped around her in an affectionate embrace.

Dale follows my line of vision.

"That's my wife and I, two years ago, not long before she died. Her name was Celia."

His voice cracks as he says the name. He turns in his chair and faces sideways, feigning a sudden interest in the river. I stare at the handsome man in the photo.

"I haven't shaved since the day she died," he says. "Or cut my hair."

"Why not?"

"Some things, I just let slip." His words are thick with emotion. "Priorities… maybe. How I looked didn't seem important anymore."

I can't seem to find the right words, so I put my glass down and walk around behind him. His body is rigid. He might be crying but I can't see his face from where I'm standing.

"This is embarrassing," he laughs weakly.

"I feel silly talking about my own situation now," I say quietly. "It seems pathetic in comparison."

Losing someone you love like this must be torture. If anything ever happened to Maggie... The notion fills me with gut-wrenching terror.

He turns, grabs hold of my arm, and the same current of electricity runs between us.

"Don't be sorry," he says. "I'm sick of everyone tip-toeing around me. It's a relief knowing I'm not the only one with problems."

He flinches.

"My turn to apologise. Sounds like I'm happy to see someone else suffering."

"No, I get it. It's hard to be around people and pretend you're okay when you're not."

"Maybe we can be sad together."

I stare into his blue eyes and have the craziest urge to lean in and kiss him. I breathe in the masculine scent and glance down at his chest, suddenly wanting to know what it looks like underneath his shirt.

I startle, as I remember we're not alone.

Inside the cubby house the girls are quiet and have been for some time. Then there's a whisper.

"Go on, show them."

"What's going on girls?" Dale asks. There's more whispering and giggling, and finally Maggie steps out of the cubby house.

With only half a head of hair.

I stare at her stupidly. Where's the rest of it? Have they tied it up somehow? I crane my neck and squint. My hand shoots to my mouth.

Courtney has cut Maggie's hair.

"Oh, shit," Dale groans.

"Do you like it Mummy?" Maggie beams.

"I'm...so sorry about this." Dale's eyes are wide and all colour has drained from his face.

"Her hair is a mess! How am I going to fix this?"

"I think it looks... good?" he croaks. "Modern?"

My heart races and my fists clench. She'll be teased! She'll be bullied! I regret telling Dale I wanted to be like him. I don't want this at all. I want us to be left alone. I want us to be safe.

I want my baby girl's hair back.

"It's all very well to give up caring about rules and responsibilities, but I don't have that luxury." My voice goes up an octave and I take three steps backwards. "I don't live in some fancy house on the river. I'm in a dumpy rental property, which I have to fight every day to pay for!"

Maggie's shoulders begin shaking and tears pour down her face. The sight of it is a million times worse than her shaggy hair.

"I'm so sorry... mu... mummy." She lets out a pitiful sob.

"Oh darling. I'm sorry too." I rush over and wrap her in a tight hug. "If you like your new style, then I do as well."

The haircut seems suddenly inconsequential.

I notice Courtney standing by quietly, her little green eyes filled with anguish. She darts away and Dale follows her out the room. When she returns, she's holding a photo and sucking her thumb. She looks so pathetically vulnerable my chest hurts.

She hands me the picture. It's her mother. Celia's hair is cut in the same, short-cropped style as Maggie's is now.

I'm so overwhelmed, it takes me a minute to speak. The room is silent and tense.

"She's beautiful," I tell Courtney. "And you're right. It's about time Maggie had a haircut."

"You know what?" Dale says. "While we're having makeovers, I think Sally should shave me. A trim wouldn't go amiss, neither."

"What?" My eyes widen.

"As atonement for my irresponsible parenting." A roguish smile crosses his face. "What does everyone think? Should Sally get rid of my beard?"

Maggie and Courtney leap about screaming, "Cut it off! Cut it off!"

"I wouldn't know how," I stammer.

"Do it! Do it!"

It seems the decision is made. A sense of excitement fills the air as Dale and Courtney fetch the necessary equipment. I'm struck by the gravity of what's about to occur.

My pulse is racing at the thought of touching Dale's face, of seeing what is underneath. Of meeting the charismatic person in the photo.

He's a handsome, successful man, who lives in an expensive house on the river. I'm a single mother living in a run-down rental property. But, I'm no longer worried about the balance of power. In the short time that I've come to know him I've witnessed more compassion, kindness, forgiveness - more unconditional acceptance - than I did in five years of marriage.

I wipe clammy palms on my skirt.

Ten minutes later I'm sitting opposite Dale, scissors shaking in my hand. I don't know if I'm nervous because I'm so close to him, or because I've never shaved anyone before. I inhale his fresh, citrusy scent. The beard is soft under my fingers. It's the first time I've touched a man in two years. My stomach is filled with butterflies. I lift my hand to start.

He grips my wrist.

"I don't want to be stuck in this place anymore." His blue eyes are almost pleading. I know that he's not talking about a physical place, but an emotional one.

I know this because I understand exactly what he means.

"Nor do I."

We inhale in unison, then breathe out slowly.

"It's time to move on." He blinks.

We nod together.

I start snipping with trembling fingers. Clumps of his beard fall to the towel on his lap. I'm so near I can see the rise and fall of his chest, but I need to get closer. I splay my legs around his knees. I'm so close to his mouth that if I leaned in a fraction, I could kiss him.

I almost do.

My breath is fast and shallow. After a while I lean back to survey my work, biting my lip in concentration. I'm starting to see the shape of his chin now. His features are strong and angular. He looks more imposing. He looks... magnificent.

"You realise I have no idea what I'm doing."

Having lost interest, the girls are eating chocolate again. My daughter looks like a scruffy, mischievous, wonky-haired pixie. Happier than I've seen her in years.

My hands shake as I glide the blade along the skin of Dale's jaw. Down at his neck, I'm careful around his Adam's apple, which bobs as he swallows. I finish the last swipe of the blade.

"Thank you," Dale says.

He's not thanking me for shaving his face but for something far more significant.

I stare at his blue eyes and see into the soul of a man I can trust.

Ghosts and Stolen Kisses

Louisa Duval

"There's a dead cat in the local pub's cellar!" my business partner panted on the phone.

"Hello, Charlie. I'm well. My mum is doing great and my brother moved back home yesterday."

"A dead cat," He repeated. "Mummified. On Halloween."

The biggest day of the year for ghost stories was Halloween and for the last three weeks, the lead up to All Souls Night had been nuts.

On top of our filming schedule, Mum had broken her ankle while out feeding the cows. I'd dropped everything to head to our family farm-cum-chocolate shop just outside Ballydoon.

Somehow, in the craziness of running Mum's shop, while helping her around the house, I travelled three hours each week down the highway to Queensland University. Taught fifteen hours of tutorials over two days and sat in on two lectures. Then back to make batches of white chocolate spider web truffles, late into the night.

"Did you get me any of your mum's pyramid truffles?" Charlie asked with a reverent whisper. "And Jaffa balls?"

"Yes. Because I'm thoughtful like that."

"Oooss! So, your mum's good, your bro is good. Focus, Matty: Mummified cat that looks to be part of some kind of weird ritual. It's going to be all over the news tonight. The archaeologist investigating the find is... eh.. Jess."

My heart-rate ramped up. Jessica Knight; historian, lecturer and, technically. my boss. Jessica Knight, the woman who'd slept with me and ran. It was a month ago, at the Faculty Ball, before broken ankles and broken hearts. The memory was still vivid. Drinking champagne together, then sneaking into a hotel storage room with her and having the best sex of my life.

I swallowed hard. "She's in my hometown?"

"Faculty email says she arrived yesterday. Media are going to want a piece of the dead puss, I tell you. Where are you? The shop?"

"I'm in the heart of the thriving metropolis of Ballydoon.

"So you're at the pub. Excellent."

"I was just on my way to the cemetery to get some stills and do a teaser for tonight."

"Look, I can handle this if…"

"I'll do it," I said, my voice rough. "It's been fine. I'm fine. Completely fine."

Too many fines.

"Get your butt inside, then." Paper rustled and Charlie's office chair squeaked. "A reporter rang asking for an interview with *The Spectre Inspector* about the Ballydoon Bandit and the dead cat. This will be great for our views on social media. We might finally get a sponsor for our channel."

"Why is Jess investigating a dead cat in our local?"

"I'm not talking about some moggy who snuck in under the flagstones. It was deliberately killed and placed with coins and a small bottle."

The metallic grind of Charlie's ancient office chair was the only sound on the phone.

"There's an old East Anglian tradition of interring a cat when laying the foundation of a building," I said.

"Yep! And you just don't find this sort of thing often in Australia. Our local pub cellar, which nobody knew existed until the revocations uncovered it a few days ago, has been a tomb for one hundred and seventy years - for spiders, rats and one moggy. Add that to the stories of the Ballydoon Bandit and you've got ghost central, mate. Are you're arguing this is, somehow, not as good as going to yet another cemetery on Halloween?"

I sighed. The Ballydoon Bandit was a bushranger who had died in a fire at the pub, years ago. Now his spirit was supposed to haunt the place, wailing loudly. Probably because of the prices. It was a nice story but it had been done to death, excuse the pun. But the cat was new.

"All right. I'm convinced."

"Shit, there's one more thing. Jan-Andrew just posted on Facebook and Instagram that he's in Ballydoon for an amazing ghost story, complete with a selfie in front of the pub."

I swore and spun around, searching the footpath and the street for any sign of the ghost hunting copycat who was poaching our audience.

"I can't see him."

"Check inside. You can't let him outscoop us!"

"Yeah. That's not a word." I hung up.

Jan-Andrew, the 'Ghost Host'. Our competitor, self-proclaimed fashionista and pompous git. He was always reminding me I had a Doctorate to his PhD, knowing full well I exited my studies due to having no scholarship and needing to pay bills and eat. Jan-Andrew had researched the Ballydoon Bandit as his PhD topic. Of all the bushrangers in all the pubs in Australia, he picked my hometown.

But my YouTube channel, 'The Spectre Inspector', had steadily grown since launching seven years ago. Right now, I'd rather meet the ghost of the Ballydoon Bandit, then let him take this story from me.

I pushed through the front door of the pub. I had to find Jess and the mummified moggy before Jan-Andrew.

Mummified Moggy, not bad. Better than a dead cat.

The bar was empty, unusual for 3.16 pm on a Sunday. Not one local was propped up on a stool with a schooner of beer.

Oh. Not entirely empty. A cat watched me from the counter.

Its markings were disturbingly distinctive. Black, save for a patch of white hair on its chest and white on its cheeks and nose, the latter the shape of a cock and balls. The cat literally had a dick on its face.

My shoulders shook as I tried to contain my laughter.

It stared at me, unblinking and unfazed.

"Can I help you?"

I jumped, spinning around to face the far side of the public bar. John Carpenter, the pub owner, strode across the room and shook my hand.

"I'm looking for Jessica Knight." My voice squeaked like a teenager, as if I was asking the father of my crush if I could speak to his daughter. Bloody hell.

"Apparently, there's a media conference about a dead cat in the cellar."

"Matty Cavanagh," he said, recognising me. "Ballydoon's very own ghostbuster."

"Strictly speaking, I'm a historian and tutor at the university. Spooky videos pay the bills, though."

John was not amused, much like Dickface McWhiskers before him.

"How's Glenys? I haven't seen your mother in a bit."

"Yeah, um, Mum's doing well."

"Heard Josh came back."

"Spent yesterday helping him move in. I'm looking forward to Josh taking over chocolate making, to be honest. My kitchen skills are average at best."

"You did good, dropping everything to help your mother," he said, "Good to have Josh home, too. So, you're involved with young Jess?

"I wouldn't say involved, exactly. It was a onetime thing and she ghosted me right after…"

"I meant, are you colleagues with Miss Knight? She said she was with the university."

"Oh! Yes." My cheeks burned. "I'm her tutor for subjects at university."

Just what I needed before I was about to do a piece to camera: a bright red face and confessing my botched attempts at romance to the towns best placed gossip.

I cleared my throat nervously.

"I'm here to record videos about ghost stories and any reported paranormal activity for Halloween. This find is of interest to our channel as the mummified cat suggests protection against witchcraft."

John's eyebrows shot up.

"The young lady didn't mention witchcraft," he frowned. "Mind you, I didn't even know I had a cellar until two days ago. You remember the Turners from school?"

"Yeah, course. Josh was in the same grade as Stacey Turner. Ran into her at the general store last week."

"Stacey's an interior designer these days. Hired her to redecorate the public bar. Found a manhole-type trapdoor when we ripped up the lino. Been pandemonium ever since."

John paused behind the bar and I couldn't help looking around for that black and white moggy. Nothing. Not even a hair on the bar where it had been sitting.

"Do you have any reported sightings of ghostly cats?" I asked

"Course not. Unless you want me to say there is." He winked at me. "Might be good for business."

He bent over a square hole in the floor.

"Looks like Jess is out of the cellar. Probably dealing with the press in our dining room." He straightened. "You with the other fella who has an internet show?"

"Tall guy? Well dressed. Wears sunglasses inside."

"That's him."

"Absolutely not."

Mr Carpenter held my gaze for several seconds.

"Good. He's a wanker."

I spluttered a laugh, but he continued in a low voice.

"Speaking of wankers, journos are all over the place. Local TV news, and ABC radio too. Bit of a big deal, this dead cat."

I followed down the hallway and into the dining room. Jess was in her dig clothes; work pants, steel-capped boots, a flannel shirt and beanie with a pom-pom on top. A far cry from the Faculty Ball. There, she'd worn a stunning red dress that hugged her every curve, with her long brown hair gathered in waves, cascading down her back.

In either outfit she was stunning.

"Should've known *you'd* turn up." A smarmy voice said.

It was Jan-Andrew, still wearing his sunglasses and sporting a pork-pie hat.

"What are you doing in my hood?" I snapped.

"Now, now," he tutted. "I'm sure we can all share a bushranger and some fossilized feline. I simply volunteered to help Jess with the press."

"Jess has done heaps of interviews before. She's a pro."

"I'm paying tribute to her," my nemesis chuckled. "She's done well."

His condescension made me curl my hands into fists. I exhaled on the count of three and loosened my fingers, as a journalist with a dazzling white smile caught my eye.

"The Spectre Inspector! Great show five weeks ago with the haunted pancake house in Brisbane. Widows throwing themselves off the roof in grief, my god!" He extended his hand to me. "Terry Schultz, local news."

I shook his hand, as Terry called out, "Jess, darling! Let's get you set up here with the ghost hunters."

"Paranormal history specialist," I muttered as Terry ushered her over.

She briefly met my eyes. I swear I saw a flash of hunger, then hurt, before she shuttered her features into a neutral expression.

Jess Knight: Ice Queen.

I still had no idea why I was getting the cold shoulder. She was the one who'd left me high and dry, after we'd had the hottest sex of our lives. Or, at least, I had. But she'd avoided me ever since.

I steeled myself and faced to the camera. Jess Knight, and Jan-Andrew were not ruining this for me or our audience.

"Live cross in three minutes," one of the crew called out. Terry preened himself in a hand mirror while Jan-Andrew moved away, talking on his phone, trying to sound important.

Jess shifted on her feet, holding a small earthenware bottle in her gloved hands.

"Congratulations on the dig," I said. "If this is a witch bottle, you've identified a momentous find."

"Thank you." She seemed surprised by the compliment. "Terry wants to do a live opening of the bottle tonight."

A waitress appeared in front of us, hip cocked to the side and ample cleavage on show.

"Want some water before your interviews?" She narrowed her eyes at me and then smiled. "Oh my god, Matty Cavanagh. I remember you from high school."

"Hey, Ash Wilde!" I snapped my fingers in recognition. "Great to see you again."

"Another waitress?" Jess grumbled "Can't help yourself, can you?"

I lowered my glass, confused. But Ash spoke before I could question Jess further.

"Excuse me but I'm happily engaged." Ash looked at me, puzzled. "No offence, Matty

"None taken."

Jess blushed and mumbled an apology but Ash had already sauntered off.

"Thirty seconds!" the cameraman trilled, adjusting his focus on us.

Jan-Andrew ended the call and took his place beside Jess with a sleazy smile.

"And three... two... one." Terry held up a finger, then pointed at us. "Terry Schultz for the local news, coming to you live from Ballydoon at The Town and Country pub, where a ghoulish discovery has been made."

His voice lowered conspiratorially.

"On Halloween, of all days."

I glanced to my left. John leant against a wine barrel with a tea towel over his shoulder, looking thoroughly bored.

"John, tell us about your discovery," Terry said breathlessly.

"Yeah, I really wanted to get the new lino down behind the bar, so we lifted the old stuff up. Found a trapdoor to a cellar and dropped me sander into it by mistake. It landed so hard it broke the floorboards. There it was, a dead cat."

He backed away, glad the ordeal was over. Terry swung his attention to us.

"I'm also joined by two ghost hunters. Gentlemen, what makes this discovery so significant?"

I wondered why the journo was asking us, when it was Jess's operation. Still, I leapt in, keen to get time on air. Grab that sponsor.

"Thanks, Terry. I'm Matt from The Spectre Inspector channel." I flashed a grin to the camera. "The significance of this find is..."

"What my colleague is trying to say, Terry," Jan-Andrew interrupted, "Is it's evidence of witchcraft. Spooky, don't you think, Terry? For Halloween?"

Terry made a 'Wooooah' sound and they both chuckled.

Jess and I stayed stonily silent. Behind me, John snorted.

"I think the best person to ask about this find is Jessica Knight." I waved to her and moved back, giving her more of the camera. She acknowledged me with a brief nod.

"The mummified cat was probably placed in the cellar to repel witchcraft rather being than a sign of it."

"Mummified?" Terry shrieked, with exaggerated horror.

"Wrapped in cloth and interred with other items, thought to protect the building and its owners from witchcraft and bad spirits. It's a good kitty."

"The cat didn't repel the Ballydoon Bandit," Jan-Andrew leaned forwards, trying to get more of his head in shot.

"You wrote a paper on the famous ghost of Ballydoon." Terry aimed his microphone at him. "A bushranger known as Freddie Blunder."

"Indeed. While I'm extremely well known as Ghost Host on my YouTube channel, I'm also an adjunct lecturer at the Queensland University, where my PhD focussed on the myth and lore of the Ballydoon Bandit, AKA Freddie Blunder."

Jan-Andrew had scored points for his PhD. and I had to salvage this interview for our channel But I didn't want to take the limelight from Jess.

"Many have said they've heard the wailing ghost of the Ballydoon Bandit." Terry flung his microphone to John. "While staying in this very pub."

"A few, I guess."

I smiled. Mr Carpenter might appreciate the publicity but he was intensely uncomfortable being on camera and had no tolerance for bullshit. I didn't think I'd never seen him get worked up in the ten years I'd been drinking here.

"As a local growing up in this area," I broke in. "I heard many tall tales about the ghost, but it seemed the only witnesses were always three sheets to the wind, Terry."

He laughed politely.

"I'll be here in Ballydoon all night. After this I'm going to the local cemetery, streaming a feed and discussing ghost stories. Who knows what we may uncover on All Souls Night."

"Meanwhile, I'll be with Dr Knight in the cellar with the mummified cat to see if we are visited by any ghosts or ghouls," Jan-Andrew purred into Terry's microphone. "You can watch my live feed with the archaeologist on Ghost Host."

I ground my teeth. Why had I set up everything in the graveyard when the real buzz was here?

"Well, folks. Looks like you need to tune in to Ghost Host to see if the spirits come out to play on Halloween in Ballydoon! But now, Dr Knight is going to elaborate on one of the finds for us. The small bottle placed with the cat in the cellar."

"I believe it's a witch bottle," Jess said.

"I beg your pardon." Terry blanched theatrically. "Did you just say witch bottle?"

"Folklore magic to ward off evil spirits, as long as the bottle stays intact. What I'd really like to find inside is rust, as evidence of pins or nails. People believed the spirit would impale themselves on the pin and be trapped. Or, sometimes a potion was made with someone's urine, nail clippings and wine or port and mixed together."

"A witch's potion." Terry shuddered.

I wasn't disturbed about witches; it was the letch beside me that had me concerned.

"You'll be in the cellar all night with Jess?" I murmured to Jan-Andrew.

"Who knows what might happen in the dark of night?" A sleazy smile spread across his face. "All alone with the lovely historian?"

Jan-Andrew stepped away.

"You lost your chance at the Faculty Ball, if I remember rightly."

My face flushed red with anger. How did this pork-pie-hat-wearing-idiot know about what happened between Jess and I?

He walked off, laughing.

"We may have just filmed the first witch bottle found in Australia. Do let us know the lab analysis of the contents, Jess." Terry smiled for two more seconds. "And cut!"

That was it. Time to confront Jess.

"Midnight in the cellar with Jan-Andrew?" I grumbled. "You said you detested the man. You don't even respect him as a historian!"

She raised an eyebrow. "Jealous?"

"Yes."

Jess blinked several times. It obviously wasn't the answer she expected.

"I honestly don't get it," I said forlornly. "Why didn't you return my calls or texts?"

"I'm not having this conversation in public." She glanced around but, with the cameras off, nobody was paying us much attention. "Follow me for some privacy."

She packed up the witch bottle and its contents in a plastic container, stomped off to the public bar and down the ladder into the cellar. I trotted after her, like the lovesick fool I was.

I hopped off the ladder and paused, letting my eyes adjust to the gloom. Stone walls covered in freckles of mould. Hardwood floorboards overhead, supported by rough-sawn wooden beams decorated with centuries old cobwebs that swayed like lace.

At my feet was the cat.

"Of all places to possibly have some privacy, it had to be with a dead moggy," I deadpanned.

"Mummified moggy," Jess corrected, hands on hips.

"Hey. That's my line." I shivered from the dank cold. "You like meeting me in enclosed spaces, Jess."

"Ugh." She paced away from me, all of two steps to the far wall.

Being in a dark room with Angry Jess and a desiccated feline was not my idea of fun. Then I had an idea. I could salvage that horrid news report by getting content for our channel. I pulled out my Go-Pro, tripod, and microphone.

"Seriously?" Jess huffed. "I though you wanted to talk."

"I do. But Charlie will be furious if I don't record *something*. You've avoided me for months, so what's a few more minutes?"

Jess didn't say a word. I didn't care. Or, at least, I pretended I didn't. Might as well get my footage before she slammed my heart into the floorboards to rest in dirt beside the Mummified Moggy.

"Do you really believe in ghosts?" she asked as I turned on the Go-Pro and sighed. The connection kept flicking on and off. The signal was rubbish down here through the stone and hardwood.

"Of course not." I pressed record but everything was frozen on screen. I sighed. "I believe in the past and the evidence left behind."

Jess sniffed.

"Streaming isn't working so I'll just record as video with a backup using my phone, then I'll be right out of your way."

She shrugged. I propped up my phone beside the Go-Pro and hit record. Leant down beside the cat.

"Welcome to this Halloween special with The Spectre Inspector, Matt Cavanagh. We promised you a tour of a pioneer cemetery and tales of bushrangers, but this is something a little different. I'm at the site of a fantastic discovery in my hometown at the Ballydoon pub. I've drunk my fair share of schooners in the bar above me with no idea that, below, was a hidden cellar, untouched for decades. With a mummified cat concealed under its floor."

I turned to her

"I'm wondering if Archaeologist Jess McKnight, who has been investigating this find. might elaborate."

Jess Rolled her eyes, then hunkered down next to me.

"Mummification wasn't considered barbaric more than one hundred and fifty years ago by those who constructed the cellar. The way the cat has been buried, wrapped in cloth with a bottle and pennies placed with it, is indicative of an East Anglian practice to bury an animal in a structure so it would ward off evil. They believed the cat protected the pub, rather than haunted it. Although many would say it was a cruel practice, which is true by today's standards, this was done in full belief that burying the cat with these rituals would keep the house, or in this case, the pub, and its residents safe."

"What's the significance of the bottle and the pennies?" I asked.

"Witch bottles will often contain herbs or dirt. The dirt especially is interesting, it may have come from home in the United Kingdom. Herbs were also thought to have properties that deter spirits."

Jess's face glowed as she told the story of her find, including how the bottle would be sent for lab analysis for plant and pollen remains.

"And are the pennies to pay off evil?"

"Not quite." Jess smirked. "Think of these as bright, shiny things to distract the attention of goblin-elvish creatures looking to cause mischief."

"The cat looks like it was buried with care. They wrapped it in good quality cloth, too."

"I'll be removing the cat to do x-rays in Brisbane to see if there are more coins were wrapped in the cloth. When we've finished our examination of the cat, it will be buried again here to keep on protecting the hotel.

She smiled and I grinned back. She was a natural at this.

"That's great," I said. "Thanks."

"I like the way you weave history, myth and rumour together about paranormal stories." Jess said. "I just hate how your fans are constantly throwing themselves at you!"

I gaped. It wasn't like I streamed shirtless or anything like that. But she was right, we had a contingent of keen fans who were always suggesting they'd like to date me. And other things.

"Are you... jealous?" I asked, mirroring her earlier question.

"Yes!" She threw up her hands. "No! I don't know. A bit? I reacted like a bitch upstairs to your school friend. She's gorgeous and I'm..."

Jess waved a hand up and down her front.

I stared, dumbstruck.

"You're beautiful, Jess. What's more, you're smart, engaging and caring. I never tired of sitting through your lectures."

I swallowed the lump in my throat. So much for convincing myself I was over her.

Jess shook her head.

"You don't believe me?" I asked.

"I'd like to. But, as soon as we'd... you know ... at the ball."

Even in this gloom, I could see the pink of her cheeks.

"Had sex," I muttered.

"Yes. Had sex." Her face hardened. "Then you tried to pick up that waitress who was all over you. You'd just been inside me and, minutes later, you were flirting with another woman and passing her your number to her."

A tear rolled down her cheek.

"Oh Jess. She cornered me at the door to the storage room and, yeah, she was a groupie. So I gave her Charlie's card. Then I looked round and you were gone."

Jess sucked on her lip, staring.

"Is that really true?"

"They're going out now."

Jess's reply was cut off by a tinny, screeching voice coming through my phone's speakers.

"It's true, Jess." Charlie said. "Lovely lass she is too."

"Charlie?" I fumbled with my phone. "How the hell do you know what we're talking about?"

"You're streaming, dude. I'm getting you both loud and clear. Comments are going nuts."

"It's... working?" I whirled around, staring at my Go-Pro.

"Oh crud," Jess mumbled.

"I didn't... I'm sorry. I thought..."

Jess cut me off, cupping my cheeks and planting a searing kiss on my lips.

"I should have talked to you," she whispered. "Even before Charlie's impressive speech, I believed you. Can you forgive me?"

"Hey! What's going on down here." Jan-Andrew began climbing down the latter. "Stop stealing my thunder!"

An almighty howl reverberated through the cellar.

"Holy Christ!" He squealed, "The Ballydoon bandit! I'm out of here!"

He vanished into the light again. Charlie's voice squealed through my phone.

"What the frack was that?"

I pulled Jess against me as I put my phone back to my ear. "Are you still streaming this?"

On cue, another howl echoed around us and cobwebs swayed in one corner of the cellar.

"Let's make this work," I murmured in her ear before turning to the camera. "It seems that Ghost Host isn't happy to put his money where his mouth is."

Jess gave a snigger.

"Dr Knight? that's an impressive ghostly sound but let's look at the evidence. Don't you think it's strange cobwebs are swaying in a breeze when we are underground?"

"Yes," Jess nodded. "There's circulation in here."

Another howl ripped through the room.

"That's a cat," she stated plainly.

We both glanced down at the mummified moggy.

"A live one," Jess added, pointing to a corner of the ceiling. "I have a feeling our answer is on the other side of the panelling."

I picked up the Go-Pro and followed her, as she pulled away a board from its rusty nails.

"Bring the camera closer, Spectre Inspector." Jess chuckled.

There was Dickface McWhiskers, with a chicken parmie in her mouth, suckling four kittens.

Dickface winked.

"I believe we've found the modern day Ballydoon Bandit with her secret family, squatting in the Town and Country Pub."

"Halloween is about the spirit realm, not love," Jess grinned.

"Well, why not both?" I turned the camera on myself and winked. "On that note, viewers, I'm taking Dr Knight to dinner and for some privacy. Have a great spooky night."

I switched off the Go-Pro and kissed her.

Fantasy is hardly an escape from reality.
It's a way of understanding it.

Lloyd Alexander

The Hat

Cassandra Kelly

Queensland 1885

The man had no neck, not like other men anyway. A great mass of flesh was piled on top of the obese body and, surmounting that, a lumpy thing passed for a head. The whole structure resembled a pyramid, sliced off at the top, leaving a small flat surface which served as a platform for the hat.

The hat deserved a better head. It was a handsome hat, artfully crafted in felt from the skins of a series of unfortunate possums. Its creator had fallen down on his luck and, with the greatest reluctance, sold it to the man with the pyramid head. There were tears in the creator's eyes as he passed it over, for indeed it was a grand headpiece and entirely unique. Clean it was too, for the creator had been diligent in its maintenance.

"Look after it mate, it's a bloody good hat." Eyes growing red with tears he turned away.

With a grunt that could have been yes or no, or merely the clearing of his nostrils, the purchaser crammed it on his head and continued on his way. The hat shuddered.

This new head was mostly bald and the remaining hair, though cut short, was filthy. The surface of his skin was covered with sweat and dust, which had slimed its way into every pore. From its aloof vantage point, the hat looked down at the mound of rolling flesh as its owner shuffled his way along the dusty town road to the coach stop.

117

The view of the feet was blotted out by the protuberance that, on anyone else, would be called a stomach. Part of this bloated surface was exposed due to a sad combination of an undersized shirt and the absence of several buttons.

The shirt had, long ago, resigned itself to fate. Once it was a gay and lively, bright-red affair, with darker stripes running vertically. It was finished off with mother-of-pearl buttons at the cuffs, the sort of shirt most men might think rather flash, and wear at a dance, to create a favourable impression with the ladies. Alas, sun, dust and time had paled it. Now, the only stripes obvious to the observer were those smeared in every direction by greasy fingers. The back was covered with a grand multitude of flies which seemed to prefer this wearer over any other. This shirt's dancing days were well and truly done and it now left quite a different impression with the ladies.

The moleskin trousers, frequently patched and mended, seemed more of an afterthought, as though their occupant hadn't quite yet decided whether he was actually wearing them. The crotch was almost around his knees and the waist band sat at an obscene level. All that was stopping the trousers from falling completely, and thus creating a visual disaster, were the braces. These, like the shirt, were too small - so bits of cord had been tied to the bottoms as extensions, tied through holes cut crudely into the waistband.

The boots, at least, fit. Though dirty and shabby, they were in reasonable condition, as they had been purchased new only a month or so previously. Unfortunately the socks were ancient and nothing more will be said about them. It's for the better.

Having arrived at the coach stop, the man was given a place on top at the back, putting him in a position where he caused the least offence to the senses of the other passengers.

"Best seat on the coach," the driver told him, Being a rather naïve and trusting sort, he believed this and was content with his small good fortune.

The coach fell behind schedule due to a bad patch of road, chewed up by teamsters forcing their loads through in the wake of prolonged rain. Gaining flatter and firmer ground the driver urged his horses on, to make up time. The coach wound its way through the sun-soaked hills and eucalypts and into a welcome afternoon breeze, blowing along the valley.

This was the moment that the hat had been waiting for. Having an intelligence greater than its wearer, it surmised it would have better prospects for the future on another head. Any other head. And so, it made its big break for freedom. At a crucial moment, when the breeze gusted strongly, it leaped from its owner's head and into the road, obscured in the swirling dust raised by the speeding coach.

"Stop!" the man implored.

But the coach rumbled on. He stared wistfully into the haze and felt despondent.

The hat, alone on the road, breathed a sigh of relief.

Many days later, a swaggy, his face world-worn and wearing a coat of dust and flies, came across the hat. He stopped and looked around. There was no one in sight. He stooped, picked the hat up and noticed its quality. He looked around again.

He placed his billy on the ground and removed his old worn out cap from his old, worn out head. He was about to set the new hat on his head but, as it passed his nose he got a good whiff.

"Whew! No great wonder you were disposed of," said the swaggy. He replaced his battered headgear and walked down the hill. He stopped by a creek bed, mostly dry, but with a few stretches of usable water thanks to the prolonged rain.

The swaggy lit a fire and boiled up his billy. Into the boiling water he placed liberal handfuls of leaves from the nearest eucalypt. When the smell from the billy was at its most agreeable, he placed his new hat upside down. Into this he poured the aromatic concoction, making sure he left enough water to soak the wide brim.

He let the hat sit until it was soaked right through; taking the opportunity to remove his boots and immerse his feet in the water hole. The hat now empty and pliable, the swaggy pushed, poked and bent it into a pleasing shape; more comfortable to his head. Taking the hat back off he placed it on a fallen tree to dry. Being an agreeable spot to camp, the swaggy spent the night there. Next morning, new hat perched aloft, he set off on his long walk to the next town, well pleased with his find. The hat, fresh and clean, felt happier too.

Some months later, the swaggy was sitting on the veranda of a hotel in Boguntungan inspecting the state of his footwear, and waiting for his mate to return from the bar, when he became aware of someone watching him. Without raising his head he peered up from the shadow of his brim.

Standing about fifteen feet away was a man, too wide for his height, and dressed in dirty ill-fitting clothes. Strangely, in a country where all men wore headgear, his pate was bereft of a lid. The man was giving him a queer look.

"Can I 'elp yer there mate, or are yer just browsin'?" asked the swaggy.

"Nice hat you've got there." The man sauntered over.

They were interrupted by the swaggy's mate, bringing the beer.

"Here yer go. Get yerself outside that." He took a seat beside Pearl. "Who's yer mate?"

"Dunno, we just met." Pearl swigged his beer, placed the glass beside him and continued inspecting his boots.

"I'm Herman," said the hatless man.

"I'm Shaky and this is me mate Pearl." Neither man extended their hands.

"I was just admiring your mate's hat." There was more than a hint of suspicion in Herman's voice and alarm bells went off in Pearl's head.

"Yeah, he found..."

Pearl brought his boot down on Shaky's toes and gave him a deadly stare.

The mild altercation wasn't noticed by Herman who was still studying the hat. It certainly looked familiar, even if it was an odd shape.

"Yeah," Shaky cottoned on quickly. "He found it in a little shop in Bendigo."

Pearl breathed a sigh of relief, and so did the hat.

"No it weren't Bendigo at all," Pearl lied convincingly. "It were Ballarat I bought it."

"No, no, no, were Bendigo fer certain. It were that little shop next to *Basil the Butcher, Best Meat in Bendigo*." Shaky warmed to the deception.

"Bendigo yer say?" Pearl put on his best puzzled look as he stared at the sky. "S'pose it could've been Bendigo."

"It were Bendigo I tell yer. Remember I wuz goin' ter buy one meself, but I didn't 'ave the two shillings."

"Two shillings?" Herman choked on the words. "I paid ten for it!"

"Ten!" Pearl feigned indignation. "I'd go and get me money back."

"I didn't buy mine in Bendigo. I got it from a man in Clermont. Said he made it himself and it was one of a kind."

"Oooh, 'e saw you comin' didn't 'e?" Shaky nodded sympathetically. They're all the rage in Victoria now, so I hear."

"That's where I'm goin' next, then. Bendigo" Herman finally accepted this wasn't his lost treasure, after all. "I loved that hat."

"What 'appened to it?" asked Pearl innocently. "Yer not wearin' it."

"Lost it off the coach. The driver wouldn't stop. Hadn't even had it a day."

"That's bad luck, 'erman," Pearl said, "Tell yer what, yer seem a decent sort of bloke so I'll shout yer a drink, help you get over yer misfortune."

"Yeah," Shaky added, "If yer do get to Bendigo, and yer plan to head back up 'ere, can yer pick one up fer me too? I'll pay yer four shillings fer it."

So Pearl kept the hat, and the hat, contented with its new head, kept Pearl covered until the end of his days.

Herman did, eventually, wend his way to Bendigo. But no one there had ever heard of *Basil the Butcher, Best Meat in Bendigo.* And no one was wearing a hat like the one he lost off the coach. Dejected, he kicked stones along the street. A Chinese fellow called out to him from a cart.

"You need a new shirt."

Herman said nothing.

"Me Wai Kee, tailor. Make you best shirt, best price."

"A good price?" Herman looked down at what remained of his top and back to Wai Kee.

"I see you sad. I make you happy price, very best ever. Best shirt, very cheap."

So Herman got another shirt made and had to admit, the craftmanship seemed rather fine. He was glad it was at the best price, though, because it still cut heavily into his savings. However, it was worth every penny.

At the coach stop to Ballarat, Herman beamed with pride as a group of ladies, standing in the shade of the veranda, admired the shirt and batted their eyelashes at him..

That's when the cord holding his trousers snapped..

Make A Wish

N e e n   C o h e n

Stella crouched by the garden bed, the autumn breeze prickling bumps onto her skin. Her voice tinkled like crystal wind chimes as she chatted to the flowers and laughed at their gentle replies. She smiled and stroked the soft yellow petals. A watering can, now empty, lay beside her on the grass.

She looked up and thanked the leaves for the shade. They shook a gently reply, dark wide surfaces pulsing with thin veins, as they sucked up her life-giving water.

Standing, Stella stroked the trunk of the oak tree feeling warmth and love returned beneath her fingertips. Humans weren't ever so kind as to openly reciprocate feelings. Definitely not her sister's friends, and certainly not her sister, Theresa.

"Why doesn't she go to school like us?" Theresa's friends flanked her, faces rigid with disgust.

"Argh, thank God she doesn't. Just look at her. She's a freak. I'm glad mummy and daddy told the school I was an only child. I couldn't imagine people knowing about her. You can't tell anyone."

The twelve-year-old glared at her friends. They cowered under her gaze, knowing what would happen if they crossed the most popular girl in school.

Stella shook the memory away. Her sister needed her, even if she never said it outright. Theresa cared about Stella, in her own way. There weren't many gentle memories lean back on, but there were enough.

The garden and its plants were her real friends, though. They kept Stella calm.

It was the only place she had ever been safe. The only place, during childhood, where Theresa forgot to torment Stella about her black hair and blacker eyes. The one place where the reminder of being adopted wasn't apparent in every photo her parents displayed around their home. The difference between the sisters was day and night.

Behind her, the house loomed, paint peeling and boards rotting. One of the windows was mended with multiple strips of plywood, all different shades. It reminded Stella of a pirate patch covering the eye of a grisly faced villain.

The doorbell chimed, echoing around the minimal furniture and dust inside, before floating out to the backyard. Stella's smile faltered. Ignoring the visitor, she took a deep intoxicating breath of the morning air.

She heard the telltale squeak of the gate and her shoulders tensed. She crossed her legs up into the seat of her chair and sat in a lotus position.

"Stella." Theresa's voice was harsh and demanding, as usual.

Stella sighed, closing her eyes.

"Hello, Theresa."

"Why bother having a doorbell, if you refuse to answer it?"

Theresa strode around the garden, feet stomping down blades of grass. If she were a dog, she would be cocking her leg and marking territory. She plucked flowers and leaves indiscriminately, squashing them between her fingertips and sniffing at the results. The petals fell, discarded and broken.

"You could make nice perfume out of these. Better than them falling to rot."

Stella ground her teeth and waited, feeling the sting of each tiny death. The cries of pain made her eyes water, as they were brutalised.

Theresa blew out a breath and collapsed into the other lawn chair, long slender limbs spilling over the sides.

A small round table stood between the sisters. The glass top was mottled and, in the right light, rainbows floated on the surface and danced for Stella. Today, it looked dirty and disgruntled. On top of the table sat a small wooden box, old and ornately carved. The patterns and lines were worn smooth from repeated tracing of Stella's fingers. It was her most prized possession. She winced as Theresa flipped open the lid.

The container was filled with glistening cubes. Beneath the first clear layer, the rest were blood red.

"Haven't seen this for years." Theresa dipped her hand in. "Are there more red cubes than before?"

"Please, don't play with them."

"What they hell are they, anyway?" Theresa snapped closed the box. "You never did say where this came from. I asked Mum once but she just told me never to touch it."

"Something of my mother's." Stella shrugged. "The only thing I had left."

She gave a bleak smile.

"Apparently I wouldn't let it go." She stroked the box, her fingertips tracing the well-worn lines. "It's like family."

"Weird." Theresa glanced around and shivered. "Why do you stay here? It's not like you liked mum and dad. You couldn't even be bothered coming to their funeral."

Theresa gave a thin laugh.

"Hell, I didn't like them, and I was their birth-daughter. I should have gotten the fuck out of town as soon as they died." She cast a calculated look from beneath long lashes. "I can help you sell, if you want."

"I can't leave." Stella looked at the box. "There are still too many… ties."

"You know, it's a little selfish. Refusing to sell, when half this place is technically mine."

"Do you need the money?"

"Yes." Theresa curled a lip. "This dump would cost too much to fix up and I need cash now. I... I need your help."

The words were forced out like a dentist pulling a deep-rooted tooth.

"Mmhmm?" Stella focused on the dappled sunshine patterning the back of one hand, resting gently on her thigh.

"Please little sis?" Theresa's eyes were cool despite the begging words. Her long fingers twirled around blonde hair, imitating the damsel in distress they both knew she'd never been. Then she gave one of her beautiful smiles and Stella found herself, as always, unable to say no.

She shifted in her seat. She would help. It was what sisters did for each other. Surely, one day, Theresa would return the favour.

"I need a wish!"

"A wish?" The word sent a small shadow skittering across Stella's heart.

"Do you think I never noticed?" Theresa's lips twisted and Stella felt fear warming her cheeks.

"What do you mean?"

How much had their parents told her? Not everything, because they knew only half the story. Stella was certain Theresa had never been trained. It took far more hours than her sister ever had to spare, what with her busy social life.

Theresa rose and stood over her sister. Hands on hips, she was queen of her very own backyard beauty pageant.

"I know what you can do."

Stella nodded, the tension in her shoulders increasing. If Theresa had only admitted this when they were children. Hinted at the knowledge, now smouldering behind her eyes. They could have talked. Been closer. But Theresa had never thought about how it would have helped Stella or their relationship.

She closed her eyes again. Theresa had only been a child and, with their parents, it was no wonder she never said anything.

"I know Mum and Dad came to you for spells and magic." Theresa stepped closer. "But you aren't a witch."

Stella let out a sigh.

"I've thought about it for a long time." Theresa placed her hands on either side of Stella's arm rests and leant forward, far enough for Stella to smell her breath, stale with cigarettes. Another attempt at quitting had failed. Theresa had even tried hypnosis this time. Was this what she needed help with?

The trees rustled sharper than the wind and she turned her head away.

"I finally figured out what you are." Theresa needn't have whispered, but she always had enjoyed a flare for the dramatic. Her fingers slipped to Stella's arm, pinching and twisting. Theresa laughed as her sister let out a cry of pain.

Memories of childhood threats sent old fears skipping through her veins. Even with her adoptive parents gone, nothing had changed. She'd been naïve to think it ever would. The garden was no longer its own kind of freedom. An anger she had never allowed herself to feel began to smoulder in the pit of her stomach.

"You're a genie, aren't you?" Theresa said, triumphantly.

"A *what?*"

"Don't play dumb. It's why mum and dad adopted you."

Stella hesitated, then gave a small nod.

"Yes, I'm a genie. Well done."

"I knew as soon as Daddy won the lottery," Theresa nodded in satisfaction. "Everything just seemed to fall in to place for them, one thing after the other."

She strutted back and forth, delighted by her own powers of deduction. Stella rubbed the red marks that were beginning to rise on her arm.

"Until they died, of course."

"Nobody can cheat fate," Stella said nonchalantly.

"I demand my three wishes, Genie." Theresa's eyes narrowed.

"What is your first wish?" Stella asked hesitantly.

The waver was mistaken for fear and a hungry-eyed smile danced across Theresa's face.

"Good girl." She patted her sister's hand before returning to her chair, lighting upon it as though on a throne. "Are there rules?"

"For you, sister, there are no rules.". Stella said. "But each wish does come with a sacrifice."

"Ok then." Theresa smiled, not forced or faked, and Stella hated the happy warmth that spread inside of her. "My first wish is for the money Mummy and Daddy kept from me in their will."

"That was for Aunt Betty."

"Oh please, Stelly. It's been so hard lately, with James out of work." Theresa's eyes brimmed with tears, reddening and making heartbreak of her face. All for show, of course.

"The sacrifice for this wish is…"

"I don't care."

"Okay." Stella pressed her lips tightly together, to hide a grin.

"Make it soon." Having got what she wanted Theresa leaned back on her heels; face clear of any sadness. "He's been so distant of late, that I…."

"It is done." Stella looked down.

She heard the footpads, heavy and stomping as they walked away from her. The gate squeaked and her sister was gone.

She breathed deeply. Theresa's scent was already fading but the smell of her garden no longer tasted quite so sweet on her tongue.

After all these years, she had finally chosen a side.

Perhaps the trees could sense it. Might they see the shift inside of her? If so, they were powerless to do anything about it.

She opened her treasure box, picked up the newly reddened cube and held it tightly in her hand, corners digging into the soft flesh of her palm.

She could feel the mental chains loosen another of their imprisoning links. Happy tears traced the curve of her cheek.

"I'm sorry Aunty Betty. You tried to be nice, but you're one of them. You knew the truth and you kept me here, just like Theresa's parents."

A month passed. Uncle Bert had called, over and over again, until Stella was forced back into the house, to answer the phone's persistent tone. He had been upset that neither sister had attended Bettys funeral.

She had assumed Uncle Bert knew. But he wasn't part of the blood line, and had obviously been in the dark about his wife's family and their heritage. Upon a time, Stella would have spent days pacing the garden, letting her teeth worry at her bottom lip, and sent pages of apologies to him for not paying her last respects.

But those days were slipping further behind her. Though her teeth still worried slightly at her lip.

Stella lounged in her garden chair, body hidden under soft layers of wool. The cold was only just beginning the touch the surrounding greenery. She had plucked off dying leaves and sent them on their way with prayers of rebirth and life. The papery caresses against her skin had changed since Aunty Betty's death, but her friends still reached out and she leaned into their love and affection. Her true father's blood was still strong in her veins.

The side gate squeaked and the plants immediately withdrew their warmth and touch. Theresa flounced in.

"I want my second wish."

"A hello would be nice. Or a please."

"Hello. I want my second wish, please."

"OK." Stella's jaw clenched

"Oh, don't be mad, Stelly," Theresa gave a brittle laugh. "I couldn't go to the funeral. Work has been so busy, I wasn't able to take time off."

"I didn't go either." Stella smiled a little, amused this was how Theresa interpreted her reaction. She still wondered how she had never seen the truth of her sister.

Theresa as remarkably beautiful, it was true. And that beauty had managed to overshadow even Stella's blood, just as it hid the darkness so obvious in Theresa's eyes.

"Maybe you should think about painting the house?" Theresa draped herself over the empty chair. The pants she wore were as tight as if they had been painted on, revealing the sculptured outlines of perfect calf muscles.

"Not that it would do much good. You really should let me sell it. It's a dump but colour might make it appealing to some poor sap."

"I can't sell it." Stella said. "Yet."

Theresa rolled her eyes and gave an angry sigh.

"What is your second wish, sister?" Stella forced out the last word.

"Oh, it's not nearly as big as the first." Theresa flashed her beautiful smile again. The one that won her all the beauty competitions of her youth, the loss of her virginity, and the crown of trophy wife. All by the time she was 21.

"What is it, then?" Stella struggled to keep the frustration from her voice.

"We're getting older, little sis."

"You don't look it."

"Thank you." Theresa preened. "You could look better too, you know. I might be able to help?"

Stella opened her mouth to object, but Theresa waved a languid hand.

"I know you aren't interested, but I don't really have a choice. It takes so much effort to look this way these days. Even your peaches and cream complexion is slipping, so imagine how much energy it takes me to look this beautiful."

She patted her cheeks dolefully

"I know I can still turn heads, but I can also see the lines around the edges, and you can too, even though you are being very sweet."

"What do you want?" Stella couldn't understand how thirty years of being perfect wasn't enough. Or why Theresa insisted on justifying herself, when Stella was ready and willing to grant the next wish.

"I want to always look like I did when James first fell in love with me." Theresa's eyes burned with an intensity that made Stella sink further into her chair.

"I'm sure he still loves you."

"Of course he does!" Theresa snapped, the slight crow's feet crinkling. "But he's been more and more distant lately."

"You want to not age?" Stella refrained from pointing out the problem was probably her sister's personality.

"Oh no, I want to age. I just don't want to look it."

Stella nodded thoughtfully and closed her eyes. When she opened them, she glanced at her newest rose bush. Its last autumn bloom was small but sweet. It had called to her, begged to be worshipped, loved, caressed and taken care of. Stella felt the thickening in her throat and the sting at the back of her eyes.

"It will take a little longer, but it shall be done. Do you care about this wish's sacrifice?"

"Does it affect me?"

"No."

"Then, go for it."

Theresa patted her sister's leg and jumped up out of the seat. Stella didn't move until the squeak of the gate faded away.

The leaves rustled, bashing against each other and screaming inside Stella's mind. For the first time in her memory, she wished they were unable to sense what lingered in the blood that ran through her veins.

Taking a deep breath, she walked slowly to the small rose bush and knelt down in front of it.

"I'm sorry, but you must understand I can't say no. I'm so close."

Stella mourned the sacrifice, watching as the flowers wilted in front of her. Rose pink turned pale and crisp, the green leaves fading into a greyness, reflected in the clouds that began to cover the sky.

Even as she drained the rose bush, she wondered if another sacrifice could have been made for the wish. Her eagerness to finally be done with it all had made the decision quick and easy. She hadn't bothered to consider another option.

Five months passed and Stella grew restless. Now the trees only responded when they had to, and that was rare. Her hands no longer vibrated with love and affection when she pressed them against the rough bark. She had never known the pain of splinters before, and the first one had made her cry, then curse at the surrounding plants. They had shivered, recoiling, as though she had threatened them with fire or weed killer.

The drop of blood that had fallen from her finger continued to stain her white shirt, no matter how many times she washed the piece of clothing.

She had known the price of her choices but convinced herself it wouldn't be this severe. Just as she had convinced herself, for all those years, that her sister was worth sacrificing time and energy for.

The squeak of the gate came at last.

Stella sucked in a harsh breath and sipped at the iced water on the table, devoid of all sheen. A second glass waited by the pitcher. She had been prepared for a long time, but fear still tiptoed up her spine and settled around her shoulders.

"Hello, little sister." Theresa waltzed in and brushed a kiss against Stella's cheek.

Theresa smelt of sweet fresh roses. Bile rose in Stella's mouth. She forced a smile and returned her emptied glass to the table.

She now understood how Theresa could smile with only her lips.

"Hello, yourself." She filled both glasses from the ice-cold pitcher. "It's been a while."

"I'm sorry." Theresa cocked her head as she picked up the drink and sipped delicately. "Things are just so busy. Did you get my sample of perfume? I have my own line of beauty products now. I simply cannot walk down the street without being recognized. Everyone wants my secret to staying so young."

She gave her sister a wink, as though the cameras had followed her into the backyard to listen and record.

Stella had nothing to say. She wanted the ordeal over with. She wanted to be left alone, to wait out her sentence. The cost of the last two wishes had been great.

"What's your third boon?" she snapped.

Theresa feigned offence. It lasted long enough for her to remember there were in fact no photographers and no one to see the true face behind the charade. Her face hardened and her back straightened. She looked down at Stella.

"I wish for a cruel and painful death to the woman sleeping with my husband."

"Which one?" Stella raised a brow.

Theresa's hand shot out and slapped. She ignored the sting and waited. For a moment Theresa hesitated. Had she finally looked at Stella, instead of right through her?

"All of them!"

Stella's mind was racing. It couldn't be this easy. Her heart raced, blood roaring in her ears.

"This will take more than the normal energy, and your intention must not waver." Stella's voice quivered in anticipation. Theresa either didn't notice or didn't care. It no longer mattered.

"What does that mean?" She put both hands on her hips.

"You must truly, genuinely want these women to suffer. Or it will not work."

"Just do it!"

"Are you certain you're willing to make the sacrifice?"

The sky darkened as they spoke and Theresa and Stella shivered in the shade. The trees were rustling, furious and angry, but Stella no longer listened.

It was too good, too easy. She couldn't continue to deny who and what she was. Her mother's blood boiled in her veins. Her father's whimpered in the flood of fire.

"Yes, whatever. Sacrifice away. Just hurry up with it."

Theresa perched on the lawn chair, the jiggling of her leg giving away her impatience. Stella felt her skin tingle with the same sensation. She wanted it over with, yes, but the years of torture were too strong for her to rush, to ignore the pleasure this was going to bring.

She opened the old wooden box, pulled out the last clear cube and placed it in the centre of the table. All other cubes were now filled with the same redness.

"Pick it up." She kept her voice calm. She could not trip now, so close to the finish line.

Theresa hesitated, eyeing the square dubiously. Stella felt a pang of unease. What exactly had her mother told Theresa when she had warned her away from the treasure box?

An oppressive hush fell over the garden. Stella could hear faint weeping at the edges of the lawn. She ignored all of it and focused on her sister.

In a tentative motion, with thumb and finger, Theresa picked up the cube.

A heartbeat passed and Stella's sister began to scream.

Oh, the screaming was a light inside Stella. Sparked the fire that had smouldered for months.

She flicked a hand and Theresa stiffened and froze; her shriek silenced. Her mouth remained open as she strained against Stella's spell, trying to stand and shake off the cube. Trying to plead for help and finding herself as impotent as Stella had been all these years.

Strength poured into Stella, warming her like the first sip of Scotch after a long cold day. The leaves rustled and raged.

Theresa's eyes were the only things capable of movement. They searched the garden but found no aid. With a little effort, Stella forced the cube out of Theresa's rigid grip.

"I grant wishes, but I am no genie," she whispered.

She opened the old wooden box, once more, and gently placed the cube on top of the twenty-three already there. Even the oldest held the blushing hue of the bled. Stella plucked three out and placed them on the palm of her hand.

"Say Hi to Mummy and Daddy." She pointed to the third cube on her palm "And Aunty Betty here…"

She replaced the cubes.

"Welcome to your family reunion. Your bloodline is finally over.

Theresa's eyes widened.

"All of them knew," Stella continued. "Everyone but you knew what I am. I guess your mum and dad saw your black heart after all. They murdered my parents. Forced me into bondage and slavery. They didn't know that their blood - your blood - was the way to free me."

Stella shrugged.

"I didn't know, either. Not for years. Even then, I refused to kill you and Aunt Betty."

Theresa's body jerked and bucked at the edge of the seat. The glasses and pitcher smashed to the ground. Stella watched, feeling nothing for a sister she had once adored. Theresa slipped off the chair, convulsing on the ground, shards of the glass cutting her exposed flesh. Her long legs and toned and tanned arms no longer perfect.

Stella leaned in close, revelling in the fear that radiated from Theresa.

"If you had loved me, I would have stayed here forever. Trapped in this garden by my father's fae half, and my love for you." She stroked the box. "But now I'm free. My mother's demon blood, the blood your parents used for their own selfish pleasure and gain, is loosed. Thank you."

Theresa made an incoherent, gargling sound.

Stella wandered inside and made a cup of tea in the last functional room of the house.

Paint and wallpaper sagged to a floor that was covered in a layer of slime and silt. It had once been filled with such pride and arrogance. The occupants had believed they were immortal, that they would always live upon the backs and magic of those they captured. Those they trapped and caged.

Stella pushed back her shoulders. Her real father's Fae blood, and his love of nature, had lost its hold. Her demon side, her mother's strength, raged.

Returning to the dying garden, she stepped over Theresa's body. Blood leaked from her sister's unseeing eyes.

Stella took a seat for the last time. The plants had withdrawn, their leaves already beginning to wilt in the heat and fear of the demon before them. She hardly glanced in their direction.

"Did I fail to mention that you are the only woman your husband slept with? The only woman he has *ever* slept with?"

Stella sipped her tea slowly. It was nice being able to talk uninterrupted.

After the last heartbeat ceased to pulse in Theresa's chest, Stella stood up and turned slowly, taking in the last view of the cage, she had once loved. Both hands caressed her mother's box.

She walked up the side of the house and opened the squeaky side gate. Her feet hesitated as she pushed against the mental barrier that had held her in check all these years. No resistance.

Stella stepped past the boundary.

She didn't turn around as she walked away. Her hand flicked up and fire surged up the dry wallpaper. The flames would not be noticed until salvage of the property was impossible.

There was nothing else to take with her

There never had been.

Ùmhlachd

Lynne Lumsden Green

Velta gave her masterpiece a final polish with the chamois cloth. Then the armourer stood back to study her latest design, hanging upon an oak stand. It was a work of art as well as craft. She had constructed a system of overlapping tiles that remained flexible, yet free of the structural weaknesses that plagued tradition armour, such as openings at the armpits and throat. She had plated the steel in copper, bronze, brass, even silver and gold, so the armour resembled a richly embroidered tunic and leggings. The tiles looked like leaves or feathers, varying in size, and the random use of colour would dazzle and confuse the eye of any opponent.

A flush of satisfaction gave Velta a warm glow. The woman who had paid for this armour would be well pleased. As a warrior, the Baroness needed sensible protection. As a noblewoman, she wanted to be a leader of fashion. Unlike many of the aristocratic class, the Baroness had paid upfront, and well. Velta hadn't needed to scrimp on materials and it had inspired her to new heights.

She sent word to the Baroness that her order was ready.

Next morning, the Much Honoured Baroness of Gàidheil, the Lady Mairead, came to Velta's smithy. The Baroness was a well-muscled woman, a good hand taller than the armourer, with a fierce patrician profile. Most people only saw the regal nose, and missed the intelligence in her eyes, the humour that danced around her lips.

The woman's expression lit up when she saw her armour.

137

"Oh my." She ran strong fingers over the left pauldron. There was a faint musical chiming as the tiles shifted. "You've outdone yourself, Velta."

"Thank you, your ladyship."

"Would you consider coming to work for me? I have need of a woman of your skills."

Most aristocrats would have simply ordered Velta to join their staff. The armourer knew the Baroness was reputed to be kind and fair, however, and her patronage would go far in cementing Velta's reputation. But there was a niggle of doubt layered in with her pleasure. Why would the Baroness look outside her own people for another smith?

Velta glanced at her masterpiece. There was her answer. No one else had her skills and expertise.

"I appreciate the esteem you are showing me, your ladyship," she bowed. "And I accept."

"Excellent. As soon as you are settled in, I would like you to start on a barding for my horse, and a helmet to go with this fine armour."

A castle looks majestic from a distance. Up close, however, it is busier and dirtier than a dead dog on an anthill. There are pantries, kitchens, laundries, breweries, workshops for tailors and candle-makers, potteries, stables and tack rooms, dormitories for the soldiers, cellars and dungeons - all staffed with their specialists. There are also maids, valets, footmen and other servants, who work in the upper reaches of the castle, where the court resides. Velta's forge and workshop were nestled beside the armoury and she wasn't surprised to find more smithies there. Two swordsmiths and a weapons master were housed around her.

The other smiths warmly welcomed the addition of an armourer to their ranks.

"We've been working long hours." Viktor, the weapons master, gestured with graceful hands, albeit the size of shovels. "Your help should take some of the pressure off."

The swordsmiths were fraternal twins, Tenney and Diot. Tenney was male and Diot female - but both were long, thin and hard as the blades they forged.

"My brother and I are excited to meet with you," Diot said. "We've seen the armour you made. Are you keeping the design a secret, or would you be prepared to divulge your techniques?"

"I'm happy to share," said Velta, pleased she would not be the only female smith.

"I want to learn how you manage to work so many different metals into your armour," Diot continued.

"And I'd like to know how you managed to get it so flexible, while it remains tough," Tenney added, with a shy smile.

Velta rode a surge of relief. She had wondered why the Baroness would need another smith and here were her answers. She was, indeed, the best.

She didn't realise, at the time, she was asking the wrong questions.

It took Velta a while to tap into the undercurrents of castle gossip. That was when she started hearing the rumours about 'Mairead's Luck'. Baroness Mairead always won her battles, no matter how badly the odds were stacked against her forces. The crops and orchards of her domain had bountiful harvests, her wells never failed, and the farmer's herds remained unbothered by wolves or bandits. Illness and plague never troubled her subjects, even when they were ravaging the rest of the country.

At first, Velta put it down to good management and superior war tactics. She was a big believer in making your own luck. Then she started hearing darker rumours of how the Baroness was much older than she looked. That she went on a mysterious journey every year to a secret location.

More disturbing was the fact that one of her retainers always failed to return from this trip. The Baroness declared the retainer had left of their own free will, but some speculated she had made a deal with demons or the Devil. That the sacrifice of an attendant was the payment for her continued success.

Velta knew the great and powerful attracted rumours the way flowers entice bees and wasps. But these were her own staff whispering these snippets, not rivals. Velta wished she had a real friend in the castle. She liked her fellow smiths but didn't know them well enough to share her concerns. Their loyalty would be to the Baroness, and truly, that was as it should be.

Velta did not share gossip. It was her own way of showing loyalty to her patron. Yet she still felt echoes of trouble to come. It was a cloud on her horizon.

The Baroness sent for her, seven months after Velta had arrived at the castle.

Velta hadn't been in the throne room until now. She was used to existing in the underbelly of the castle, with the other servants, drudges, and craft specialists, a different world to the court upstairs. The room was used to impress visiting dignitaries or hold judgements - a vast, cold space decorated with prizes that the Baroness had taken in battle: varied weapons, blood-stained and torn banners, cleaved helms, and battered shields. The trophies spoke clearly of her strength and leadership.

Anxiety made Velta's pulse beat faster. Why would the Baroness need to speak with her here, of all places? When she wanted to discuss armour, she came down to the smithy.

Velta had expected the room to be packed with courtiers in their colourful clothing, but the only other people present were Miles, second in command in the Gàidheil army, and two of her captains. Anxiety escalated into fear. Velta went down on one knee, head lowered.

"My liege," she said.

"Oh, Velta, do get up. I have something to request, and would prefer it if I could ask you eye to eye."

Velta raised her head but remained kneeling, arms crossed in front of her.

"My liege?"

Mairead sighed and rubbed her eyes. "I imagine you've been here long enough to hear about my missing vassals?"

Velta suppressed the urge to bite her lip. She picked her words with care, as she answered. "I have heard whispers to that effect, yes."

"Have you heard that I make a bloody sacrifice every midsummer? That I consort with witches?"

"Truthfully, I heard that your bargain was with the Devil."

Velta was expecting Mairead to throw back her head and laugh.

"No," she replied solemnly. "I have made a deal with the Fey, the spirits of this land. But it isn't a blood sacrifice. I volunteer a hostage, an Ùmhlachd."

Velta didn't know what to say.

"More than once," the Baroness went on. "I have offered myself. However, as the deal is with me, it is always refused."

"Did you hire me with this bargain in mind?"

"I did not. You were taken on because I really do think you are a superb armorer. But you are also one of the few people in my employ without close family or friends. I've been informed you haven't even taken a lover."

"Are you asking me to die for you? I've taken your coin and accepted your patronage, so yes, I would... in battle." Velta hesitated. "But as a sacrifice?"

"The Fey insist all volunteers are unharmed."

"And the volunteers confirm this?"

"None of them have ever come back," the Baroness admitted. "Therefore, if you do accept this challenge, I would be most grateful if you'd promise to return and ease my concerns.

She paused for a moment and, when she spoke again, her voice was rough.

"I have no choice but to trust the Fey. They give their word, but all know that they are as clever as lawyers, when it comes to promises."

"My grandmother told me that the Fey always keep their word," Velta shrugged. "There was no mention of lawyers."

"Milady, this woman is not one of your soldiers," Miles spoke up. "I still feel you should request one of them to volunteer."

"We both know every single person in our army would say yes," Mairead sighed. "Including you. They would see it as their duty, and it feels unfair to ask."

"Isn't it my duty as well?" Velta piped up. "After all, I've accepted your protection. In a way, that means I've also accepted your bargain with the Fey. I've benefited richly from it too."

"Unknowingly."

"Yet, I've still prospered." The armourer made her decision. "I will go. If the Fey really do keep their promises, I will come back. I swear."

On midsummer's day, they arrived at a space between two ancient oak trees, large enough for a person to walk through, but too small for a horse. At noon, the gap turned into a mirror, shining and shimmering. On the other side of that mirror was the realm of the Fey.

The Baroness and Miles watched Velta step through.

Emerging from the portal, she found a woman waiting on the other side. She had expected the Fairykin to be tall and fair. Instead, the woman was so short Velta towered over her. Were all fairies this small?

She realised she was staring, quite rudely.

"Oh... um... Hello. My name is Velta. I've been sent by the Baroness as this year's Ùmhlachd."

"My name is Heulwen," the woman replied. "I will be your guide and protector while you visit with us, since you gave me the gift of your name."

She waved her hand and a table laden with food and drink magically appeared next to them.

"May I offer you something to drink or eat?"

"If I eat anything, will I be trapped here?"

"You are in no danger of being trapped here, or anywhere, while I am with you," Velta's companion laughed. "Even if you were alone, you would be safe enough. Our food can be dangerous, but you have fairy blood and, as such, are not at risk. Did you expect to starve for a year?"

"I have fairy blood?" Velta was stunned by the news.

"Very watered down," the woman confessed. "But it's there."

Relieved and feeling a little braver, Velta asked another question.

"You said my name is a gift?"

"Don't think me impolite, but the sharing of names is a very important ritual in this place. You surprised me when you gave yours so freely, and I felt compelled to return your trust."

She held out a silver goblet.

"Heulwen means 'sunshine' and you are now my honoured guest."

Velta took a sip of the proffered wine and it was wonderful. The buns were delicious as well. She wondered if she was eating dry bread and water, and the infamous fairy glamour was making the meal seem so good. She supposed it didn't matter. She instinctively trusted Heulwen not to let her eat anything that would cause harm.

"This is the land of the Queen of Summer," Heulwen said. "Her palace is near. I shall go and inform her you are here."

Now she had time to look around, Velta studied her surroundings. The twilight didn't brighten or darken. There were no sun, moon or stars to be seen. Instead, the sky glowed with the flowing colours of the aurora. It was never the same for two minutes in a row and Velta was hypnotised into a trance-like state, after she had watched it for a while.

The trees around the glade appeared to be the same sort found in the Welsh woods. Velta had, somehow, expected there would be palms and tropical vines. She associated summer with sweat, the tang of wind-borne salt, and sand chaffing in bodily orifices. The reality was a pleasant surprise.

"The Queen of Summer is ready to meet with you." Heulwen strolled back into the glade. "Follow me, please."

The Queen of Summer's palace was a pavilion, part temple, part tent, the sides left open to catch the breeze. It was every shade of the season, sky blue, sunset red, sunflower yellow, and a thousand colours, glowing like butterfly wings. Instead of a formal garden, there was a profusion of each summer-flowering plant in the world.

The Queen and her throne were even more impressive.

The throne was a massive knot in the trunk of an oak - the biggest tree Velta had ever seen. It was living wood, yet had grown into remarkable sculptures, that mimicked carvings.

Sitting upon the throne, lovely and as regal as the full moon, was the Queen of Summer. Velta was amazed by her incredible colouring. Her complexion was the green of the sun through leaves, and her hair changed constantly, from leaf green to dust red to wheat yellow. Her robe was a dragonfly shimmer brocade, rich with gold thread and decorated with beads of emerald and yellow topaz, while her crown was crafted from the same gems. Beside her stood a sun-gold mare, majestic as a lioness.

"The horse is Epona, her companion and main advisor," Heulwen whispered behind her. "The mare is also an oracle. When we are announced, bow first to the Queen, then to Epona."

Heulwen led Varia to the Queen's throne.

"Haf, Queen of Summer, also known as Sul, goddess of the Sun and Moon, Amaterasu, the Bringer of Light, Habetrot, the Spinner of the Wheel of the Year, and sister to Cailleach Bhear, Queen of Winter. May I present Velta, the tribute."

Velta bowed as deeply as she could manage, then hastily curtsied to Epona. Close up, the Queen was even more glorious, back straight yet pliant as a sunflower, her radiance overpowering.

She gestured to the human.

"I can see my mark upon you, Velta." Her voice contained the honey buzz of bees, the boom of surf and the rattle of leaves in a cool breeze. "It is always a pleasure to discover kin that has been lost to us."

"How kind of you to say, your majesty," Velta muttered.

"I just need to make sure your heart is pure. Please look into my eyes."

Velta stared into the gaze of Summer and was enveloped. White-hot sunshine, storms chained by lightning, freshly mown hay, ripening grain, a goat dying in drought and the pollen-heavy wind dancing with blossoms danced across her vision. Tens of thousands of sensations battered her, then were gone, leaving her alone and bereft.

The Queen spoke to her, her voice sounding far away.

"If that was painful, I'm terribly sorry, child. You *are* kin. That means more here, especially in this place, at this time, when I am in the midst of my duties. A ruler has more responsibility than her subjects and is confined by her own enchanted laws."

She swept an arm around.

"With full summer upon us in Gàidheil, I am at my most powerful. Yet so are my limitations. I give my word you will be never be harmed or imprisoned and this promise I cannot break."

Velta could see the sense in this. If the Queen couldn't keep her own law, how might she be expected to give judgement on any transgressor?

Still, there were still so many unanswered questions about the Fairykin.

"Could you clear something up for me? My mother used to tell me the Queen of Summer is also the Queen of Winter. How can that be?"

"The Queen is not a person," Heulwen interrupted. "The Queen of Winter and the Queen of Summer are the same force of nature, as you cannot have one without the other. It might be better to think of them as twin sisters, born at the same time, but only half of the one true thing. Opposite and equal, one cannot exist without the other."

"Like night and day? Is there a Queen of Autumn and a Queen of Spring?"

"The seasons are not that simple. In temperate climates there is a spring and an autumn, but in other places there may be a wet and a dry, or a time when the winds blow or periods of light and dark. Human beings recognised these as seasons for sowing, growing, harvest and fallow time."

"And the sacrifices?"

"We need a human to give us a sense of this time passing, for we do not work the land or count the years. You aren't a sacrifice. You are a necessary guide to these shifts. But, as we've found, the longer a mortal being lingers in our realm, the less they can detect the changes in seasons. This is why we need a new Ùmhlachd every year."

"What about the others who have come before me?"

"If they wanted to leave, they could. But no one ever does."

"I can see why." Velta was still overwhelmed by the beauty around her. "May I speak with them, though?"

"Of course."

Velta enjoyed her year living with the Fey. She travelled and undertook many adventures, for theirs was a realm of wonders. Yet she deliberately made no friends and built no ties.

One week before she was to return to the mortal realm, Velta was again allowed to meet with the Queen of Summer. This time, her throne was in the middle of a field of wildflowers. Insects hummed in every blossom, and her court lounged around her, looking like a garden of strange posies.

"Well, young one," said the Queen, when greetings and other pleasantries had been exchanged. "Do you wish to remain in my realm or return to your own?"

"If it pleases your majesty, I would prefer to return to my duties with the Baroness of Gàidheil, the Lady Mairead."

"You are the first of the Ùmhlachd to request this." The Queen looked genuinely surprised. "Are you certain? Once you leave, you can never return."

"I am sure. It was delightful to visit your realm, but my place is beside my Baroness."

"You have done your duty by us," The Queen smiled. "There are few gifts I can give you that would survive the portal back into your world, but here are two. First of all, you have my heartfelt thanks. I will keep the memory of you alive for as long as there is summer in the world. Secondly, I can strengthen the fairy blood in your veins, so you will live a long and healthy life."

"I'm overwhelmed by your kindness, majesty," Velta bowed.

The Baroness was standing with the new Ùmhlachd, when Velta stepped back into the mortal world. Both their faces lit up with relief.

"Well met, milady." Velta raised a hand in greeting. "I look forward to getting back to my tools and forge.

"Well met, Mistress Velta. The sight of your sonsy face gladdens my heart. In truth, I was not expecting you to return."

"The world through that door is wondrous, but there is no iron or steel in the Fey realm and I am married to my work."

The Baroness nodded gratefully.

"Besides," Velta said. "I gave you my word."

And those with Fey blood never broke a promise.

A Promise of Ash And Blood

Caitlyn McPherson

Kazumi had always known she'd been born different. Even without her mother's dark whispers of forest spirits, yokai, and fox-magic, she'd understood she was not quite human. So it really wasn't a surprise she'd ended up in the bowels of the fortress dungeon, beaten and bruised, her kimono covered in ash and blood, awaiting judgment.

Something in the corner of her cell scurried towards her, paused, then scuttled away. Likely another rat. It was impossible to tell in the pitch black, but her keen hearing and sense of smell was rarely mistaken.

How long had she been down here? It could have been hours, maybe a day? Two?

She didn't care anymore.

Further up the hall, whimpers echoed off cold stone. Someone had been quietly pleading for food since Kazumi had awoken. More than once, she'd tried to call out to them through the darkness, but there was never anything more than a strangled moan in reply.

Kazumi had fallen silent after that. Her throat was raw and dried out from inhaling smoke during the fire. She'd given up groping blindly in the dark for the water bucket that should have been supplied. Apparently, her jailers had neglected to give her one.

"Mama was right." she rasped between gritted teeth.

No matter how hard she'd tried to lead a normal existence, how hard she tried to fit in, Kazumi would never truly be one of them. It didn't matter that she'd been a dutiful daughter and loving wife. In the end, all they saw was a creature less than human. A monster.

She slumped against the damp stone wall then curled forward again, as pain lanced through her abdomen. Even now, the ache lingered. At this rate she was just as likely to die of infection as she was from thirst. Or, would they drag her into the middle of town and execute her before a crowd, like they always did with her kind?

No. Surely Takuma would rescue her before it came to that. As the lord's second son, he had the authority to stay her execution. If they could just talk, if he could see her and hear her out, he would realize how different she was to other yokai. After all, she was half human and still his wife.

The soft pad of feet down the stairs alerted Kazumi to a visitor before the flickering glow of a lantern broke through the dungeon. She shielded her sensitive eyes behind the shadow of her hand. After hours locked up in the dark, even the softest light was blinding.

A few heartbeats passed before she lowered her arm and saw who had come to visit her.

"Takuma!" Kazumi gasped and stumbled up to the bars, reaching a hand out towards him. She wanted to feel the warmth of his calloused fingers entwined with hers. Feel the weight of those familiar arms around her. Kazumi broke into tears before he could respond. She hadn't thought she had any more tears to give, but something about her husband's presence drew more heartache to the surface.

"Y-you came!" she sobbed, wiping tears on her charred kimono sleeve. "Takuma, I... I..."

There was so much she wanted to say to him but the words wouldn't come. How could she explain? Everything that had happened since she'd left his embrace that morning had turned from a dream into a nightmare. Kazumi sank to her knees, face in hands.

"You can stop with the act." Takuma's voice was so low and soft it was practically a growl.

Tears still blurring her vision, Kazumi looked up in confusion, trying to make sense of the cold words. The golden lantern light did little to soften his sharp features. The shadows under his eyes only darkened his expression further as he scowled down at her.

How could he look at her like that? As if she were his enemy? He might not be wearing his samurai armour, but he was ready to battle.

"Please, Takuma, you don't understand!"

"What's to understand?" He gritted between clenched teeth. "You're a liar and a murderer."

"W-what?"

"Don't play innocent. Did you think bewitching me and making me fall in love with you would somehow save you from your fate, kitsune?"

Kazumi recoiled, as though she'd been slapped. She hated that word with her entire being, hated the way it slid like poison from those same lips that had once kissed her with such tenderness. How could he think such a thing! As though she were the one betraying him and not the other way around. She couldn't help who her mother was, but she did have control over her actions and the way she decided to live her life. She had always chosen her papa, to live as a human, despite the maddening call of the forests.

"Don't say such horrible things! It's never been like that. I love you, Takuma."

His knuckles turned white as they tightened around the hilt of his sword.

"Save your honeyed lies, Kazumi. I am no longer the fool I was. I saw the bodies. Who do you think dragged you out of the blaze before the place collapsed? Those men were in pieces."

He glanced pointedly at the deadly sharp claws that still protruded from her fingers and the bushy fox-tail that swished behind her back.

Even hours after her initial transformation, she still hadn't worked out how to shift back to normal. Not that she intended to hide what she'd done from Takuma. If there was anyone who'd understand, she thought it would be him.

"They got what they deserved." Kazumi snapped. "After what they did to papa. To me. To our…"

The words died on her cracked lips and she stared at the dark stain down the leg of her kimono. The bleeding had stopped hours ago, but the loss of life from her womb was a scar that would never heal. Kazumi's fingers curled into fists and she bit back the anguished howl bubbling in her throat. No matter how angry Takuma was, or how unfair, she didn't want to break his heart with the news.

Their baby was dead.

Takuma scanned her head to toe, tracing each bruise and scratch, each smear of blood. Then something clicked and his eyes widened.

"The child?"

Lips trembling, she dropped her head and nodded.

Takuma inhaled sharply.

"No…" He slid to the ground and buried his face between his hands, lantern and sword forgotten. He was silent for a long time, his chest shuddering with each breath. But, when he spoke again, his voice held firm.

"Tell me what happened. From the beginning."

It had been late in the afternoon when Kazumi had left for her papa's little textile shop on the edge of town. The sun hadn't yet set and the sky was darkening to a beautiful shade of purple, much like the wisteria that grew in gardens of Takuma's family estate.

By now, most of the merchants in town had begun to shut up shop, save a few restaurants opening for the night crowd. Kazumi hurried past those. The smell of roasted pork and boiled egg-noodles churned her stomach these days.

She was pregnant.

She'd suspected for a while, but doctor Watanabe had confirmed it this morning. Nearly two months along, if he was correct. Takuma had radiated with joy at the announcement. He'd picked Kazumi up by the waist and swung her around, promising neither she nor the baby would ever want for anything. She'd laughed and kissed him in return.

Takuma left to share the good news with his parents and brother, while Kazumi set off to her papa's. She smiled as she gently pressed a hand to her stomach. Papa would be beside himself with joy. She wouldn't be surprised if he threw a celebration for her. After all, he had always spoiled her with gifts. Anything from elegant kimono to pretty hairpins, like the one she was wearing today. She'd never worked out how he'd managed to afford such expensive presents, but it wasn't her place to question such generosity. If he wanted to shower the baby with similar gifts, she wouldn't stop him.

When Kazumi reached the shop, she was perturbed to see the door open. But Papa was getting old. Perhaps he'd forgotten to close up before heading out back to his quarters.

"Papa?" she called, expecting him to saunter around the corner and greet her with open arms.

When no reply came, Kazumi called a little louder.

"Where are you?"

Still nothing.

Kazumi entered the premises and took in the disarray, eyes widening with shock. Had there been a fight?

She ran over to the counter. Papa's paperwork was scattered over the floor and his favourite Inari ornament was broken in two. Why? He might sell some of the finest wares in town, but hardly made enough profit to garner the attention of thieves.

Panic rose in her chest. Should she run and call for help? Try to find Takuma or one of his men?

She never got a chance to decide. A set of heavy footsteps crunched behind her.

"Well shit…knew I shoulda closed the door earlier."

Kazumi spun around and screamed. Before her loomed a giant man, bulging with muscle and covered in nasty scars.

She leapt for the door but he was quicker and stronger. His hand shot out and grasped her hair, yanking her backwards and smothering her scream with a calloused hand.

"Geez woman! Shut your mouth already." He dragged her out back, kicking and flailing, until they reached the screen door that led to her Papa's private rooms.

"Let's try again shall we, Mr Sato? Where is my money?" the question was punctuated by hard thumps and a breathless wheeze of pain.

Were… were they beating her father?

The shoji door slid to the side and Kazumi was jostled into the room.

Her Papa, Satoshi Sato, lay prone in the centre of the room, arms tied behind his back. Bruises were purpling around his left eye and his lip and nose dripped with blood. His clothes had been torn and hung loosely from his chest, showing off more dark marks. He was clearly in pain yet, when he looked at her, the fear in his eyes was for her.

"Found this one sneakin' round the front, boss." Scar-man said gruffly. "Want me to deal with 'er?'

"L-leave my daughter out of this. P-please Daichi, I beg you..." Papa's plea was cut off as the man next to him drove a foot into his ribs.

"It's much too late for that, Mr Sato," the one called Daichi sighed. "Such dirty business when family gets involved, but you were warned what would happen if you didn't get the money to me in time."

He lounged back on a cushion, chin propped on a hand. His black and grey yukata was decorated with an eagle and snake locked in battle, talons and fangs clashing. Even without the irezumi tattoos peeking from the shadows of his sleeve, Kazumi could tell this man was a member of the Yakuza. Not just any member. He was clearly their leader.

Yakuza were notorious for their ruthless and brutal dealings. How had her sweet, hard-working Papa become involved with them? Her stomach dropped. Was that where he'd gotten the money to afford those gifts over the years?

Suddenly, the hairpin she wore felt less of a gift and more of a curse.

Daichi's pitiless gaze slid to her. It felt like centipedes crawling over her skin but she refused to look away. She wasn't going to give him that satisfaction, no matter how much he terrified her.

"Bring the girl here." he commanded.

"N-no! Daichi, p-please!" Satoshi begged. "I'll get you the money, I-I just need more time!"

"Mr Sato, your time is of no value to me. I've come to collect and I'm not walking away empty handed."

Kazumi barely had time to brace herself as she was thrown at Daichi's feet. Her palms and knees smacked against the hard floor and her hair fell in disarray about her shoulders. Daichi leaned in and grabbed her chin between thumb and fingers. Forced her face side to side, then up and down.

"A little on the plump side, but still…" he chuckled. "Bet those lips would make me a lot of money, if put to proper use."

Bile rose in the back of Kazumi's throat. This man was beyond disgusting. Bracing her hands against the floor, she pushed backwards and yanked her face out of his grasp. How dare he touch her? How dare he suggest…

"I am the wife of Takuma Yamamoto, the Wolf of Izuki." Kazumi took a shaky breath. "Touch me again and you'll be lucky if he lets you keep your head."

She forced confidence into her voice. These men might be merciless criminals but surely they knew where to draw the line. And if they didn't… Takuma would gladly draw it for them with his blade.

Daichi stood slowly, his lips twisting into a cruel smile. Without warning his foot slammed into her chest. Kazumi cried out as the force of it knocked her flat. She blinked up at Daichi, as he loomed over her.

"You should've kept that pretty mouth shut." He shoved his bare foot roughly over her mouth. "Your ransom should more than cover the old man's debt and the time I've wasted in this shithole."

Daichi nodded to his men. The scarred one sauntered over to her Papa, untied his ropes and flattened Satoshi's left hand on the ground. The shorter one, missing an ear, drew a butchers knife from his robes.

"But, it's no longer just about money. Your old man needs to be taught a lesson."

Daichi made a show of inspecting each of his fingers.

"How many should I take? One? Two?"

Kazumi's eyes widened in horror. No. No he couldn't mean... She frantically twisted, dug fingernails into the soft skin at Daichi's ankles and scratched with the ferocity of an animal.

"Argh! Crazy bitch!" Fast as a viper, he retaliated with a crushing stomp to her stomach. The air left her lungs and pain exploded through her body. It twisted her abdomen and shot up her spine, setting every nerve on fire. Black stars swam across her vision.

She was vaguely aware of sticky wetness soaking through her kimono and staining the floor.

Her baby...

Anguish ripped through her chest and tore out her heart. She wanted to scream and scream, until her throat was raw, but couldn't. She and her Papa were still in danger.

Kazumi curled onto her side and surveyed the room. Daichi and his men had returned their attention to her Papa. They'd shoved his face into the floor and splayed his fingers out beneath one-ear's knife. Clutching her stomach, Kazumi clambered to her knees. Agony laced every movement and blood slowly trickled down her legs, but she had to stop them from mutilating her Papa.

Time slowed as the blade came down over Satoshi's fingers.

She was going to kill them.

Every. Last. One of them.

All her life, Kazumi had feared giving into her yokai blood. But these scum were creatures far worse than her. They preyed on honest, hard-working people. Hurt those weaker than themselves simply because they could. They enjoyed it.

And they had killed her baby.

Kazumi pushed herself up slowly, letting rage and grief burn away the pain. The floorboards groaned beneath her fingers, then splintered as long, sharp claws gouged through the timber.

"Err, boss…"

She was done being weak. Done being at their mercy. Done playing by their rules.

Done keeping the wild animal locked up in its cage.

Daichi swung back around, his eyes widening.

"Kitsune!" Daichi spat. The word echoed through the room like a curse.

Not human.

A monster.

Kazumi didn't need a mirror to know she looked the part. Her lips peeled back over elongated fangs and she let loose a vicious snarl.

"Don't just stand there, shitheads," Daichi ordered. "Kill her!"

Kazumi crouched, her muscles taught as a bowstring ready to fire. She had no idea what she was doing, so she let instinct guide her.

Scar-man was the first to lunge. He'd been faster and stronger than her before her transformation, but not anymore. Kazumi launched herself at him, sidestepping his fists and slashing her claws from hip to armpit. Fabric, skin and muscle tore in long ragged lines and he screamed. He swung at her again, backhand whooshing through the air. Kazumi ducked, pivoted to the side and thrust with all her strength. Blood spirted through the air in an arc as she ripped out his throat. He clutched at the ravaged flesh and collapsed.

From the corner of her eye, Kazumi caught the glint of silver rushing towards her. She twisted to the side, narrowly avoiding the butcher's knife as it flew through the air. His lips split into a wicked grin as he drew a second knife from his belt.

"Here kitty kitty." He taunted.

Ignorant asshole. She was a kitsune.

Kazumi shifted into a low crouch. She'd have to attack low to avoid getting cut.

One-ear leapt at her, stabbing and slicing. Kazumi rolled beneath his reach, swivelled and clawed through the tendons of his ankles. One-ear buckled under his own weight, falling face first with a howl. Kazumi pounced on his back and pinned him down. Her fingers curled around her hairpin and she thrust the needle-sharp point into the soft flesh of One-ear's neck. He bucked and flailed beneath her, squealing in terror, but she didn't stop. She stabbed again and again until the shrieks turned to gurgled choking and his body went limp.

Panting heavily, Kazumi crawled off the body and staggered to her feet.

One more to go.

She snatched up One-ear's discarded knife and rounded on Daichi cowering in the corner. His face drained of colour as she ran a claw along the blade.

"How many should I take?" She repeated his words back to him. "One? Two?"

Sweat beaded on Daichi's forehead, as he started to back away. One step. Two steps. Kazumi smiled broadly, flashing her fangs. Now that the snake had shed its skin, she could see him for what he truly was. A worm. Daichi spun on his feet and sprinted for the door but blue-white flames exploded in front of him, blocking his path.

Kitsune fire.

Another conflagration sparked to life in the palm of her hand, growing in size as she fed her fury into it. She flung it at Daichi and the fireball slammed into his chest, blasting him into the wall. He shrieked and thrashed wildly as his yukata ignited and the flames quickly engulfed him. Kazumi turned away. He might deserve it, but that didn't mean she could stomach watching.

Ignoring Daichi's dying screams and the awful stench of burning flesh, Kazumi dashed across the room to her Papa. He lay unconscious in a pool of his own blood.

"You have to get up! I'm not strong enough to carry you. Wake up Papa, we need to get you to a doctor."

The crackle of flames caught Kazumi's attention. Daichi's smouldering corpse and her first fireball had taken on a life of their own. The conflagration was burning through the thin shoji screens and climbing the wooden beams to the ceiling rafters.

The whole place would be engulfed in moments. Rolling her Papa over, Kazumi slid her arms under his armpits and slowly dragged him towards the door. Sweat trickled down her back and her muscles ached but she kept moving. Smoke was starting to smother the room, rolling overhead like storm clouds. Breathing was getting steadily harder, each inhale scorching her throat.

Overhead the timber groaned and creaked.

"Come on, Papa!" she wheezed, eyes watering from the smoke. "Wake up!"

She yanked him closer but the doorway was still so far away. The haze was getting thicker and her body weaker. She couldn't seem to get enough air into her lungs and everything was getting... fuzzy.

There was a thunderous crack, as one of the burning beams came crashing to the ground in a shower of embers. From somewhere beyond the blaze, Kazumi heard a voice calling to her. It was hard to tell over the roar of the fire. Black dots swam behind her eyes. She couldn't focus.

"Kazumi! Where are you!?"

It sounded like Takuma.

Kazumi crumpled to the floor and the world went dark.

"My Papa's dead, isn't he?" It was a statement rather than a question.

Takuma's grim expression gave her the answer she dreaded.

"I couldn't go back for him." His tear-reddened eyes connected with hers. "I'm sorry, Kazumi. For everything."

The beginnings of hope flickered to life in Kazumi's chest. He understood.

"But none of that matters now." He growled. "I see now, those men got a cleaner death then they deserved. But you're still half kitsune. My father has ordered your execution."

Kazumi's hope turned to ash in her mouth. Claws cut into her palms as she clenched her fists. It wasn't fair! She'd played by everyone else's rules, lost and somehow, she was still the villain?

"I never chose this," she snapped. "Never wanted any of this to happen. If I hadn't done what was needed, I would be dead. Are you going to blindly accept your father's command? I didn't realize I married a coward."

Her shoulders shook with barely contained fury.

"You married a samurai, Kazumi! How the hell did you think this was going to end? That you and I would get a happy ending, simply because you chose to keep your head in the sand."

Takuma dug the heels of his palms into his eyes.

"If I'd known from the start, I would have slain you where you stood."

Her heart lurched at his reply. She had been a fool to think Takuma would pick her over his responsibilities as a samurai.

"Why don't you just be done with it, then! Go on!" She drew a claw in a cross over her heart. "There's not much of it left, but it still beats."

"You think I wouldn't have already, if I could?" He ran a hand over his face. "Do you have any idea of the torment you've placed upon me? I'm sworn to hunt and kill yokai like you, but what kind of man kills the woman he loves?"

Kazumi didn't know whether to laugh or cry.

"Then don't! No one else needs to know what I am. We can go about our lives as if this never happened."

"Stop living in a dream Kazumi." Takuma shook his head sadly. "There is no reality where you get to walk away from this. You can't imagine how furious my father is that someone like you married into the family without anyone realizing you were Kitsune. If this were to go public, my entire clan would be disgraced."

Her gaze dropped. Her flesh and blood were gone and her only remaining family had turned on her like wolves. When would the sting of betrayal stop?

"Kazumi..." Takuma's voice was soft, the way it had been before the fire. "This is where we part ways. Tomorrow you will be brought before my father for execution."

Numbness spread over her body. The hope that Takuma would see past his prejudice and acknowledge her for who she was, not what she was, wilted and died.

Jaw clenched, Kazumi turned her back on Takuma and the light. Her silhouette stretched ominously before her, foxtail lashing back and forth. With a sigh, Takuma got to his feet.

"Maybe in the next life, we can meet again under different stars."

She really hoped they didn't. Because if they did, it would not be as lovers but as enemies. Takuma had made his choice and in doing so taken away hers. A viscous growl rumbled up her throat and her shadow rippled with anger.

"Farewell, Kazumi," he whispered.

Then he was gone, footsteps disappearing up the stairway along with the lantern light. Kazumi shuddered as the darkness swallowed her once more. It seeped into every pore, into the marrow of her bones and settled in her broken heart.

If I'd known from the start, I would have slain you where you stood. Kitsune.

I'm sworn to hunt and kill yokai like you.

Monster.

How the hell did you think this was going to end?

Cursed.

There was no point resisting anymore. No going back to the life she'd had or the person she'd been.

Kazumi spread her arms in an arc. A ring of blue-white flames blazed to life at her bidding. Focusing her energy, she clawed the air and tugged. Shadows and smoke coalesced around her, slithering up her legs and arms.

If they wanted a monster at that execution tomorrow, she would give them one.

She was done being human.

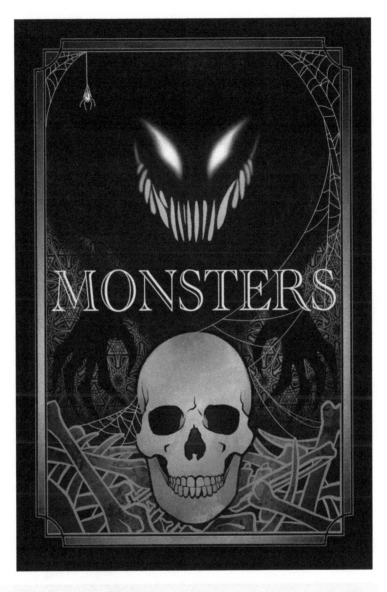

Whoever fights monsters should see to it that in the process he does not become a monster. And if you gaze long enough into an abyss, the abyss will gaze back into you.

Friedrich Nietzsche

A Monster Circles the Wreckage

Jan-Andrew Henderson

Serial killers are not radicals: they have enthusiastically embraced the established order only to discover that it offers them no place they can endure. Encalculated with an ambition which they are either unable to attain or cannot feel at ease living.
Dr Elliot Leyton. *Hunting Humans.*

I didn't think or realize I would ever do these things... I never really wanted to hurt anybody... what drove me to do this? I don't think I was born like this. Why did I start?
Albert De Salvo, The Boston Strangler.

"You know. There are two types of criminals." Miles Harrison was seated in the captain's chair, though the oxygen tank strapped to his back meant he had to perch on the edge. "Some think their biggest mistake was getting caught. Others believe it was getting born."

He glanced at Stuart.

"Aren't you going to take notes?"

"Oh, very droll." Stuart's arm was missing just above the elbow. "Don't worry. I won't forget this shit-show in a hurry."

A slow spiral of blood floated up from the ragged stump, diluted by water. From behind his mask, Miles could see the cabin had taken on a rose-tinted hue.

"Due to the circumstances, I'm going to be fairly direct," Stuart said. "I don't wanna... just circle the subject."

165

"Not like our friend outside, huh?"

As if on cue, a huge dark mass drifted past the window, momentarily blocking the weak light. Miles was almost out of air, but he had no intention of venturing beyond the cabin while that creature lurked in the gloom. Stuart followed it with his eyes.

"Looks like this is your last chance to come clean."

"You want to know why I killed these women?" Miles thought for a while. "I think it was cause of a novel I was trying to write. Or maybe there wasn't much on TV these nights. In the end, all roads lead to Rome, Stuart."

He checked the cylinder gauge. Well below the caution zone. And he had so much to say. The two men obviously couldn't hear each other, yet communication didn't seem to be a problem. Maybe because of encroaching Hypoxia. Maybe because Stuart had died half an hour ago.

"Nazis!" Miles decided a tirade would fastest. "Let me tell you about Nazis, Stu. Wore nice uniforms. Invaded Poland. What about those former blue-eyed boys?"

He put on a cut glass English accent.

"How could the rotten Jerry persecute those poor homeless Jews? Bad form. Filthy Hun. Only Jews aren't poor or homeless anymore, says Facebook. No. Now they're controlling America or persecuting poor homeless Palestinians."

"That's Israelis. There's a distinction."

"Don't muddy the waters." Miles laughed mirthlessly. "Every man on the street knows, if we all gave an itsy bitsy, teeny weeny yellow polka dot bit of our wages to the Third World, we could wipe out famine. Cheese off our little suburban dicks. Do we do it?"

"I guess not," his companion admitted.

"Course not! We've endless excuses. I don't wanna be encouraging these people to have more kids - not with a global famine on! They overpopulate their world and next thing you know they're over here overpopulating ours. Turn back the fuckers' boats! Let 'em drown!"

He gave the instrument console a muffled thump.

"How do you think this nasty old tub ended up down here? It was already a grave before I discovered the wreck. I just added to it."

"How efficient of you. Also, a bit simplistic in the analogy department."

"Aw, don't tell me you people can't see the big picture. You're all sitting high enough up on white, middle class, picket fences."

"I wasn't going to," Stuart began. But Miles was on a roll.

"There's always a war going on somewhere, so you might have to become a Nazi, or you'll end up skulking in the ghetto. But you gotta be careful, eh? When a soldier fires at the enemy, he's a patriot. By the time the bullet has reached its victim, yet another ceasefire has been declared and he's a murderer. Ends up on death row, waiting for the state to execute *him*."

The oxygen gauge gave a bleep and Miles forced himself to calm down.

"We're allowed to kill, Stuart. I just didn't get the proper permission."

"Right. Thanks." Stuart's face remained impassive, but a slight eddy caught his wispy hair and wafted it upwards. It gave the impression that he was horrified and trying not to show it.

"I should have had you over for a Xmas lunch. Not just a provocative raconteur but an expert on carving. We could have eaten spleen with a nice bottle of Chianti."

"Call it the times, or genetics or our upbringing, but we're as much a mass product as the processed meat on any supermarket counter." Miles ignored the sarcasm. "Future generations will probably look back on us eating animals with the same disgust we have for people who kept slaves."

"So... You were writing down your fantasies." Stuart refused to be side-tracked. "Then you acted them out. Would that be right?"

"No. Not at all."

"What then? Your pencil snapped and you did too?"

"Once things are down on paper, they come a little closer to being real, yes. But what I wrote didn't make me want to kill anyone. Course not. It just set my mind on a certain track. See, I stopped asking myself *what makes people kill* and started asking *what stops them from doing it?* Y'know? I seriously thought about it."

"And what stops them from doing it?"

"Circumstances mainly. And another reason."

"What's that?"

"They never seriously thought about doing it."

Outside the window, the leviathan made another pass, looking for some way to reach them. But the aluminium and fibreglass of the fishing boat's cabin had held up well, despite years under the sea, though the wooden panels were rotted and covered in barnacles. The compass was overgrown with moss and the steering wheel had fallen off long ago and lay on the floor like a spiky tarnished halo.

"Awright." Stuart flourished an imaginary pen. "An awkward question. For an... ah... obviously intelligent guy. Well... your jobs..."

"Shit, huh?"

"Not exactly rocket science."

"I got bored easily. What's the difference between cleaning a toilet and curing cancer? One takes a lot longer. You never felt like that?"

"I suppose."

"Well, I'm more unsettled than you and you had a better job than me."

"I didn't, really." The man looked abashed. "I didn't make a lot of money."

"Shame. You would have, after this."

"What would you like to have done?"

"Avoided killing people, mainly."

"Ehm... apart from that?"

"I dunno. Something creative. Not writing, though. I gave that up. It's too cerebral. Too many notes, Mozart. That's why I asked you to tell my story."

"But you pinned your hopes on writing at one time?"

"I figured if I could get things published, that would set me up in a lot of ways. I could earn money and still not be stuck, y'know?"

"But you never got anything published."

"Nothing," Miles chuckled. "Not even my novel about a goddamned serial killer. Guess it didn't ring true."

His head had begun to ache and he checked the gauge again. It was firmly in the red. His arms felt sluggish, though he was hardly in the same boat as Stuart. Then again, he was. Miles began to giggle.

"Around the time you went... off the rails," Stuart said tactfully. "You were seeing a woman. Ally Stone. 28 years old."

He glanced at imaginary notes.

"Pretty young."

"Thank you. There were a couple of others, but they were casual."

"You shittin me?"

"I'd got that 'deep but fun' thing down pat. The 'hint of badness' that girls love."

"Yeah. If you're still living in the 1980s."

"Perhaps I was. Upshot of my environment and all that. Guess those girls didn't take the hint."

"I'm surprised you could get it up so often." Stuart's eyebrow arched and a couple of small bubbles drifted off, as if he'd had a cartoonish thought. "You could... couldn't you?"

Miles raised his own eyebrows in return.

"Forget it." Stuart grimaced. "I don't need to know every tiny little detail."

"Specially not if you're gonna phrase it like that. And don't be simplistic. My motivations were... complex."

"Was your sexual relationship with Ally a good one, then?"

"I'd say so."

"But... something must have been missing."

"You still think the adoring public has to know the size of my member?" Miles pursed his lips.

"No. You keep that under your hat, metaphorically speaking." Stuart gave an annoyed snort. "Besides, nobody's gonna read about you now."

Miles let the barb pass.

"I don't know. I guess sex was never a be-all and end-all for me. I mean, there's a brief period after the initial nervousness and the eventual... boredom, when screwing someone is great." He hesitated. "All right, boredom's too strong a word. Having nothing new to show them and them to show you."

He raised a hand to his brow, as if scanning unknown horizons.

"The first few times you're both explorers. After that..."

"New lands to explore?"

"That's right. But I was getting old Stuart. Way past my prime. A salty old dog with nothing but stories of previous encounters, slowly turning into a ruin of his former self."

"With a lover 20 years your junior." His companion sounded envious. "Doesn't sound so bad."

"She'd find a younger me, eventually. Too many wrinkles, Mozart." Miles patted his face. "Don't underestimate the call of the sea. Plenty more fish there."

"And what do explorers do when the only new lands left are hostile?"

"They attack and subdue them."

"Much as I appreciate these nautical metaphors, you gonna kiss and tell?"

"Nothing to say. I loved Ally and she loved me. She even asked me to go to America with her. But the age gap was huge and she wasn't the settling down type either. Then what? I... I... had a job here."

"That's right. You were head of Microsoft."

"In the end, she wouldn't want some old guy hanging on her coat tails." Miles flicked his flippers and rose a few inches, hovering over the seat. "You know what happens when you try to be Peter Pan? People stop believing in you and you fade away."

He sank back down and looked around. There were five female corpses in the corner of the cabin, weighed down by chains round their necks. Prey to every passing marine animal, none of them had faces. Miles tried hard to think but most of their names eluded him. Due to lack of air, he presumed. Or perhaps he had never known. His lungs were starting to hurt.

"Tell me about the women, Miles." Stuart broke into his reverie. "It's time."

"Let's see. If you took all the girls I slept with and laid them end to end, about a dozen would get run over on the highway."

"Being flippant isn't helping your case."

"I didn't mean to kill the first one, you know." Miles shrugged. "I was just getting my own back and it spiralled out of control."

"Getting your own back. You wanted revenge on society."

"I wanted revenge on her." Miles searched his memory. "I was at an ATM with Ally. She was being too slow or too flamboyant, I don't know."

"How can you be flamboyant at an ATM?"

"Ally could, trust me. Anyway, there were a couple of young girls behind us. Tall, blonde, out for the night. Cleavage like the Bermuda fuckin triangle. Started slagging Ally. Maybe it was the way she was dressed. Or just trying to cause trouble. I told one of them to shut it and, bang, the boyfriend was there - looking like he should've been on top of the Empire State building swatting planes. Right up in my face, he was."

Miles leaned forwards and rasped out a Brooklyn accent.

You looking at me, huh? You fuckin looking at me?

"You were attacked by Robert De Niro?"

"He's the only tough guy I can imitate."

"Did you get into a fight?"

"Nah. I hate violence. Anyhow, couple of months later, I saw one of those girls again, going into her apartment. Then I knew where she lived. I kept watch on her house a couple of times, sort of like a game."

"A game?" Stuart frowned.

"I kinda thought I could use it as research for my book. To follow someone and secretly watch them? I wanted that novel so much to be a success. Thought I had a unique perspective."

"I'd certainly go along with that."

"I needed to really experience what a fledgling killer would. You're writing about me, after all. Don't you want to be accurate? But you won't understand how I feel, no matter how much I describe it. You'd have to..."

"Let's stick with the narrative," Stuart interrupted. "I'll live."

He glanced at his missing arm.

"That was a dumb thing to say."

"All right, maybe I was thinking of some way I could get back at her." Miles' face crumpled. "I only wanted to frighten her. Take some money. I was broke. She hurt other people without a second thought. Why shouldn't she have the tables turned? She gave up her right to safety, picking on Ally like that. I don't know. I had a million reasons."

"Too many notes, Mozart?"

"Yeah. Anyway, she came home late one night. Short skirt. Staggering a bit. I'd been drinking. She'd been drinking."

He clenched his fists and pounded his head.

"To this day I still don't know where I found the nerve. I wish to God I hadn't. But I crawled through the window. Slammed into her coming out of the bedroom and there was no turning back."

He closed his eyes.

"I tied her to a kitchen chair and gagged her. I had a mask on and I went looking for cash. She was making whimpering noises in the next room, reminding me she was there. I only wanted to let her see what it's like to be threatened. I leaned over her, pretending like I was going to do something to scare her. I moved my hands down over her breasts. To show her what it's like being abused by a stranger."

He looked at the floor.

"And... maybe cause I wanted to feel them."

"Miles..."

"I just... kept going." He raised his head defiantly. "You play dog eat dog and a bigger animal might just come along and gobble you up. Too many dogs, Mozart."

"Don't start telling me you ate your victims." Stuart looked distinctly queasy. "I'll probably barf."

"Not at all. I always knew I wasn't quite right, though." Miles seemed properly reflective for a second. "I mean, I could act like the nicest guy in the world but my best friend might be pouring her heart out to me, and if there was a song I liked on the radio..."

"Half your brain would be listening to that."

"All of it. Then again, I'm a big music fan."

"And a complete sociopath."

"Well, duh! That's why you have to cover up your flaws." Miles gave a charming smile, though it was hidden by his mouthpiece. "Nobody likes flaws. Everyone pretends, to some extent. No honey! You're not too fat... ya big sweaty beast. Of course I wouldn't fuck your sister... unless she let me. We all think horrible thoughts and pretend we don't, so why not go for broke? Why not do exactly what we want to do and pretend we don't? Not hurting someone's feelings is much more important than truth."

"I'd say killing these women went a damn sight further than hurting their feelings." Stuart was stone faced. "Don't *you* have feelings to hurt?"

"I know how to feel lots of things," Miles retorted. "I know how to feel like an outsider. I know how to feel like a failure. I know how to feel incomplete. I know how to feel scared. I know how to feel useless. I know how to feel cheated. I know how to feel lonely."

He grunted sourly.

"And I know how to pretend that I don't."

"You want to tell me about the other killings?" Stuart asked.

"Do I have to?"

"Yeah, Miles. It's sort of what makes you interesting to the general public."

"Shame, that, isn't it?

"Why victim two? Any particular reason?

"I worked for her years ago. She was a complete bastard. I can honestly say the world would be better off without her. Eventually, I took her out."

Stuart looked astonished. Miles made a slashing movement with his hand.

"No. *Took* her out."

"What... eh... What... was it like?"

"I don't have words for it, Stuart. A feeling of absolute power. A release from everything that makes you human or, at least, part of the human race. It's disgusting. Sickening. But... your head spins."

Miles' head was spinning right now, and he felt sick. He sat up straighter and sucked hard, trying to coax more oxygen from the tank.

"You'd have to try it to understand."

"I don't appreciate comments like that."

"Victim three? I'd never seen her before. Aw, there were a thousand pretty girls passing me by on the street, every day. Too many women, Mozart. I was getting older. My hair was thinning. My time was ending. But I couldn't let it be over. Picking up dames was the only thing I'd ever been good at."

"Why didn't you just..." Stuart began. But Miles wasn't finished.

"I saw a woman. She was young, beautiful. She'd never look twice at me now. Never try to know me. So, I decided I would have her. I could do anything I wanted. Why not? Why the fuck not?"

"Cause.... it's horrible, Miles."

"I know. That's why I killed her afterwards." Miles levelled a finger at Stuart. "See... anything is acceptable as long as you don't have to stare it in the face. Like when you ignore those starving people all over the world. Or the ones risking their lives to get to another country."

Miles summoned a last burst of energy.

"Death. Taxes. Your life slipping away. The shit this world is in. The pointlessness of it. Your pointless, shitty, mundane little life, slipping away before your eyes. Anything at all. Don't you realise that? Anything is acceptable as long as you don't have to stare it in the face."

"No. No... no. I'm not taking that." Stuart shook his head. "I'm not taking that."

"Why? Cause it's not true or cause you don't fucking well want it to be true! If you're so squeamish, you're the wrong man for this job."

"I know the truth about you. You're a heartless killer."

"Simplistic! You realised that before you started! You were a struggling writer, just like me. And you jumped at the chance when I offered you the scoop of a lifetime. Believed me when I said I wouldn't harm you. That I'd show you where the bodies were."

"I wanted proof before I handed everything over to the police, you ass."

"I figured that. I didn't figure a fucking Great White was gonna tear your arm off on the way down to the wreck, then trap us here." Miles glanced at his watch. "I should be on my way to the bloody airport to catch a flight to the USA."

"I thought you might have contacted me because you secretly wanted to be caught. You'd have been tracked down if I'd survived. No matter where you went."

"I'm a master at hiding myself, remember? Maybe I just wanted to understand what it's like to be hunted. Give myself a scare, so I'd throw out the anchor a bit and get a grip."

Miles peered through the cabin windows. There was no sign of the shark. He would have heaved a sigh of relief but couldn't spare the air.

"Let me ask you a question, Stuart." He decided to turn the tables. "Suppose there's someone you know and don't like. What stops you from killing them?"

"Some moral code I guess."

"Would this be your own moral code?"

"Yes, it'd be my personal moral code."

Miles smiled thinly, ready to pounce.

"So, in that case... you could change your mind whenever it suited."

"Not at all," his companion protested. "I think we're also conditioned from childhood to adulthood, enforced with a decency the church or society, at one time or other, has put upon us."

"OK. Therefore, if you could get rid of the conditioning of church and society your personal principles could be totally flexible. Wouldn't that follow?"

Stuart considered this before shaking his head.

"I think there is an atavistic fear in all of us about taking the life of someone else. We still subscribe to some arcane ideal we can't get rid of."

Miles leaned forward, hungrily.

"Suppose you could take all the morals out of the world. Exorcise yourself from their hold. What would you replace them with?"

"Common decency?"

"That's a concept, Stu. Stop being coy."

"You'd replace them with the law of the jungle, I guess. Survival of the fittest."

"Dog eat dog." Miles shifted his gaze to the gauge. The tank was completely empty. "Thank you."

"Why don't you stop baiting me and fucking well ask them?" Stuart waved his good arm at the corpses. "You might get a different response."

One of the bodies lifted its head. The jaw was slack, held to the rest of the skull by a few loose tendons.

"My name is Jennifer Hillcross," it rasped. "I like typefaces and waltzing and drawing with fine art pens. I'd like to be richer; I'd like to be thinner. I used to live in Bundaberg but didn't like *that* much. I've got rats, three of them, though I don't keep them in a cage. They make me laugh. They do the funniest things. They were car sick last week because I moved to a new house. All three of them, holding onto the seat leather with their little claws."

She turned empty sockets towards Miles.

"I was looking forward to having my own place. I'd bought a new dress and I was wearing it to a party when we met. Damn you to hell."

"I think this interview is over." Stuart sank onto his side.

"That's right. Cop out now!" Miles sucked as hard as he could, taking in one last lungful. "Where's the rule that says you can't do whatever you want? There's laws, sure, but why should you abide by a law if you don't want to? What if you don't want to do what other people tell you? There's no moral code out there in the ether everyone has to follow. There's no God and, even if there was, we don't have to obey him."

Both fists drummed on his knees

"What did I do? Eh? Eh? I want to grasp what I did that was actually wrong!"

The other women began to crawl towards him, pieces of flesh drifting from their decaying, bitten bodies.

"I didn't know you!" Miles tried to push them back. "You mean as much to me as these starving kids I don't send money to help. Yes, I'm filled with self-loathing. Do I hate myself? Too right, I do. But I try to find some fucking rule to condemn myself and I can't find one! There's nothing to actually stop me!"

"It's the way the world works." Jennifer rasped, clawing at his leg. "That's what stops you."

"*I don't like the way the world works!*"

Miles inched away from the advancing women.

"We're just dogs slavering and straining at our collars. Pavlov's fucking dogs, that's what we are. And I slipped my leash! Broke away! Bad dog. Slap his nose! Slap all our noses when we shit or fuck or act in any way that's not deemed acceptable. Eh? What we want to do but we're not allowed to do!"

He slid off the chair and shook his companion, releasing another plume of blood.

"Maybe that's what we need. Maybe we need more training, more conditioning. But, for Christ's sake, we need taught to show affection, not to attack. How many times do rabid dogs like me have to turn on people? How many do we have to put down, when we should just stop breeding them?"

He kicked out at Stuart's motionless body, but his flippers got in the way and all he could manage was a penguin like slap.

"Maybe you should have written a book about dog training." Stuart opened one eye. "You are remembering I'm dead, aren't you?"

"Of course," Miles grunted miserably. "Surprise, surprise. I'm trying to justify myself to myself. Me, me, me, eh?"

"No, you moron. It means I don't need my air tank anymore."

Miles goggled at him. Then he struggled out of his harness and clumsily swapped the man's scuba gear for his own. He switched masks and air from Stuart's cylinder flooded his lungs. Miles sat on the wooden floor for a while, breathing in sweet oxygen.

He looked around.

Tattered, chained bodies were scattered across the floor of the cabin, no longer moving. Miles swam to the window and looked out. He could see no sign of the predator. It had to have gone by now.

"Thanks, Stu. You've given me some much-needed perspective."

Miles still felt lightheaded but was refreshed enough to have a fair chance of reaching the surface. He shook Stuart's good hand then let it drift away.

"I would have happily stuck to society's conventions, know that? But everybody twists them to suit themselves, so I ended up doing the same. Go big or go home, mate."

He opened the cabin door and cautiously ascended, recalling - just in time - to stop halfway up. It would be beyond ironic to get the bends this close to freedom.

Miles hung in the translucent water, watching the light filtering down from above. He had always loved diving. He was comforted by that sense of being cocooned and shut off from everything, alone in a silent, muffled world.

He was about to begin his journey again when the Great White emerged from the gloom. Must have measured 20 feet from tip to toe.

Miles tried to flee but was gripped by a terror more overpowering than anything he had ever experienced. He thrashed wildly but his arms and legs refused to comply. It felt like he was moving through soup.

"Please. Please, no! Don't hurt me!" he screamed. "I'm sorry! I'll do anything!"

The mask stopped any sound from escaping.

The creature opened its mouth, revealing two rows of vicious jagged teeth. It looked like it might be smiling but the blank, emotionless eyes were devoid of pity. It slowly moved towards him, a killing machine moulded by a million years of evolution. No rules. No compassion. No choices.

Miles continued to beg and plead, though he knew it would do no good.

"Ah," the shark said. "*Now*, you understand."

Half Truths

Jem McCusker

Peace could be found in the most unlikely of places if one found enough courage to claim it.

My daddy found peace in the darkest corners of his mind. Its protective shell, cocooned with half-truths, made livin achievable. Not to be confused with enjoyable. Enjoyment and its neighbouring emotions, contentment, happiness and hope. became off limits to the likes of him.

The only man worth havin' is a broken one. My step mumma used to say,

I can't deny, when I was young, this confused me. But I came round to understandin her way of thinking. At one time, my daddy would have flown me to the moon on his back, using sheer will power. But, with time, and a good breakin' in, mumma made him durable to the servicin of her purposes. Namely, keeping her in the lifestyle to which she'd become accustomed. This also involved makin sure I was attributed no more importance than you'd give to shit on your shoe. A swipe across the grass, to get rid of the lingering scent of unpleasantness.

He'd sat and listened to my stepmother, eyes closed and head resting against the recliner chair. All the while noddin subtly in agreement to everything she said.

The carping went on until, finally, he accepted half-truths as reality. Acted on her demands, and did so without the guilt a mentally well father might experience.

My stepmother, Gloria had never mentored me in life. No midnight chats of motherly guidance, as I navigated high school. No shoppin adventures. Constant complainin about my behaviour. I learned the hard way that, in order to make a lie believable, it must include a seed of truth.

"How long are you going to let her control our lives like this Richard?" Gloria said. "We're decent people who need to get on with the business of living."

"I'll deal with it," he replied.

My daddy took the stairs two at a time, with an authority I knew was not his own. I crept back to my room, away from my crouched position behind the newel post.

He didn't knock. The door burst open but his figure, now so slight, failed to fill the door frame as it once had. He cast a meagre shadow of failure. The part of me that still held a grain of love for the man he once was, recoiled.

He didn't look at me. He never did. He looked through me, as if I were glass. Easy to break, difficult to clean.

"Gloria and I want you out. You've no business being here any longer."

It wasn't the first time we'd had this argument. I shifted from the bed, walked over to him and placed my hand on his shoulder. He flinched, as if I had burned him. I backed away and he breathed a sigh of relief.

"I've nowhere to go." I replied.

He turned his back on me and opened the window, his elbows restin on the frame. A cool breeze swept greyin hair back from his face.

"I can't live like this," he whispered.

"So, don't."

He didn't respond, just stared out that damn window, because it was easier than lookin me in the eye. Gloria had broken him and he would never be whole again. He was simply a stranger I shared genetics with.

I slunk from the room, without so much as a goodbye or possession to my name.

I made sure to slam the front door behind me. It was the only way they would know I had left.

I walked around the side of the house. My father opened the window and looked down at me. I waved good bye and this seemed to please him.

He should have known better. While they slept, I'd sneak back in. I liked to think he left that window open, so I had a way to return. But he probably just needed the fresh air.

The truth is no defence against a well told lie. The best ones are simply repeated until they become so real, they replace memory with a story that fits better.

"I'll never forgot the way she held that knife, Richard." Gloria pressed a hand to her chest.

"Come now, love," he rubbed a hand over her back.

"I thought I was going to die." She looked up at him, face tear streaked.

"She's gone now You never have to worry about her again."

"Am I being silly?" Gloria sobbed into his shoulder, the performance deserving of an Oscar. "I can't even stand in my kitchen without being haunted by the memory of her attacking me."

She was steamrollin toward the crescendo of her performance.

"I'm so thankful you chose that night to go hunting. If you hadn't had the rifle in your hands, she'd have done me in."

Richard pushed the hair back from her face and kissed her forehead.

"There was something not right with my Tilly." He clasped her face in his hands. "I'll never forgive myself for not listening to you. You urged me to get her help and like a fool, I ignored you."

"We'll move." Gloria said.

"To what end?" Richard replied wearily. "I'm pretty sure she's gone for good."

"That's what you always say." Gloria pushed up from the chair, her heavy weight making this simple goal challenging. "If she decides to come back, I don't want us here."

"This was the only home she's ever known."

"Then give it to her. Let's live out the rest of our lives in peace."

"It's mine too!" Richard's face briefly turned an angry red.

"Oh, for heaven's sake." She rolled her eyes. "I've had enough of your simpering. It wasn't your fate in her hands, it was mine."

He fell back into his seat, like a balloon bein deflated.

Love makes some folks happy. Others, well it sucks the life out of them, until they are shadows of their former selves. My dad was no exception.

"We can't move with things as they are," he said.

"No one's stopping you from changing them. It's your weakness that keeps us here and her returning."

I'd only sneaked in a few minutes ago and already I was growin tired listening them.

"Tonight," Richard said. "I'll do it tonight."

"Well, praise Jesus," Gloria threw her hands in the air. "The man has grown a backbone."

Richard put down the bread he was butterin. The knife clattered on the bench before fallin to the floor. He bent down slowly, picked it up, and straightened his shoulders.

"You could help me."

"I've helped you these past fifteen years. This is something you'll have to do on your own."

"All right." Richard put the dirty knife in the sink and abandoned his sandwich. His shoulders squared and a light sheen of moisture filmed his eyes. "No time like the present, eh?"

"There's the man I married." She winked at him and he gave a smile in return. The first genuine one I'd seen him offer in some time.

"I'm going to the shed to get my tools."

I positioned myself behind the curtain and peeked out the window. My father returned a short time later, pushin a wheelbarrow filled with bed sheets, a hand saw, garbage bags and bricks.

"I'll make a celebration meal while you finish up." Gloria gave him a lingering kiss. "Something to rejoice in our new freedom.".

I knew the work Richard would be doin. I slunk down the staircase, mindful not to make a sound. I climbed the ceiling beam, so I was positioned above the chest freezer. The basement had grown dusty with misuse. The far wall was lined with fishin rods, tackle boxes and paring knives. Stacked boxes filled with Christmas ornaments and dated clothes lined the other. Faded memories of happier times.

Richard took a key out of his pocket and inserted it in the padlock. He opened the lid, and peered in. His legs gave out beneath him, as they always did when he managed to get this far.

I could climb down, sit on his lap and tell him it was goin to be okay. However, the more time passed, the less inclined I became.

I'd tried before. I thought he might sing me a song, his lyrical voice bringing the stars and the moon to me. But I was lyin to myself - daydreams of the small child who still lived within me. With every passin year, she had died a little more.

It was time to lay her to rest and embrace the woman she had become.

I climbed down, my movements sure and steady. He lay on his side now, legs tucked up to his chest.

"What have I done?" he cried.

I knelt beside him and placed my hand on his arm. This time he didn't baulk. This time he saw me, not just my frozen body squished into a freezer. It was no longer a spirit he sensed, but his daughter. The daughter he murdered.

Tears I promised I'd never shed again flowed. He used his thumb to wipe them away. I hoped to experience an explosion of joy that he was finally connectin with me. Instead, I felt nothing. If my eyes had been closed, I never would have known he was there.

"I tried to stab her because she was beatin me black and blue, yet again," I whispered. "I was defendin myself."

"I should have known," he sobbed. "You told me over and over but I didn't believe Gloria would do that."

For the first time in a decade, I had his full attention, I wouldn't waste this opportunity. I clasped both his hands, draggin him away from the freezer and toward the wall. I made him take down the fishin knife and cupped it in his hands. He looked through me again, I was losing traction.

Quickly, I pushed him up the stairs, and he didn't protest.

Gloria was makin pie. The sheet of pastry in her hands dropped when she saw my father.

"Richard?"

He froze and looked down at the knife in his hand, puzzled. I couldn't lose momentum now. I clasped my hand around his, pushed him forward and rammed the blade into her belly.

Gloria dropped to her knees and so did my father. He turned the knife in his hands, so the point faced toward him. I reached out to stop him, but it was too late. The knife pierced his chest and blood wept onto the floor. My father groaned and rolled onto his back.

Blood pooled at the side of Gloria's lips and her complexion grew waxy. Her mouth formed a soft -O- shape.

"There was always something bad about your daughter." Blood filmed her teeth. "I ignored her. Shunned her. Hated her, even. But I never laid a finger on that girl."

My father's last expression was one of doubt and confusion. I took his dyin hand in mine.

"Sorry dad," I whispered. "The truth is no defence against a well told lie."

Heed the Piper

Megan Badger

The shadow slipped through the house. It didn't hold any shape for long but shifted and reformed like a cat, a pig, a dog, a snake, a rat. It floated above the dirt floor and drifted to the cot where I and my brothers and sisters slept. I lay stiff as a board while it hung over me. It smelt of smoke and snow and something else I couldn't place. I watched its pointed nose quiver and turn away from me. It moved to my brother and repeated the action, but this time its head moved back and a horrifying grin cracked its face. The shadow formed into a figure crouching on Enolf's chest. Teeth closed on his throat, almost tenderly, and the smoke of its tail drifted in tendrils into his mouth and nose. Enolf tossed in his sleep and his brows furrowed, but he didn't wake.

All night the shadow fed on my siblings, one after the other. Then, in the grey light of twilit dawn, it slunk to hide in the darkest corner of the room. My kin all bore the mark of the bite, two small pierced holes, on neck, shoulder, face. Mutter shook them and asked what was wrong. I tapped her shoulder and made the sign for rat. I didn't know how to describe what I'd seen. Mutter put down black hellebore with the barley meal and burned the seeds of oregano, celery and love-in-a-mist as incense. It made our eyes water but did nothing against the shadows.

More of them came, rolling mist through the valley. They feasted at night. The town children, always pale, grew grey and weak. The marks spread in a pattern of double spot scars, like pox. Baldram was loath to let me and Everold out of his sight. We sat together using hand taps to talk. Everold had heard his sister moan and grumble in her sleep. A

187

quiet sucking sound, as soft as the wind through spring leaves, but horrible instead of beautiful.

Baldram had tried to beat the creature with his cane. He cut the
smoke in half but it reformed and snarled at him. The shadows fought
over the children, bared their teeth and swirled around each other, sometimes knocking over a lamp or candle.

My father, Vater, called a town meeting. The rat traps remained
empty. The children were wasting away. He sent missives to the Mo-
nastic Island of Reichenau, begging for help.

*All medicinal and herbal treatments have failed and we can only
assume that the devil is responsible.*

He made the messenger repeat the phrases back three times, before
sending him on his way. All adults were ordered to work the farms.
Every hand was needed.

"We have to come together as a community," he said, his lips in a
hard line as I watched the words form. "No baking, home keeping,
weaving or brewing. No hunting, butchering or leather working. If we
don't pull together now, we will starve come winter."

The townsfolk's shoulders were rigid under the weight of his orders.
Vater sent missives to towns as far reaching as Augsburg, Regensburg,
Trier and Cologne, requesting aid and supplies. He raised the taxes.
That spring I watched as the added responsibility slowly bent his body.
Every day the adults worked the farms and each night they went to
church and prayed. And we waited.

Sermon the first

Two men, simply clad, but not without guile, came to Hamlin.
Though they feigned the greatest piety, they were ravening wolves dis-
guised as sheep. Pale and thin, they went about barefooted and fasted
daily, did not miss a single night the matins in the cathedral, nor would
they accept anything from anyone, except a little food. When, by such
hypocrisy, they had attracted the villager's attention, they began to
vomit forth their hidden poison, preaching to the ignorant new and

unheard-of heresies. In order, moreover, that the people might believe their teachings, they ordered meal to be sifted on the sidewalk and passed over it without leaving a trace of any footprint. Likewise, walking upon the water, they could not be immersed; also, they had little huts burnt over their heads, and after those had been reduced to ashes, they came out uninjured. After this they said to the people,

"If you do not believe our words, believe our miracles."

The bishop and clergy, hearing of this, were greatly disturbed. And when they wished to resist those men, affirming that they were heretics and deceivers and ministers of the devil, the pretenders escaped, with difficulty, from being stoned by the people. Now, that bishop was a good and learned man and a native of our province. Our aged monk, who told me these facts and was in that city at the time, knew him well.

It was the start of summer and the leaves were glowing green, when a man came from the river. He didn't arrive by boat, but they leave that out of the stories. His long hair and beard were twisted like water weeds and the ends looked green in some light. The hems of his clothes were always damp. His coat was patched in red, gold, purple and green, and he had one leg of his pants lime and one yellow.

Only Baldram and I were there to see him. He didn't make for the tavern like other travellers but, instead, went to the square and sat beneath the willow tree. He paid no heed to the shut-up buildings and empty streets but took out a set of reed pipes and played. Bertram smiled when he heard the music. A few grey skinned children peeked through the curtain doors of their cruck houses.

Baldram, always the bravest of us, was the first to approach the man.

"Herr Pfeifer, your presence is welcome in these dark times. From where have you come?"

The piper looked at the way Baldram faced, so I could read the conversation on their lips, and gestured to us. I squeezed Everold's arm and tapped we are called on his palm. Together we walked forward, Everold holding my arm and waving his stick before him.

"You are an unusual group." His mouth was shaped kindly when he spoke. "How did you come to be friends?".

"Everold's eyes do not see." Baldram spoke for us. "Galiana cannot hear. I have a body that doesn't work. Together we make almost a whole person."

He smiled at his own joke.

"You seem much more to me," The man raising the pipes to his lips. I thought for a moment I heard the tune, light and twittery like a bird.

But that is impossible I told myself.

Not impossible. Magic. A voice came to my mind, clear and true. I gasped.

Ev? Gali? Baldram grabbed our hands and started tapping. *He has bewitched me, I imagined you spoke inside my head.*

I hear you, I cried, the tears cold on my cheeks and my smile stretched wide. *I hear you. I hear you.*

Everold looked at my face, his own taut in concentration.

Gali? Can you hear me too?

The three of us hugged and laughed, words flowing free and fast from mind to mind and we giggled, as though it tickled. Speaking had never been simple for us. We revelled in it. The piper let us have our moment before interrupting.

"I don't mean to intrude but I was drawn to this place because of the reek of dark magic. Can you tell me what has happened here?"

We told him of the shadows, and for the first time I was able to articulate how disturbing they were. I shared images in his mind of the shifting shapes. Everold conjured the sounds they made and Baldram revealed the sticky fog-like feeling of them.

"Alp." The piper scowled. "They don't normally gather in such numbers. What of the children? Are they the only victims? Let me see."

We showed him the slender pale skinned perfection of the children. Showed them singing and playing and dancing in the meadows. The piper sat back and shook his head.

"Why here?" he mumbled, lips pursing "Why this place?".

"What is it Herr piper? What's wrong?"

The man looked startled, as though he'd forgotten we were listening.

"Could I tell you a story from my folk?" He said in our minds. "It might be simpler than trying to explain."

"Oh yes, do." Everold's face lit up,

It was less a story, more a history that played out.

A parade of creatures, magical and mundane, human, and other, growing, shrinking, outgrowing, disappearing, working together, then divided by war. Creatures with skin of bark and leaves, or grass and sod. Creatures bent and creaking, like branches rubbing together, part man part monster. Creatures of the land and sea, and some of rivers. Creatures of fire. Creatures of darkness. The shadows and a figure cloaked in black with a withered hand, pointing toward the mountains. Death spread before his fingers in a browning wave.

And, in those far-off hills, fair skinned and slender folk, with voices like bells and hair of spun moonlight. The hand reached to the borders of their land but no further. The figure hissed, retreated, and watched. The fair skinned creatures prospered, their numbers growing, until the mountain realm could no longer sustain them. By night they crept into the village, our village. The human infants were plucked from their cots and dropped in the river. Long-limbed infants were gently set down in their place, their cheeks stroked tenderly.

A younger piper appeared in the water, surrounded by a swirling hole, through which we saw a meadow filled with flowers, chirping birds and beings, part human and part horse. The babes who had been discarded were gently passed through to the waiting arms of those beyond, who held them gently. The piper tossed a silver coin into the water each time. I supposed it to be payment for taking the children. Then the hole closed.

"Is that what happened here? Our brothers and sisters are gone? Taken? Traded?" I sensed the gravelly anger in Baldram's voice. "And those... those things left here?"

"They were babies too," the piper answered. "Whose desperate parents wanted only to protect their children from starvation and suffering."

He showed us the hooded figure again. Its gaze turned and focused on our village. Black tendrils of smoke billowing from under its cloak and took form, shifting shape, hissing, growling, rattling. The hand directed them here. They had no eyes nor ears, only noses, and they sniffed and snuffled for the scent of the intruders. As the shadows fed, the pointing hand became plump and the creature laughed. Hair stood up on my neck and Everold whimpered.

"This is not about the village; but a far older battle being fought in your homes. I will do what I can to help and rid your town of these Alps."

Baldram and Everold were well pleased with his promise, but something niggled at the edges of my thoughts. The cloaked figure, the shadows, seemed the work of an evil force. Were we, too, being taken in by a servant of the devil? For what was magic but the illusion of sin?

When the adults returned from their fields, they glanced furtively at the strange man. Baldram told me they called his music unwelcome and immoral, after the trouble the town had seen. Still, the man sat every day in the square. Each night he slept under the stars. Mutter called him a fool; her mouth twisted with scorn.

On the third day after his arrival Vater called the stranger to an audience. Villagers crammed into the hall, craning to see this odd fellow with his outlandish clothes.

"Traveller, you come to us during a time of great duress. What is your purpose here?" Vater puffed out his chest and crossed his hands behind his back. "If you have none, be on your way, as we have no resources to spare."

"I am called Alfhelm Piper and I am a rat catcher. I believe I can help rid you of the blight on your children."

Vater looked down his nose,

"And how will you succeed when so many have failed?"

"I can't very well reveal my secret, now can I? How would I stay in business?"

"And how can we judge your capability?" Vater huffed, looking like a mountain goat.

"The proof is in the act, not the word. I require payment of one silver piece for every rat I dispatch. You can make payment after the deed is done, if it will set your mind at ease."

Vater looked around at the gathered villagers' desperate faces. I thought of the empty coffers. The missives. The money dispersed for supplies and aid. It was wrong to promise funds we didn't have, but we sorely needed assistance. Vater didn't know that the rats he feared were of a magical nature. He didn't believe in enchantments but did believe in the devil. He would burn the piper if he found out. But who else could help? I looked away and stayed silent.

"I will give you the opportunity to prove yourself. Rid us of this plague upon our village and you shall be compensated."

"Will you shake on the deal?"

Vater stepped forward and presented his hand. The piper pondered it. Turned the hand over and stroked its palm. His lips turned down at the corners, but he shook, nodded to the congregation, and strode out.

Sermon the Second

The bishop, seeing his words were of no avail and that the people entrusted to his charge were being subverted from the faith by the devil's agents, summoned a certain clerk he knew, who was well versed in necromancy.

"Certain men in my city are doing so and so. I ask you to find out from the devil, by your art, who they are, whence they come, and by what means so many wonderful miracles are wrought. For it is impossible that they should do wonders through divine inspiration, when their teaching is so contrary to God's."

"My lord," the clerk said. "I have long renounced that art."

"You see clearly what straits I am in," the bishop replied. "I must either acquiesce in their teachings or be stoned by the people. Therefore, I enjoin upon you, for the remission of your sins, that you obey me in this matter."

The clerk did as instructed and summoned the devil, who asked why he had called.

"I am sorry I have deserted you," the clerk responded. "And, because I desire to be more obedient to you in the future than the past, I ask you to tell me who these men are, what they teach, and by what means they work so great miracles."

"They are mine and sent by me, and they preach what I have placed in their mouths.

"How is it that they cannot be injured, or sunk in the water, or burned by fire?"

"They have, under their arm-pits, sewed between the skin and the flesh, my compacts in which the homage done by them to me is written," the devil said. "By virtue of these, they work such miracles and cannot be injured by anyone."

"What if those should be taken from them?"

"They would be weak, just as other men."

Having heard this, the clerk thanked the demon, saying, "Now go, and when you are summoned by me, return."

He went to the bishop and recited these things to him in order.

I avoided the piper. I thought he would see the guilt on my face. I laundered my father's clothes and performed the usual household chores. I couldn't catch the music as it drifted between the huts. Didn't hear the whisper and whoosh of the shadow as it passed behind me and under the door. What I heard was Baldram's voice in my mind.

Gali, you should see this.

I walked through the door and watched shadows peel themselves from buildings, rolling like mist along the ground. I followed, careful not to let them touch me. They writhed like serpents. They looked, for all the world, like something a demon would dream up to torment the innocent and pure of heart. At the river a large swirling hole spun in the water and the shadows flowed into it. The edges went dark and blue sparks crackled around the edges.

The piper stood in the river, up to his waist, eyes closed and face strained. Baldram and Everold sat on the shore, their faces lit as though in rapture. I envied them their hearing. The silent scene played out before me. The shadows drifted into the water until the last flickering tail of darkness flicked and was gone from the land. The hole closed and the piper lowered his arms and turned to face the shore.

"It is done." His face was haggard and his eyes troubled. "I will rest a moment before speaking with the mayor."

He lay on the grassy bank and fell into a deep sleep. Everold sat and stroked his hair.

"He did it Gali. He saved them."

Sermon the Third:

The Bishop, filled with great joy, summoned all the people of the city to a suitable place and said,

"I am your shepherd, ye are my sheep. If those men, as you say, confirm their teaching by signs, I will follow them with you. If not, it is fitting they should be punished and that you should penitently return to the faith of your fathers with me."

"We have seen many signs from them," the people replied,

"But *I* have not seen them," the Bishop protested. "Why protract my words?

The plan pleased the crowd. The heretics were summoned. A fire was kindled in the midst of the city.

My stomach was in knots as I stood with my father before the piper.

"You called for an audience, Piper. For what purpose?"

"I have rid the town of rats as you required and am here to receive payment."

"So say you, but where is the proof?" Vater circled the piper and faced the gathered villagers,

"The rats are gone, what more do you need?"

"Bodies. Tails. Something more than your word.

"This is preposterous. You shook on the deal and must now honour your part."

"I made a deal under the misrepresentation that you were a rat catcher. Yet you brought no traps or baits nor any tools of the trade. You have deceived me, as you have deceived this village."

A wave of anger swelled in the crowd. Fists clenched, jaws gritted and heads shook from side to side. I looked at the piper, expecting to see denial or anger. Instead, his face was frantic.

"Mayor, I need the silver."

"How do we know it wasn't you who released the rats, under some foul plot to rob this town of their taxes? We need the money to order supplies, as your infestation has led us to the precipice of ruin."

"Mayor," the piper pleaded, his eyes swimming. "You don't understand..."

"Are you calling me, in the honourable and respectable position of Mayor, a simpleton?"

"No Mayor, I..."

"Do you presume to rob me?"

"I do not." The piper wrung his shirt and water trickled to the ground.

"I call those gathered here to attest that this man, Alfhelm Piper, must leave. Should he return, he will stand trial on the traditional date of the twenty second day of June. All those in favour?"

"Wait..." the piper stepped forward

Most of the town motioned *Aye,* eyes lit with fervour.

"All those against?"

Only three shaky hands rose. Mother Green, whose children had all begun to show colour in their cheeks and a farmer who was known to still follow the old ways. The third was mine, but nobody paid attention.

"It is decided."

"You're making a mistake," the piper pleaded with the crowd. "I must have the payment."

"For the wagon fare away from here." Vater threw down three coins at the man's feet. "You'll get no more."

"You must heed me. Your troubles will return threefold if you will not give me the silver you promised."

"Enough." Vater held up his hand, "Any claim you make can be aired should you return for your trial. Good day."

That night a storm rolled into the valley. Thunder shook the walls of the manor house and I feared for my friends in their stick and daub lean-to's. Horizontal rain battered the town. Rivulets with rafts of mud and dung wended their way to the river. I imagined I saw the piper, standing below the whipping branches of the willow, untroubled by the deluge and scowling at my father's house.

The storm raged for days that turned into weeks. The pale children lost the pallor in their cheeks and regained the sparkle in their eyes. They ate, drank, and laughed and despite the howling of the storm outside, the villagers felt hope.

The day of the trial arrived, with no sign of the piper. Early morning service was called. All men and women were instructed to put down their tools and gain the grace of God. The morning sun rose and brightened the clear washed sky. Yet, something didn't feel right. The piper's enchantment had allowed me to continue to speak to the minds of my friends. They told me not to fret.

Baldram and Everold watched the water eagerly, as they were sure the piper would return. Talked on and on about magic, giving silly names to the creatures he had shown us. They play fought the cloaked figure, Baldram with his cane and Everold using his stick. Neither of them could balance without them, so these mock battles ended with one or the other of them falling on their buttocks. I scratched at my arm. There was something in the air, some threat hanging in the bright daylight.

Of course, when it came, I didn't hear the splash of displaced water or the sloshing steps striding towards the town square.

"Come on, Gali." Everold was giddy with excitement. "He's here."

Baldram dragged us along, Everold stumbling now and then, to keep pace with the piper. He walked with stoic purpose, back rigid, the green tips of his hair flicking with every step.

"Hey piper, hey piper, we missed you. Where are you going, piper?"

"I have to save them, can't you see?" Her turned, eyes blazing. "The portal won't seal without silver. I must take the children home."

He put the reed to his lips and, for the second time, I heard distant high trilling.

Children slipped into the street, swaying and smiling, eyes lit from within. They danced grotesquely after him, arms swooshing like willow boughs, while we three followed as well as we could.

The adults were working in the fields and, at first, did not even realize they were gone.

Everold was the first to fall by the wayside, tripping on a stone and cutting his leg. Baldram looked torn between staying with his friend and continuing along the path.

"Go on, go on." Everold urged, tears in his eyes. "You can tell me what you see."

The path got rougher, winding and turning until, eventually, there was no path at all. Scraps of clothing caught on vicious shrubs that scratched our skin. Baldram couldn't navigate the rough terrain with his cane and threw it aside. He continued for a few more feet, then dropped to his knees, holding his head in frustration.

"It's up to you Gali. Only you can show us what waits in the mountains."

I was shaking with thirst, itching with sun and wind burn, bites of insects and layers upon layers of scratches. The piper stopped at a cave, gathering the children around him. I craned to see past them, to glimpse the realm they would call home. Green. Pink. Yellow. Red. Colours so vibrant the world here looked faded as oft washed linen. I wanted to go to that place and stumbled toward the portal.

"It's not a place for you." The piper blocked my way.

But why? Why do they get to live in my world for a time, but I cannot live in theirs? I stamped my foot and started to sob. *It's not fair.*

"Life's not fair human. Your kind saw to that. You wanted this world, now you can keep it."

I was startled out of crying. The piper's skin grew greener and his eyes became deep pools.

"Enjoy my gift." Then he ushered the children through the portal. It closed and he was gone.

Sermon the Final

Before the heretics entered the fire, they were secretly summoned to the bishop, who said to them,

"I want to see if you have any evil about you."

Hearing this, they stripped quickly and said with great confidence,

"Search our bodies and our garments carefully."

The soldiers, following the instructions of the bishop, raised the heretic's arms. Noticing some scars that were healed up, broke them open with knives and extracted the little scrolls which had been sewed in. Having received these, the bishop went forth with the heretics to the people and, having commanded silence, cried in a loud voice.

"Now shall your prophets enter the fire, and if they are not injured, I will believe in them."

"We are not able to enter now," the wretched men wailed.

Then the bishop told the people of the evil which had been detected and showed them the compacts. Furious, they hurled the devil's ministers into the fire, to be tortured with the devil, in eternal flames. And thus, through the grace of God and the zeal of the bishop, the growing heresy was extinguished and the people who had been seduced and corrupted were cleansed by penance.

Baldram, Everold and I limped back to the village. It was past sundown when we arrived, greeted by a sea of burning torches.

"They're calling for the children," Everold said. "When only we three return, they will think we were in league with the piper."

He was right. Vater had a wagon secretly waiting and had me spirited away, with only the clothes I wore and a letter to the monastery, asking them to take me in, as my deafness made me unable to work.

I woke to the rattle of the cart and my sore buttocks and back from lying so long. Screams echoed inside my head.

Baldram showed me the trial. They were guilty before the vote was cast, according to the villagers. His mother lit the pyre. Then Everold screaming, calling my name, Baldram's name. Calling for the piper.

More screams, from Baldram this time. Then silence.

My name means silence. It was a blessing I didn't appreciate until I spent eternity, or what felt like eternity, with the shrieks of my friends echoing in my head.

I do penance every day. I do my work.

I pray.

There are crimes of passion and crimes of logic. The boundary between them is not clearly defined.

Albert Camus

Murder at Lavender Manor

Nicole Harvey

A blood-curdling scream echoed down the hall.

Amelia's gaze snapped from the window and its picture-perfect view of lavender flowing beyond. She leapt from the window seat, away from a sudden gust of wind, then hurried out of the guest room. Her footsteps sank silently into the thick, purple carpet.

Amelia entered the lounge and found Brit, tears in her eyes. At Brit's feet, a man lay on his stomach, head turned to one side. Blood pooled at the back of his skull, its metallic scent leeching into the air and seeping into the collar of his checked shirt. There was only one person here who wore a checked shirt every day.

"It's Landon," Brit's gaze was transfixed by the body. "He's dead."

Amelia put two fingers to the man's neck for confirmation. A glint caught her eye and she noticed a shiny silver statue, in the shape of a duck, alongside the blood pool. The body was still warm.

There was a killer close-by.

"Come, dear." Amelia guided the young woman away. "There's no point looking. You'll only upset yourself more."

"What are we going to do?"

"What's going on in here?" Aaron's gravelly voice came from the hall. "I heard a scream."

He appeared in the doorway, sweat stained running clothes clinging to his body.

"Oh good. You're here, Aaron. Come sit with Brit while I let the owner know and call the police." Amelia pushed him towards the

203

woman. "Mind the body, dear, and don't touch anything. This is a crime scene."

She looked back as she left the room and saw Aaron pull Brit into his arms. Even sitting down Brit barely reached his shoulders. Looked like there was definitely something going on between them.

Hmmm. They would make a comical couple.

Amelia flung the door to the kitchen open, harder than intended. The owner of the manor was chopping mangos and dancing along to *Jingle Bell Rock.*

"I'm sorry to interrupt, Frank, but something dreadful has happened to Landon. He's been murdered."

"Murdered? How do you know that?" Wind rattling against the window almost drowned out his voice and the volume of the song didn't help. "Maybe he had a heart attack."

He turned off the music, looking panicked. A suspicious death would be bad for business.

"I used to be a forensic pathologist." Amelia said. "When you've been around as many crime scenes as I have, you get a feeling. Plus his head's bashed in."

"What can I do?"

"Nothing, dear. You just keep working. I'm sure your lovely wife will be back soon with the rest of the guests."

"Officer Daniels here." He picked up the phone on its second ring.

"It's Amelia."

"I thought you'd gone on holiday."

"I have. I'm at the Manor on Lavender Island. One of the other guests has been murdered."

"Of course they have," Daniels sighed. "Death seems to be attracted to you. You can't even go on holidays without someone getting bumped off."

His voice dripped with exasperation.

"Look, there's a storm coming in fast. The Regional Harbour Master has banned all boat travel, so there's no getting my men to or from the island. I'll need you to relay all the information you can to me."

"A young lady found the deceased in a pool of blood with a statuette beside him. Seems to be the murder weapon."

"See what else you can find and ring me back. Suspects, photos of the crime scene. That kind of stuff."

"Well, here's one thing," Amelia said. "I spotted a security camera in the hall. Pretty well hidden, so I doubt anyone else noticed it."

"Excellent," Daniels grunted. "I'll check that out. And Amelia?"

"Yes."

"I'm only asking for your assistance because of the storm. You're retired and not meant to be helping with cases anymore."

"Whatever you say Detective." A smile spread across Amelia's face.

Back in the sitting room, Aaron was still comforting Brit on the lounge. They looked up as Amelia came in the door.

"How'd you go?" Aaron asked.

"I spoke to Officer Daniels on the mainland. He says there's a squall coming, so they won't be able to make it out until it has passed."

As if on cue a howl echoed through the window.

"Since I used to work alongside him, he's asked me to do some investigating to give them a head start. Why don't you two go to the dining room while I search for evidence?"

Brit glanced toward the body and shivered. Aaron put his arm around the woman's shoulders and steered her from the room.

Amelia took some photos of the body on her mobile and emailed them to Officer Daniels. There wasn't any blood past the main pool so the body hadn't been moved. There was a gash down the back of Landon's head. Using an intricate doily she folded from the coffee table, Amelia picked up the duck and turned it in her hands. It matched the gash perfectly. Click, click. More photos off to Daniels.

A flash in the corner of her eye startled her but it was just the lights on the Christmas tree coming on. They must be set with a timer. Looking at her watch she saw it was 5 o'clock. The darkness outside made it seem much later.

"She's not a cop, so you don't actually have to tell her anything."

Amelia overheard Aaron and stopped outside the dining room.

"She's only trying to help."

"She's an interfering old biddy with nothing better to do. Telling her about Landon won't change what happened. It'll just make you a suspect."

Amelia entered the dining room and the conversation stopped. Brit looked at Aaron, alarm written across her face. Amelia acted as though she'd heard nothing and asked to talk to them separately.

"Why should we?" Aaron folded his arms and sat up straighter.

"Just think of me as the police assistant."

"But you aren't actually a cop. You don't have any authority."

"No, you're right. I'm help…"

"Then I don't see any point in talking to you."

"How about you, Brit?" Amelia realised she wouldn't get anywhere with Aaron, so focused on his companion. "Could we have a quick chat?"

"I guess so." Brit gave Aaron an apologetic glance.

"Wonderful, dear. Let's head down to my room." She turned coldly back to Aaron. "It'd be best if you stayed here."

Amelia offered Brit the seat facing the window before rounding the table. Brit claimed to have been sunbaking on the beach all afternoon. With the rest of the guests away on a daytime excursion to the mainland, there was virtually nobody remaining on the island. No one to corroborate her story. Amelia noticed the woman's skin seemed redder than earlier but there was still the matter of Aaron's warning. Brit fidgeted with a placemat and avoided eye contact.

Amelia brought out cookies she had baked before coming to the island and offered one to the girl. Explained any information could help lead to Landon's killer. The only reason to hold back, she added casually, would be if she was the one who did it.

"You think I murdered him?" Brit's eyes widened.

"No, dear." Amelia soothed. "I'm just trying to gather any information I can. Anything you might be able to recall about Landon's movements today would help."

Brit opened her mouth as if to say something, closed it again and stared out the window. Amelia placed a hand on her arm and Brit jumped.

"I can see something's troubling you." She gently pulled her hand back. "Please let me help."

"This morning, I..." Brit hesitated. "Landon... he tried to... assault me."

"Go on, dear." Amelia gave her most trustworthy old lady smile.

Suddenly, the words flooded out. The older man had cornered her, breath stinking of rum. Forced Brit against the wall and reached beneath her dress. If Aaron hadn't passed by, at that moment, and pulled him off, Brit didn't want to think about what would've happened.

Landon had zig zagged drunkenly down the hall, while Aaron gently held Brit and told her everything would be alright.

"Try to get some rest, dear," Amelia said kindly. "Landon can't hurt you now."

"Amelia." Daniels didn't bother to answer the phone properly. "I've been waiting for your call. What have you got?"

"I take it you received my photos. The duck statuette's definitely the murder weapon. It's an odd shape and it fits the wound. The blood is fresh, so he hadn't been dead long."

"Good work. What about suspects? I imagine you ignored me and started investigated."

"There are only four people here, besides the deceased. Most of the guests went on a day trip to the mainland with one of the hosts, so that rules them out. There's me, of course, and Sandra's husband Frank. He couldn't have done it, because he was in the kitchen the whole time, preparing for tonight's big Christmas feast. I was in my room across the hall and could hear him banging about and singing at the top of his voice all afternoon."

"What about the other two?"

"Young things in their 20s. Brit and Aaron. I've just had an interesting chat with Brit. The deceased tried to assault her this morning. Would have succeeded too, had it not been for Aaron catching him in the act."

"Are Brit and Aaron connected?"

"They weren't before coming here but they seem pretty close now."

"What's Brit's alibi?"

"Claims she was sunbaking down on the beach but there isn't anyone to back that up."

"What has Aaron had to say for himself? Seems to me he's the most likely suspect."

"He's not keen on speaking to me. Says I'm not a cop."

"How very helpful of him." Daniels grumbled. "Though, technically, it's true. Can you put him on the phone?"

"I'll try. Let me go find him."

Amelia returned to the dining room and found Aaron engrossed in something on his mobile.

"Officer Daniels wants to speak with you, young man."

Aaron looked up and reluctantly took the phone. He listened, his face turning ashen. Nodded. Amelia could hear Daniels rough voice on the other end but couldn't make out the words.

"Ok, Officer." Aaron handed the phone back. "I'm ready to talk."

Amelia blinked in surprise.

"Thank you." She sat down at the table, across from him, as if this was an official interrogation. "Brit told me what happened this morning but I'd like to hear your side of the story."

"I'd been for a run after breakfast and was heading back to my room. When I turned the corner Landon was holding Brit against the wall. I pulled him off her as fast as I could. He smelled strongly of booze, even though it was 9:00am. Who drinks *that* early?"

"Do you think it was alcohol that made him do it?"

"I don't know." He sounded sceptical. "Isn't that behaviour some-thing that's ingrained in people? The liquor might have made him freer but the instinct was probably already there."

"You think he could've done something like this before?"

"Perhaps. I didn't know him."

"By my reckoning the murder took place a couple of hours ago. Where were you then?"

"Went for another run, cause I assumed he'd be sleeping it off. I jog morning and afternoon. I was going to have a proper go at Landon when I got back. Instead I found you and Brit in the sitting room."

"Where did you go?"

"Into the forest. I jog along the beach of a morning, but it's too hot in the afternoon. The forest is shaded."

"See anyone?"

"There's nobody left on the island to see."

"I know, but I have to ask. Thank you for answering my questions." Amelia gave him a motherly smile. "I really appreciate it and Officer Daniels will too."

"Landon was a nasty man." Aaron paused at the door. "I think he deserved what he got but that doesn't mean I killed him. I just don't know how anyone could do that to a woman."

"I agree with you there," Amelia said grimly. "By the way, what did Officer Daniels say to persuade you to talk?"

"He told me he'd kick my head in if I didn't."

Dinner that night was a sad and stilted affair. The storm had prevented everyone else from getting back and there was a corpse in the next room. After all Frank's hard work, there was no merriment as the four of them ate the Christmas Eve dinner he'd prepared. Their host was silent and sombre and who could blame him? He'd had to clear out one of his freezers to store the body and a murder was never good for business. Amelia wondered what would happen to Frank and Sandra's livelihood.

Aaron looked over at her between bites, chewing nervously. A couple of times Amelia noticed him put his hand on Brit's, in an awkward attempt to comfort her.

Brit fidgeted with her napkin and pushed the potatoes around her plate. Amelia didn't see her put a morsel of food into her mouth throughout the entire meal.

Amelia picked at the meal too. She tried to initiate some conversation but knew she was wasting her breath. Nobody felt like talking. After a while the guests drifted off, without so much as a goodnight to each other. Amelia had hoped to draw them out a little, but that would have to wait until morning.

Amelia awoke to the sound of her alarm and got to work. There was a lot of material and not much, all at the same time. She took a quick shower and looked at the clock. 7:56.

Not long left. The storm had abated and Daniels would soon be on his way.

Amelia kept her ears pricked as she brushed her hair.

8:00. Footsteps leaving the Manor as Aaron went jogging. Brit was probably still asleep and Frank was cleaning the kitchen. Amelia tied her grey hair in a tight bun. The sergeant wouldn't be happy if he found out what she was doing, so she'd have to be careful to leave no traces behind. She waited five minutes to make sure Aaron hadn't forgotten anything, then slipped out of her door.

On light feet she snuck around the corner to Aaron's room. Pulled the spare pins from her pocket and picked the lock.

She glanced around the room to get her bearings. It had a similar layout to her own. She crossed to the window. The sky remained dark and the wind continued to blow - but the rain had died down. Leaves, branches and lavender flowers were strewn across the beach. There was no sign of Aaron so she turned away from the window. She knew he took an hour long run but still wanted to be quick.

A heavy duty laptop sat open on the table. Amelia moved the mouse and a lock screen appeared. She tried some basic passwords but didn't know enough about Aaron to make informed guesses. A rapid search of the rest of the room revealed no evidence linking him to the crime. Amelia glanced outside to check he wasn't on his way back early, then slid back out the door. He'd never know she'd been there.

As Amelia entered her own room, she noticed her phone vibrating on the bedside table.

"We've caught a break," Daniels said, in his usual brusque manner "I've got something I need looked into. I want you to measure the heights of everyone at the Manor, yourself included. Also the height of the top and bottom of the painting outside the lounge."

"Why so?" Amelia was intrigued

"I contacted the security company and got hold of footage from the hall camera."

"That ought to clear things up."

"No. It's cheap and the quality is crappy - but that checked shirt the deceased wore is unmistakable. He entered the lounge and someone else followed him. They were dressed in a hooded coat, so we can't see any distinguishing details. It *is* enough to give us the murderer's height, though."

"I'll get that data for you."

"Thanks. Call me back as soon as you're done."

Amelia found Frank in the kitchen. Despite everything, he still intended to serve breakfast for the three remaining guests. Brit sat at the dining table with a plate of toast. Amelia was glad the young girl was eating something.

Once Frank had returned with a measuring tape Amelia had them line up and jotted the details down on a piece of paper.

Frank - 185cm

Brit - 152cm

Amelia - 157cm

As Amelia finished adding Aaron's name to the list, he walked in and headed for the coffee pot. She let him make his brew and take the first sip, before explaining what she needed. It seemed last night's conversation with Daniels had really affected him and he didn't hesitate to stand against the wall.

Aaron - 195cm

Amelia thanked them and walked down the hall, tape in hand. The base of the painting sat at exactly 100 cm and it reached up to 182cm. She called Daniels and relayed the height of each person.

"Are you sure?"

"Of course. Why?"

"None of those measurements match the person in the security footage."

"How could that be?"

"I don't know, Amelia. I don't know."

"Might there be someone else on the island?"

"I guess it's possible." Daniels went quiet for a moment. "But if the culprit had a boat, it's unlikely we'll find him. I'll organise a search when we get there, nevertheless. The weather's cleared so we won't be too long.

"I look forward to it."

"I can't see why we'd need to keep the guests once we've conducted official interviews. Can you inform them?"

"Will do, Officer."

She returned to give Brit and Aaron the good news. Both seemed relieved to be off the hook and went down to the beach to escape the manor.

Amelia shuffled back to her room to pack before the boat arrived. She flipped her suitcase open on the bed and opened the wardrobe. Reached into the back of the drawers to make sure she hadn't forgotten anything, her hands landed upon a newspaper clipping.

SCHOOL TEACHER AQUITTED. INSUFFICIENT EVIDENCE.
Former teacher, Gary Marsden, was acquitted of the assault and murder of schoolgirl Julie James yesterday. The prosecution's case collapsed after a serious error by the coroner, Amelia Robertson, was discovered.
Ms Robertson has now retired from the police department, for mental health reasons

Below was a photo of a young man in a checked shirt. The caption said Gary Marsden but the picture was of the man who called himself George Landon.

Amelia pulled the drawer open further and discovered a black, hooded coat wrapped around a pair of platform boots.

At the sight of them, memories flooded back. Landon on his hands and knees, grievously wounded and pleading

Why?

I know who you are, Gary.

My name is George Landon.

It's Gary Marsden. The schoolgirl you killed was my niece, Julie. I failed her last time but now justice will be served.

Amelia thought about all the diagnoses she had refused to accept.
Dissociative Identity Disorder. Fugue state. Split personality.
"Oh, my God," she whispered. "What have I done?"

Don't Open It!

Mandy Chandler

It all started when Mary took the notebook. Not that she'd stolen it. *He* had foisted it upon her. Right after he'd almost run her down. The big oaf was marching along the pavement, full of his own self-importance, and barged straight into her.

Or so she thought.

Admittedly, Mary had been daydreaming, as she trudged along the sleet-covered streets. She'd been Lady Violet, the flamboyant 16-year-old heroine of a novel she'd been trying to write for the past two years. Unsuccessfully.

Violet lived in a luxurious mansion on Cheapside Common, where an endless stream of suitors came to woo her. But Violet's heart belonged wholly and completely to her best friend and confidante, Colette, a French girl fostered by Violet's parents. In the daydream, Violet and Colette sat side-by-side in their favourite spot, beside a fountain in a forgotten part of the garden, Colette pretending to be the latest Lordling to have put his suit to Violet. They were nose to nose, giggling. Then the mood had sobered and intensified. Colette tilted her head. Violet leaned in. Soft lips brushed hers…

Then… bang! The collision had knocked Mary clean off her feet. Large hands grasped her waist, strong arms raised her into the air and set her firmly back down.

"Oh dear, do excuse me!" A young man doffed his cap. Piercing green eyes sparkled at her from beneath the wildest mop of red hair she had ever seen.

Momentarily stunned, Mary gaped at him. She should have been outraged at his impertinence but, instead, felt oddly aroused. Perhaps it was because of her daydream but she was transfixed by those emerald eyes, until her indignation at being manhandled broke the spell. Blood surged to her face. She snorted and attempted to move away.

"Wait." He grasped her slender wrist. "Are you okay?"

"Quite fine," she said primly. "And no thanks to you, Sir. You should look where you're going."

"You are absolutely right, my dear," an easy smile made her relax, despite herself.

"Please accept this small token, by way of an apology." Before she could object, he thrust a moleskin notebook into her hand.

Mary's anger rose and her cheeks flamed once more.

"You're much mistaken, Sir, if you think I'm the sort to accept gifts from someone so impudent."

He gave a Gallic shrug.

"Keep it. Sell it. Throw it away, if you desire." After a quick glance to make sure no one was watching, he leaned in, and hissed a dour warning in her ear.

"But, whatever you do, DON'T open it!"

He bowed and stalked off. Mary hitched her skirts in an attempt to pursue him, but he had already vanished around a corner.

If she'd known then, what she knew now, she would've raced down the road and forced him to take the damned thing back.

Instead, she stood stupidly staring at the book. As the shock wore off, she succumbed to the sensual feel of the moleskin leather beneath her fingers, a gorgeous golden band enclosing the cover and the gilt-edged pages. It was exquisite and thrummed with the promise of secrets longing to be revealed. She licked her lips, slipped the notebook into her coat pocket, and continued on her way.

Mama would be waiting and Mary would get a tongue-lashing for her tardiness. She smiled, thinking of how scandalised Mama would be if she ever found out about the young man and the unexpected gift.

Papa, on the other hand, would share her joy at the stunning craftmanship. He'd tease her about the fellow, of course. But he'd share her curiosity.

"Go on, open it," he would say. "What harm could there be in it?"

They were kindred souls, her and Papa - adventurous natures driving them to peel back the shroud of the ordinary and expose the unexpected in everyday life.

"Senseless risk takers the pair of you!" Mama often chastised them. She would never understand.

Despite the warmth of the hearth in their tiny home, Mama's mood was predictably icy. Her rage at Mary's tardiness was as expected and Papa had already retreated to the sanctuary of his print shop, two blocks away, on the less fashionable side of Fleet Street.

"Would you look what the cat dragged in," Mama snatched the herbs she had sent Mary to fetch and set about making her brew.

"Took your sweet time, didn't you girl?" she continued angrily. "Never mind that your poor mother has to suffer the agonies of this damned rheumatism, while you're off gallivanting! And that no-good Papa of yours disappeared with barely a word of thanks for the supper I slaved over! You two would leave me here to die on my own, if you had your way. Don't think I don't know it. You with your new-fangled ideas! Gives you notions above your station, it does. Think you're better than the likes of me. Pshaw!"

Finally spent, Mama settled in an armchair in front of the fire and nodded off. Seeing her serenely sleeping by the firelight, Mary felt a pang of sorrow, a nostalgic yearning for the bright, carefree mother of her childhood. Before the disappointment of giving birth to four stillborn babies in as many years had turned to bitterness. and her joints had seized up with disease.

Mary ate a cold supper, washed the dishes and cleaned the kitchen. Around midnight, she crept to her cloak by the door and quietly extracted the notebook from its pocket. Stowing it in the folds of her skirt, she climbed the rickety ladder to her gable room.

She loved her tiny garret with its floral wallpaper, pale pink bedcovers, and her most prized possessions - a wooden rolltop writing desk and chair. The set had been a gift from Papa on her sixteenth birthday. She had spent many hours since on the pink velvet seat cushion, trying to imbue Violet and Colette with life.

That night, the moleskin notebook took up centre stage on her desk. Its burnished gold band gleaming in the lamplight was fastened by emerald fish shaped clasp. Its eye was a tiny ruby and a golden hook protruded from the mouth, a key dangling from it like a lure.

"Whatever you do, DON'T open it!"

Had there been just the hint of fear in the stranger's voice, as he delivered his warning? Surely not.

Besides, it was unfair to thrust such a superb thing upon her, then bid her not to use it. He had given the journal to her, and she was within her rights to do with it as she pleased.

She felt the familiar rumblings of battle in her soul as her conscience (bless the dear relentless thing) waged war on her intractable nature.

In the end, as always, her craving for a taste of forbidden fruit won out. She extracted the key, inserted it into the intricate lock, turned it, and... nothing.

Mary stared in disbelief. Tried again, with the same result. She shifted the notebook into the full light of the lamp and examined the clasp closely. The eye seemed to wink at her.

She extended a slender finger toward the ruby and pressed it ever so gently. There was a satisfying click and the clasp sprung open. Mary stifled a whoop of glee. An odd sense of destiny, the notion she had set things in motion that could not be stopped, threatened to overwhelm

her. Mary pushed it down and opened the cover, eager to see what forbidden mysteries it contained.

She was a little disappointed to find the pages were blank. That ridiculous young man had wanted to scare her, nothing more. There were
no horrors, no obscenities - not even a hint of what Mama would call
the 'works of Satan' in these pages. It was just a pristine notebook. She
hesitated a moment before giving in to the urge to write.

The moment her nib kissed the paper's soft surface, a queer feeling
came over her. The light grew dim and the room seemed to fade away.

Mary found herself in a fashionable home. She realised, with a
shock, that this was Violet's parlour, exactly as she had imagined it,
down to the tiniest detail. She took in the sumptuous wallpaper, the ornate fireplace and inhaled the rich warm aroma of roasting chestnuts.

"Good morning, Lady Violet." A young man approached and gave
a small bow. In one palm, he held a squirming ball of grey fur

"For you, dear Lady." He thrust it towards her with an awkward gesture. "A token of my... hmmm... erm... high regard."

She embraced the kitten, and it gazed up at her with wide green eyes.
It wore a blue satin collar from which a silver heart dangled.

"He's lovely!" she cooed. "Thank you ever so much, but you really
shouldn't have!"

"'Tis but a poor gesture." He leaned in to kiss her cheek.

Aghast at his nerve, she took a step backwards, tripped on the edge
of the rug and tumbled to the floor. The kitten leapt from her arms,
scurried across the room and shot out the front door.

White with shock, the young man extended his hand to help her up.
Violet's heart swelled as Colette bustled into the room. She waved the
man away, with a typically French gesture, and pulled Violet to her feet.
She then escorted the apologetic offender from the house and slammed
the door behind him.

"What is zis?" she purred, as Violet straightened her dishevelled pet-
ticoats and smoothed the silk of her robe.

"Oh, tis nothing." She couldn't help giggling. "He gave me a lovely little kitten, then tried to kiss me. I fell over."

Colette joined her and they sank onto the couch in fits of laughter.

"What 'appened to ze poor little kitty?"

"It ran out into the street, I'm afraid."

"It will catch its death out zere. I will go look for it." She stormed out in a way that was all Colette when she was on a mission.

Violet sat back among the soft cushions and, before she knew it, was fast asleep.

Mary woke to the cold morning light, streaming in her garret window. She had fallen asleep at her desk, quill in hand.

In front of her was the notebook. Filling the pages in her neat script was the opening chapter of a story. Her story!

She got dressed, grabbed the journal and ran down the stairs, in such high spirits that not even Mama's sarcasm could dampen them.

"Mornin' milady," sarcasm dripping from every syllable. "This is a fine time to finally get out of bed. A right little lay-about."

"Morning Mama," Mary chimed. "I'm sorry! I was up late writing my novel."

"To think we've had the next Dickens living beneath our humble roof all this time!" She feigned a swoon. "Snap out of it, girl. Stop dreaming, grow up and get to your chores."

"But Mama, this time, its... its... well... better than anything I've ever written before. Where's Papa? I must show him."

"Where do you think?" Mama sneered. "His Lordship's up to his old tricks again, printing pamphlets for those evil suffragettes! Blasphemous, that's what it is, to be unsatisfied with your God-given role. Voting is men's business and, if you ask me, they're welcome to it. Mark my word, no good can come of this."

Seeing that Mama was about to work herself up into full sermon mode, Mary said a hasty goodbye, grabbed her coat and hurried out the door.

She hadn't gone far when she bumped into Papa. He'd been up all night and it showed. Yet his tired, ink-stained face creased into a broad grin when he saw her. She enveloped him in a hug.

"Woah, Hang on." He pushed her away gently. "Don't squash little Smudge."

"Smudge?"

He gave an impish smile and pulled a tiny bundle of grey fur from inside his coat. A pair of familiar green eyes stared up at her. She shivered and drew back from the kitten.

"Are you alright? You've turned a might pale."

"Fine. I'm fine, thanks Papa."

"I found him cowering among some sacks at the print shop. Must belong to someone, though. Look at the fine satin colour and silver pendant."

Mary hesitantly took him, unable to shake the dread clawing at her heart. Could this innocent kitten be some sort of ill omen? She shook her head to clear it of such foolishness. She was a modern woman who had no time for superstitious nonsense. Leave that rot to the likes of Mama.

Remembering her news, she put the cat into one voluminous coat pocket and pulled her notebook from the other.

"Oh Papa, I can't wait to show you what I've written."

They moved into an alcove, out of the hustle and bustle of Fleet Street. She stroked the little kitten between the ears, while her father read what she had written.

"Well?" she asked.

"This is good." He stared at her. "Really good!"

"Better than anything I've penned before, I know." She glowed with pride. "It's weird, but I can't help thinking it has something to do with this notebook. It seems to have unlocked my creativity."

"It is very fancy. Where did you get it?"

"Walk with me and I'll tell you all about it."

They linked arms and made their way through the crowded street.

Mama almost had apoplexy when she laid eyes on the kitten.

"Of all the selfish, unthinking, stupid things to do," she snapped. "Just like the two of you to bring me another mouth to feed. Who's going to take care of it and pick up after the damned thing? Me, that's who."

Papa's attempted to placate her, suggesting that the kitten might earn its keep by catching rodents. It only added fuel to the fire.

"So, I don't keep the place clean enough, is that it? My housekeeping is so poor you need to bring in a cat to keep mice at bay."

She continued ranting well into the evening, until Mary finished her chores and took the offending pet upstairs. As she closed her door, she heard Papa heading back to work.

"Off again, are we?" Mama said acerbically. "To bring out more blasphemous suffragette nonsense."

"Beatrice, you know we've no choice," Papa soothed. "The big publishers are gobbling up all the smaller printers in Fleet Street, like greedy Cuckoos preying on chicks."

"That's no excuse for printing the devil's own words!"

Papa shook his head and walked silently out the door. Mama huffed and settled back down into her armchair.

Mary gently placed Smudge into his basket and, with eager anticipation, took out the notebook once more. Tonight, she would tackle the tricky scene where Colette is left paralysed after being run down by a carriage. It pained her to put her beloved characters in harm's way, but without drama there would be no story.

Next thing she knew, it was daylight and she was standing in her father's print shop. The smell of fresh ink and paper surrounded her. She could hear the shuck, shuck of the printing press and the clatter of typesetters setting up the pages. Papa and Adam, his apprentice, went about their daily tasks, unaware she was there. They were printing a news broadsheet to sell and she glanced over at one of the sheets, still glistening with wet ink. Her breath caught as she read the headline.

Young Woman Injured in Tragic Carriage Accident.

The drawing beneath this horrifying announcement showed an elegant young woman with pale features and locks of hair tumbling down one side of an oval face. A face that Mary knew all too well.

It was her best friend Jasmine.

Mary jolted awake. Her gable room felt cold and dank. She stared down at the notebook and its pages were filled with words that most eloquently described the details of the carriage accident – only this time the victim was Colette. Her skin prickled and she was covered in a fine layer of sweat. What a horrid nightmare!

Jasmine must have been on her mind, as they were having lunch together tomorrow. That was all. It would be good to see her friend again. She could show her the notebook, let her read what she'd written and introduce her to Smudge.

She got into bed and a smile crossed her face, as she drifted off to sleep.

Next morning, she awoke elated at having had two nights of excellent progress on her novel. Even Mama's unchanging frosty mood couldn't bring her down.

When she was done with her chores, she put on her coat, snuggled Smudge into one of her pockets and headed out to meet Jasmine.

Halfway down Fleet Street, she caught sight of a flash of red hair protruding from an emerald cap. The outlandish combination was instantly recognisable - the mysterious young man who gave her the notebook.

Damn it! What if he had changed his mind? Well, he could forget it. She would not return the notebook, now that it contained the precious opening scenes to her novel. She slipped into a doorway and he passed by without spotting her.

Silly girl. It was a gift. An apology. Obviously, he wanted nothing more to do with her or the stupid book. Breathing a sigh of relief, she went on her way.

As she approached the teashop, a tug on her pocket caused her to look down. The grey ball of fluff landed daintily on the sidewalk and darted towards the busy street.

Time seemed to slow down and speed up, all at once. Mary let out a shrill scream and dashed forward to grab the runaway kitten. It scampered into the road and she lunged towards it. Fur brushed against her fingers as Smudge scampered away again.

Someone gave her a mighty shove. She sailed through the air before landing clumsily on the sidewalk. Her head cracked against the icy pavement and everything went black.

When she came round, there was chaos in the street. Men shouted. Women screamed. Children ran hither and thither. Dogs barked.

As the fog lifted from her brain, a horrific yet horribly familiar scene unfolded.

A glossy black carriage with a buckled wheel stood in the middle of the muddy road. Beside it was the blood-soaked figure of a girl in a pale blue dress.

"JASMINE!" Mary struggled to her feet and ran towards her friend. Jasmine had pushed her out of the path of the carriage, only to become trampled beneath its wheels.

Mary struggled to get to her, but strong arms caught her and would not let go. Eventually, she stopped struggling and began to sob. When she looked up, a pair of emerald-green eyes peered at her from beneath a familiar shock of fiery hair.

"I see you ignored my warning about the notebook," the man said.

"What?"

"You opened the notebook, didn't you? It's my fault. I should never have given it to you."

"What are you talking about?" Mary tried to get free. "My friend is hurt, let me go!"

"A passing Doctor is working on her There's nothing you can do for now." His grip tightened. "Did you open that notebook?"

"Don't be ridiculous!" Mary snarled.

"My name is John Priestly." His green eyes held her blue ones. "The notebook brought me nothing but heartache and appears to be doing the same for you."

"That's the most ridiculous thing I've ever heard! It's just a book!" But she could not prevent a barb of guilt piercing her heart.

"Just give me it back before more trouble befalls you."

The thought of being parted from the notebook awakened in her a burning rage, the like of which she had never experienced before.

"You insensitive bastard! How dare you stand here questioning me about a notebook while my friend could be breathing her last!"

"It's for the best, trust me." He remained unmoved by this remonstration. "Now where is the damned thing."

"I no longer have it. It... eh... burned in a fire."

"Did it now?" Suspicion tinged his words. "A fire, you say."

"Yes, a fire." With that she pulled herself free of his grip, spun on her heel and stormed off, hot tears spilling down her cheeks.

In the weeks that followed, Mary was wracked by guilt. She threw the notebook into the furthest corner of her closet and tried continuing her story in a different journal. But the words did not flow, the characters were flat and uncooperative, and the narrative went nowhere. She gave up in frustration.

The doctors said Jasmine was lucky to be alive, and would almost certainly be paralysed for the rest of her life.

Just like in your story. The insidious thought tormented her.

To escape the agonies of self-reproach, she spent long hours with Papa in the print shop, helping him with the suffragette pamphlets. Rheumatism forgotten; Mama spent the same amount of time at her anti-suffrage meetings. Her fervent, almost obsessive, passion for the cause appeared to be an antidote for her private suffering.

Ignoring Mary's protests, Papa sent her home early on the night of the final print run.

"Go on. Adam and I can take care of this lot. You're exhausted."

Stacks of boxes, the culmination of weeks of hard work, lined the walls. Tomorrow, Mr Hall would collect them, and they could finally pay their bills. Mary's spirits lifted for the first time since the tragedy.

To her relief Mama was out when she got home. After a quick supper, she tidied up the kitchen and headed upstairs.

To her surprise, the notebook lay open on her desk. Cold fear gripped her heart. Mama must've found it in her closet and read it.

Even as she stood, staring in horror at the thought of what Mama would do to her for writing such a scandalous story, the creamy white pages called. The desire to write her way back into Violet's world was almost palpable.

Mary hesitated. The solemn face of that red-headed stranger appeared. He was convinced the book had been behind the tragedy and his concern for appeared to be genuine.

Don't be silly! She scolded herself. Books did not have the power to make things happen in real life. But how to explain the appearance of the kitten, and the tragedy of Jasmine's accident?

She had a flash of inspiration. She would write the notebook out of her story. What if Violet destroyed it? In the unlikely event that what she wrote in the book did come true, the journal itself would be destroyed in real life and she would be rid of it.

It was worth a try. She had the words memorized and could easily transfer them to another journal. Tomorrow, perhaps.

She set pen to paper and felt the, now familiar, sensation of drifting into another world.

Lady Violet Landry stood before the fire, the notebook in her trembling hands. Her beloved Colette lay in hospital, fighting for her life.

At the very least, she would be paralysed. And it was all Violet's fault for letting her go on a fool's errand to find that darn kitten.

She gazed down at the notebook, eyes awash with tears. They had crafted their future in its pages. The faraway places they would visit. The great adventures they could have. All the hopes and dreams of youth. All gone now, and all her fault. In rage and frustration, she began tearing out the pages and laying them on the fire, a pilgrim offering sacrifices to appease a dispassionate god.

An odd aroma filled Mary's nostrils. Roasted meat? No, more like charred flesh.

She struggled to pull herself into the present. The smell intensified until she thought she would gag. With it came heat and flames. Fire! She was surrounded by fire.

Mary spun around. To her horror, she was back in the print shop, and it was ablaze. Through the windows, she caught a glimpse of angry women with torches.

"End suffrage." they shouted "Let women know their place. God's way is the right way. Destroy the pamphlets."

Mary's mouth gaped as she recognised Mama at the head of the crowd. In one hand, her mother held a flaming torch and, in the other, the notebook.

Revulsion at this vision propelled Mary out of her fugue. She peered around the familiar setting, reassuring herself that it had all been some dreadful dream. She looked down to see what she had written, but the notebook was gone.

Then she heard bells, shouts and screams from the street below.

She ran out of the front door and tore down the street, in her night-gown. Yet she hardly attracted attention, for the crowd was engrossed in the goings-on two blocks down.

"FIRE! FIRE!"

She rounded the corner into Fleet Street, and a nightmare tableau lay before her. The London fire brigade had arrived and men had formed a bucket line. They were dousing the flames, but it was clear that Papa's print store was lost. Mama stood on the corner opposite, hands covered in soot, a dead torch lying beside her. The look of dazed fervour that had burned in her eyes, was replaced by confusion and desolation.

Mary ran over to her. There was no cutting greeting this time. Mama stared sightlessly at the burning ruin.

"What have you done?" Mary whispered.

"I had to burn those evil diaries and that notebook you've been scribbling terrible things in, night after night. God willed it so."

"How are we going to survive without the shop?"

"I had promises from members that we would be taken care of," Mama replied listlessly.

"Where are Papa and Adam?" Mary grabbed her by the arms and shook.

"They weren't supposed to be there."

"What do you *mean*? They were doing a last print run! Where *are* they, Mama?"

Her mother lifted a shaky soot-stained arm and pointed towards the shop. Four men carrying a pair of stretchers emerged, carrying two bodies covered in white sheets.

"PAPA, NOOO!"

Mary staggered towards her father's burned corpse. Once more, a set of strong arms caught her. She didn't need to see his red hair. She knew instinctively who it was.

"We need to talk," Priestly said.

She made no sound for the fight had gone out of her. Priestly placed his coat around her, lifted Mary and carried her home.

He put her down in an armchair and set about making tea, while she did her best to stop shaking from shock and cold.

"Why ever did you give me that wretched book?" she sobbed.

"I can't explain it," he replied sadly. "The notebook goes where it wants, destroying one family after the next. It seems to be drawn to pride, ambition, and wilfulness."

She started to protest but he patted her hand.

"It came to me too," he sighed. "I did try to warn you."

"It wasn't much of a warning," she snapped.

"Would you have believed me, if I had told you everything?"

"No," she admitted. "So, you hoped I'd be a good little girl and do as bidden?"

"That's of no consequence now."

"I've lost everyone I love because of you and that damned book!"

"I know, and I am truly sorry. It did the same to me. Everyone and everything taken because of my ambition and pride." He looked around. "Where is it now? Be truthful this time."

"Mama said she burned it in the fire."

"If it were that easy to destroy, I'd have done it myself." Priestly helped Mary to her feet. "How I wish I had never given it to you! I don't know what came over me."

"Too late for regrets now. We must go after it."

They were soon trudging back down the sludge of Fleet Street.

"See what I mean?" Priestly pointed.

Amid the ashes of the burned-out print shop, despite having been ravaged by fire, doused with water and covered in mud and sleet, the book lay unblemished. Priestly gingerly picked it up. No sliver of mud or ice dared stick to the moleskin cover.

"You're right, it can't be destroyed," Mary wept. "What do we do now? Bury it?"

"I think it has to be passed on, or the curse on your family will never be lifted," Priestly said dolefully. "I would offer to take it back from you, but I don't think it works that way."

"Perhaps, if we gave it to someone who can't read or write," Mary suggested. "That might…"

Before she could finish, a small cutpurse darted from the shadows, grabbed the notebook from Priestley's hand and sprinted off down the street.

Priestly and Mary glanced at each other. Then both yelled as loudly as they could at the boy's retreating back.

"WHATEVER YOU DO.... DON'T OPEN IT!"

Cat Fight

Aletia Johnson

It was a dark and stormy day. Or, at least, it was trying to be. Grey clouds were clumping together, heavy and pregnant. Zoe Meredith Morningside Evans, sitting atop her Harley, looked up at the sky and sighed. Checked the GPS again. The engine thrummed underneath her.

Yep, this was the right place. She was exactly where she was supposed to be. She keyed off the ignition and kicked out the kickstand.

"Wait for me, Lucy." She patted the bike's shoulder. "Hopefully I won't be *too* long. I'll try to get you home before the rain hits."

The bike pinged in reply, as its engine cooled. It didn't believe her.

"You'll be fine, girl. Stay safe." Zoe patted it again, as if she understood. "Don't get stolen."

Zoe loved her bike. It was a 2017 Harley-Davidson CVO Street Glide 114. She loved its 1868cc 4-stroke engine. She loved its shiny red paint, black stripes, ABS brakes, leather seats and 12 inch chubby handlebars. She loved that it had two saddle bags, also red with black stripes. They were practical, and you could never have enough storage. Most of all, she loved that it was hers. After three years of scrimping and saving, working second and sometimes third jobs, she'd finally managed to pay it off and start her own private investigator business. The Justice business.

Problem was, it had left her seriously broke.

That was why she had taken this commission. Was it dangerous? Probably. Was it a good idea? Probably not. Were there any better options? None that she could see. She took a deep breath, removed her

231

helmet and shook out her hair. Then she headed into the forest, alone, to catch a monster.

Just think of it as another job, she told herself.

Nothing out of the ordinary. Find the person. Ask the person nicely to come with you. Make the person come with you when they refused. Bag and deliver them to the client. Collect the reward. Don't ask questions. Keep your big mouth shut. Don't be a jerk. Do *not* let your temper get the better of you. You know what happens when you let your emotions run things. It never ends well.

The forest floor was soft under her feet, and the smell of pine needles comforting. Wasn't so great on her six inch spike boot heels, though.

Zoe mentally slapped herself. They were good in a street fight and made her taller and look like a badass. But, sheesh, they were *not* great on uneven ground. And what if she had to run? Now that was a troubling thought. Good thing she wasn't the type to flee from a fight. Even walking was hard.

Cold laughter echoed around her, snapping Zoë's attention back to the present.

"Hellooooo, little mouse," came a voice. A beautiful voice. Female. Lilting and musical, seductive and sultry. "Have you come to catch me? Or have you come to… play with me?"

There was a soft rustle, warm breath on the back of Zoë's neck and a light tickle in her ear,

"I hope it's play, little mouse. Because I'd love to play with you."

There was a high pitched cackle, followed by a rush of cold air. Zoe jumped and let out a shriek. She snapped her head around, almost tripping over her feet. There was nothing behind her but trees and air.

"Ow!" she complained. "That was *sore!*"

The voice laughed.

"It's not funny!" Zoe gritted her teeth. "It really hurt."

"Oh no. Poor little mouse." The voice cooed, sarcastically. "Would you like me to come and kiss it better?"

"Not especially," Zoe answered, truthfully. Her heart was hammering and her breathing shallow. She needed to get control of this situation before things escalated. She kept her voice calm. Game face on.

"I'm spoken for." She paused, listening for movement. "But could you come out so we can talk?"

Silence.

"My name is Zoe," she continued. "Zoe Evans. I'm a consultant. Been asked to come and chat to you about something."

More silence.

"Please?"

"They don't want you to talk to me, little mouse." More laughter, bitter this time. "They want you to catch me, so they can kill me. And then dissect me, to see how I work."

"You've no idea who hired me," Zoe protested.

"It doesn't matter." The voice snarled angrily. "They're all the same. Do you really think you're the first?".

Zoe could tell the anger came from being hurt. From being wronged. From being judged. Zoe knew a little something about that.

"You're not the first," the voice sighed, and now there was sadness and pity. "And you won't be the last. They'll keep coming. Keep sending people to murder me."

The harshness was back. Angrier. Clearer. Closer.

Above her.

It was in the trees.

"Perhaps I need to send them another message," it snarled. "Perhaps I need to send them your head!"

Zoe blew out a breath. Don't react. Think, then act. Ignore everything that isn't important, right now. You can't run away. You're too slow in these heels. You're wearing leather and Kevlar and you have a gun, so you should fight. But first you need to freeze. Stay still. Listen. Absorb all the information you can. Make a plan. You don't have to stick to the plan, you just have to *have* one. She's obviously an ambush predator, so she'll wait for you to move before she attacks. Use that time. Catch your breath. Calm yourself down. Breathe.

"Bitch, please," she snorted. "My head's far too pretty where it is. Just come out and talk. Be a grown up. Stop acting like a crazy person."

"Crazy? I didn't come, alone, into a forest, to try to capture a monster."

"Maybe you're not a monster. Jut a nice lady who's misunderstood."

"Oh, I'm a monster, little mouse. A genuine, shape shifting monster. And now I'm hunting you."

"Look, kiddo, I don't want to fight you, but I will if I have to."

"In that outfit? You won't last five minutes."

"Hey, what's wrong with my outfit?" That was just mean. "This is genuine Italian leather."

"Exactly. You're going to overheat in three minutes. You won't be able to move and I'll rip it off and eat you. And you shan't be able to hide, because it squeaks like a cheap whorehouse mattress every time you move."

"Oh, *that's* why I'm a mouse? Very clever."

"No darling, you're a mouse because you're tiny and adorable. Maybe I'll keep you as a pet instead. What do you say? I'll take good care of you. Clean out your cage and give you fresh straw every day."

"Know what?" Zoe released the safety on her gun. "Maybe I *will* just shoot you."

"With that monstrosity? It's far too big and I'm betting you don't even know how to use it. Sure it looks impressive, but the kick back will break your wrist if you're not careful. What kind of charlatan would sell you something like that?"

"It was my father's." Zoe kept her tone steady but inside she was fuming. Was the woman psychic? How did she know so much about all her insecurities? Of *course* she didn't know how to use the gun. The idea was to intimidate people so they ran away first. She didn't even know if it was loaded.

Something rustled overhead and a thump came from behind. Zoe whirled around and squeezed the trigger. There was an almighty bang, she let out an involuntary scream and landed on her back. Spike heels and uneven ground. Damn it! The kickback had thrown the weapon from her grasp and the base of her thumb was throbbing. She probably should have been holding it with two hands. But her wrist was fine, so psycho lady was wrong. Ha!

There was no sign of the mark. That was something, at least. She checked herself. Head? Fine apart from a few extra leaves in her hair. No loss of consciousness. No concussion. Just a bit of deafness. Arms and legs? All present and accounted for. Hooray for bike leathers. Suck it, crazy tree lady.

Something was wrong though. Why hadn't her assailant struck while she was down? It's what Zoe would have done. Maybe she was just enjoying playing with her. She should be grateful for small mercies, she supposed.

"Look, love, I haven't got time for this." Zoe got to her feet, shakily. "I've got places to be and so do you."

She clenched her fist and stepped into an attack stance.

"Come out and face me, bitch. Let's get this over with."

Temper, Zoe, control your temper. Don't let her rattle you..

"Now, why would I do something stupid like that? I've got all the advantages. I see you but you have no idea where I am. Do you think insulting me will make me throw that away? Maybe I should start saying hurtful things too. You know, just to even things up."

"Do your worst, then."

"Alright. If it's a bitch you want, I'm happy to oblige. Are you ready?"

"Bring it on, sister."

"You're wearing far too much eye makeup. It doesn't suit you and you're going to get panda eyes when I make you start crying."

The voice was coming from in front of Zoe. No... behind. To her left? Hell, the assailant was moving too fast.

"When I'm finished, your corpse will be very unattractive. The police will think you're a worthless little two dollar hooker and nobody will try very hard to find out what happened to you. Just some cheap slut who deserved what she got. How's am I doing?"

Wow, that was oddly specific. And cruel. Not to mention, misogynistic. Zoe could feel her ire rising. It had taken ages to put on makeup that morning. Also, some of her best friends were sex workers.

"It's sad nobody has ever told you not to wear so much lipstick with that colour of eye shadow. Looks like you're trying too hard. Plus your eyebrows are pretty thick."

"I've changed my mind." Zoe felt her hands tingle. "You're not a nice lady and I'm going to enjoy beating you to a pulp."

"I'm sure you'll try, little mouse."

The whisper came from right behind her!

Zoe screamed and spun again. This time she didn't fall over, at least. She struck out with a backhand, but the woman had moved back out of reach. Also, she was holding a sword. Because, of course she was.

"Let's make this interesting," she purred seductively. "If you can beat me, I'll go with you, no fuss. I think it's about time I had a little talk with my pursuers, anyway. It really is unfair of them to keep sending such sweet little mice against me. You do know how expendable you are to them, don't you? What did they offer you? Fame? Glory? The chance to make the world a better place without monsters like me in it?"

"Money, mostly," Zoe answered. "Though you've made it kind of personal."

"Shame." The woman puffed out an annoyed sigh. "In another life, we might have been friends."

"Not after your crack about my eyebrows. Are they *really* that bushy?"

"What if I said that I was lying?" She lowered her sword. "And that they were perfectly lovely."

She almost sounded sincere.

"I'd say, I don't care. My girlfriend loves me the way I am, and her opinion counts a hell of a lot more."

Zoe regarded her. The woman was tall. Probably six foot. Her long blonde hair was tied up in a simple ponytail and looked like it had been professionally styled. Salon grade utensils would have been involved. Her legs were muscular, arms lean, but well developed. That meant she was used to gripping things and lifting heavy objects. She would be good with her hands. She would be strong.

She was wearing a simple cotton wrap dress, tied at the waist. No belt. No bra either. Some people would be distracted in a fight. Not Zoe, of course, but some people. There'd be jiggleage. She looked like she'd be comfortable in heels, but was barefoot. If Zoe had to use one word to describe her, it would be *elegant*.

Her makeup was light and her eyebrows were bloody perfect.

"Enough with the flirting," Zoe growled. "Let's get this over with."

"Now, now, little mouse," When her opponent grinned, there were far too many teeth. "Niceties must be observed. We're not savages, after all. Let's be ladylike."

"That is an antiquated term designed to oppress women and make us conform to patriarchal stereotypes."

"Said the cute little red head in black leather facing the hot blonde with a sword."

"Oh, you think you're hot, do you? You must have spent a lot of money to get all those tickets on yourself."

"I do not apologise for it. It is both a gift and a weapon like any other." She smiled smugly and bowed slightly. "I celebrate my hotness. As you should."

"I told you to stop flirting with me." Zoe didn't know why the words were making her so angry. But this needed to end before she lost control.

Zoe charged. She would take the stupid cow down in a tackle before she had a chance to use that stupid sword or make any more stupid jokes.

She took three steps before tripping and falling on her face. By her outstretched arm was another sword.

"I told you, little mouse, we must be ladylike. That means a fair fight. You no longer have your gun, yet I have a blade. Therefore you must have one too. Otherwise it wouldn't be any fun at all, would it?"

"You want me to use a sword? I'll use the damn sword." Zoe picked it up and sliced off the spike heels on her boots. "Let's see what *you've* got."

"En Garde!" Zoë's adversary was grinning like a maniac. Beautiful and graceful she may be, but she was missing a few screws for sure.

Blondie thrust out her sword. Zoe parried, just in time to block it from slicing into her shoulder. She pushed all her weight against it, lifting it up and tossing Blondie's blade up in the air, throwing her off balance. Then she charged, taking her enemy down in a bear hug and sitting on her. She wrenched Blondie's sword away and tried to get her in a choke hold.

The woman grabbed her hands and held them against her jiggalicious chest. Zoe tried to pull back, but Blondie kicked up one knee and sent her sprawling. Grabbed her around the waist and rolled, reversing their positions. Now she was on top, and Zoe was trapped. Blondie grabbed her by the hair with one hand and yanked. Zoe screamed. Blondie used her other hand to push her head into the ground and begin choking her.

"Honestly, darling, has no-one ever taught you to use a hair tie? You really do need training."

"Get off me, you Amazonian *bitch*!" Zoe gasped.

"No need for that sort of language. Just accept defeat with grace and humility. You fought well, for a rank amateur, but I have bested you. Yield to me now, and I will let you walk away."

"Argh! Let me *go*."

"For the record, I'm not a bitch." Her eyes narrowed to slits, "I'm a pussy."

Her voice lost its lilting quality and became a growl. Zoe froze as claws began to dig into her neck. Her assailant's eyes glowed golden, and her face began to change. The nose elongated and her cheeks sprouted tawny golden fur. The lips turned black, splitting up the middle as they parted to reveal sharp, jagged teeth.

Zoe panicked. What in the actual hell was happening?

"Fear not little mouse." Tiger lady purred seductively. "You have fought well. As a reward, I will kill you swiftly, before I eat your heart."

Zoe screamed again. With terror, but also with rage.

Does that line ever work on people? She thought. *Could you be any more of a cartoon villain right now?*

"Last chance," she rasped. "I'm warning you."

"I'm sure you are, little mouse." Claws pressed into Zoë's cheek, drawing blood.

"Fine. Just don't say I wasn't *ladylike* about this."

Blue lightening coursed in Zoë's eyes and around her finger tips. The air crackled with static, as energy erupted from her body. Tiger lady was thrown back, flying through the air into a tree trunk, then bouncing off and landing, face first, in the pine needles. Out cold, she morphed back into her human shape. Her hair was no longer immaculate, and Zoe found that oddly gratifying.

Her throat felt crushed, both eyes were streaming and her hair looked like she'd stuck her finger in a power socket. With shaking hands, she unzipped one of the pockets in her jacket, pulled out the zip ties she'd stored there, and cuffed the unconscious woman's hands behind her. She sank down on the ground, exhausted, and burst into tears.

An air horn sounded. She jumped back into her fighting stance.

"Who's there?" she demanded.

Suddenly, she was surrounded by a ring of men in black fatigues, all pointing automatic weapons at her. She dropped to her knees and put her hands on her head.

"Whoever you are, I surrender."

She knew when she was beaten.

A man appeared, dressed in a suit and tie. He nodded to his men, who rushed over to Blondie and untied her. She groaned and rolled over to stare at the sky.

"Well done, candidate." The man raised his hands in a gesture of calm and smiled at Zoe. "It's been a long time since someone's gotten the best of our Cat."

"Huh?" Zoe frowned, still breathing hard.

"It was a test, Miss Evans, and you passed. Welcome to the organisation." He looked around at the forest. "Although, you do need a lot of practice with your hand to hand combat."

"What?" she blinked.

"Katarina, are you ok?"

"No," Blondie groaned and sat up. "I feel like I've been hit by a truck."

"I did brief you that she was a witch, Cat. You should have expected something like this."

"You didn't tell me she could throw fricking lightening."

"What do I always say, Cat? Expect the unexpected."

"So you didn't know either?"

"I did not." He smiled. "It's absolutely fascinating though, isn't it?"

"Not from where I'm sitting."

"If it's any consolation, I didn't tell her you were a tiger."

"Um, what the hell is going on here?" Zoe tried to keep her voice steady.

"I apologise, Miss Evans. My name is Roger and I'm the founder of our little organisation. This was your entrance exam."

"Say *what*?"

"When someone applies to join us, we obviously test them. We like to see how they act under stress and find out what kind of person they are. We want to make sure we aren't hiring thugs or psychopaths who shoot first and ask questions later. We need responsible, intelligent, flexible people, who can fight, but also think and act rationally under duress. You have proven you are such a person, Miss Evans.

He looked her up and down.

"Though you do require training and your attire needs tweaking."

"Hey," Zoe protested. "Don't be hating on my leathers. They're protective and spell proof."

"Also heavy and impractical. Cat here went easy on you, today. If she'd actually being trying to hurt you, you'd have been a greasy smear on the ground. We'll have to work on that."

"Are you saying I fight like a *girl?*"

Roger laughed. It was rich and genuine but went on for longer than Zoe thought polite.

"Oh my goodness," he exclaimed. "Heavens, no!"

He wiped tears from his eyes with the back of his hand.

"No, Miss Evans, Cat fights like a girl. You fight like a baby giraffe learning to walk."

"Steady on, Roger," Cat wobbled as she tried to stand. "I think she did pretty well for her first time."

She limped over and stuck out her hand.

"Hi," she said. "I'm Cat. Sorry I was such a bitch to you. I didn't mean any of it. Just acting."

"Very dramatic acting, Cat." Roger added wryly.

"Shut up, Roger. I was playing a role." Cat tried to hide a grin. "You said I had to be a vicious monster, so I was being a vicious monster. Didn't you hear the things I was saying? Words hurt more than swords, Roger. I use all my weapons."

She winked at Zoe.

"Most of the time I can destroy people before I've lifted a finger."

"I'd agree with that," Zoe grunted.

"You still look a bit frazzled. I was the same at my initiation." As she bent down to help Zoe up, she winced, clutching her side. "I need to get checked over by medical, but let's get a drink after, yeah?"

"Um, sure?" Zoë's head was spinning. It always left her a bit foggy when she had to zap someone. Plus Cat's chest was right in her face now. She didn't know where to look.

"Just so you know, I'm taken."

"Just so you know, I'm happily married with three kids. You're safe."

"Married?"

"You think I can't be in a happy, long term relationship, because I look like this and I'm a badass?" She winked. "Just messing with you, kid. I get it all the time. Just like you and short jokes.

"I'm not *that* short."

"People always think I'm too hot to handle." She waved a hand over herself, "They look at this and make assumptions about these," She pointed to her heart then her head.

"Says more about them than it does me - and it gives me another weapon in my arsenal."

"I shouldn't have assumed," Zoe stammered.

"I'm living the dream. Husband's a cat person, plus he cooks. Had to lock that down before anyone else tried to snag him."

"Lucky you," Zoe smiled.

"Luck had nothing to do with it," Cat smiled, seductively, "I used my feminine wiles. Poor man never stood a chance."

"Sorry for throwing you into a tree trunk," Zoe blushed

"I did threaten to eat your heart out so I totally deserved it."

"Probably."

"Plus I had just turned into a tiger while I was sitting on you."

"True, I've never been attacked by a feline in a dress before."

"At least I wasn't wearing a bra. Tiger me has six nipples. Try finding one to fit that. "

"I hadn't noticed," Zoe lied.

"Yeah, you did." Cat shot her a wry look. "Like I said. Lots of weapons in my arsenal."

"So, what happens now?" Zoe blushed and looked away.

"If you still want to join us, come to the office first thing Monday." Cat's tone turned serious. "Roger and I will teach you how to fight properly. In return, we'll subcontract some of our less... controversial operations to your agency.. If it works out, you can take on some of our more well-paying jobs. Maybe even join us permanently. It's been a long time since we've had someone like you on the team. Not since we lost Maggie."

"What happened to Maggie?" Zoe gulped

"Maternity leave. Woman breeds like a meerkat."

"No-one outside needs to know about me do they? *That's* something I try to keep private."

"Nothing to be ashamed of, Zoe. It's who you are."

"I'm not ashamed. Just... cautious. It isn't always safe to be out of the broom closet, as they say."

"Literally nobody says that."

"We do. You just don't know about it. That's how cautious we are."

"But you're still keen?"

"Definitely. I'll be there first thing."

"Just out of curiosity, what would you have done, if this hadn't been a test? Would you have really handed me over to be dissected?"

"Of course not." Zoe answered quickly. Then she thought about it.

"Well, probably not. You did say some really mean things back there. I might have locked you up until I could find out more about what was actually happening. Once I'd calmed down, anyway."

"That was a good answer." Cat nodded seriously. "Ethics are important and you can't always trust the information you're given."

She brightened.

"Go home and get some rest. I think we're going to be good pals."

"Will do."

"And get some barrettes. All that hair in your face distracts from your beautiful eyebrows."

Zoe laughed and gave her the finger. She'd made a friend today.

She reached the bike, pulled her helmet out of the saddle bag and started the engine. For the first time in a long while, she felt right where she was supposed to be.

That meant something when you were a witch.

Frogman

Jan-Andrew Henderson

It was a nice night for a murder. Nothing much on TV, plus the local drugstore had a sale on stain remover.

And murder was Harlan Macfarlane's business. Not that he killed people. At least, not very often.

He was, in lieu of the fact, a private dick - though his personality hadn't much to do with anything. *Smarter than the average bear* was his slogan, because he had been abandoned in the forest as a baby and had to survive by raiding picnic baskets.

Harlan was rummaging around in a garbage can when a short, rotund man in an overcoat strolled over. This was his associate, Fats Norbett. If crime was a fairy-tale, Harlan liked to say, Fats would be the Duke of York. Neither had any idea what that meant but it sounded good.

"Looking for clues, buddy?" Fats asked.

"I saw someone throw a Subway foot-long meatball sandwich in here." Harlan shook his head in disbelief. "Only had a couple of bites taken out."

But I digress.

In a way, the pair got into this whole crazy mess - which I am about to describe at great length - because Fats had a birthday coming up. If he had never been born, none of it would have happened.

"Sorry," Fats apologised, forgetting I was the narrator, and he wasn't supposed to know I existed.

"Not your fault," I replied. "Your parents should have thought their actions through a bit more, that's all. Now leave me alone. I'm writing a story about a serial killer and a shark."

For Fats' birthday, Harlan decided to give him a surprise. This involved driving to New Jersey, which was a surprise in itself, since they lived in Australia.

As Harlan and Fats approached their destination, Bad Boy Blobby's Sinister Clown Museum and Aquatic Trailer Park, they saw a plethora of police cars parked outside a nearby mansion.

What's a private eye to do in circumstances like that? Harlan took Fat's blindfold off and they went to investigate

It turned out to be the scene of a horrible mass killing. The police had no suspects, so they arrested the duo and tried to get them to confess. Fats confessed he was wearing his girlfriend's underwear and Harlan admitted to secretly liking Eric Roberts movies.

Eventually the police let them go but, by then, Harlan was intrigued and offered his services. After all, he pointed out, he and Fats weren't doing anything important.

The troopers relented and showed them the crime scene. Out on the highway were five unidentified bodies in fancy dress. A witness claimed they had run from the house and thrown themselves under a passing truck. Inside the mansion was the corpse of aging millionaire playboy, Bruce Payne.

"Isn't he the person everyone suspects is secretly Batman?" Fats hopped around with a hand in the air.

"That's Bruce *Wayne*," Harlan corrected. "Though I personally harbour the suspicion Batman is actually Eric Roberts."

If Bruce Payne ever had a secret identity, however, it would remain a clandestine one. His head had exploded.

Behind a couch in the living room lay the body of Bruce Payne's daughter, Lois. Beside her lay a blood-stained egg whisk.

"Looks like she's been beaten to death," Fats giggled. "Get it?"

"Try to show some decorum," Harlan sighed, helping himself to the contents of the fridge. "Ooooh. A jar of pickled eggs."

Strangest of all, in the bedroom were a pair of diving flippers - size nine - with the feet still inside.

The cops were baffled, mainly because one of them had brought along a box of Chupa Chups and they couldn't work out how to get the wrappers off. There was no sign of forced entry at the dwelling, which belonged to Lois Payne, and no clue as to what had happened.

However, after seven cheese daiquiris and a sherbet dip-dab, Harlan deduced exactly what had occurred and recounted the story to Fats. Which saves me having to do it.

"It all began this morning," he stated. "In the offices of Payne Industries."

The glass of the window exploded and Bruce Payne, wearing a furry onesie, landed on top of the nearest filing cabinet. It wobbled alarmingly, so he attempted to leap onto a large executive desk. But his back gave out, so he sat there looking miserable and holding on for dear life.

A younger man entered, sporting an expensive suit with a DC comics tie. He glanced at the intruder and groaned loudly.

"Shall I order my secretary to fetch a ladder? Or she could bring you coffee, if you intend to sulk up there all afternoon."

"Hi Donald," the man said sheepishly.

"Hello, father. Want me to help you?"

"No, I don't. I can manage."

Bruce climbed gingerly down, using the drawers as steps, hobbled behind the desk and lowered himself painfully into a leather executive chair. He fiddled with the levers and it sank several inches, until all Donald could see was his head.

"It's no surprise to me that you should arrive at this precise moment," he grinned. "Want to know why?"

"Not really."

"Superpowers, Donald. Your untapped abilities sensed I was in trouble and this caused you to rush to my office, exactly when I needed aid."

"This is *my* office, father. I just went to the toilet. You came through the wrong window again."

"Shut up and take my money! Nothing gets past you, eh?"

"Why are you so obsessed with the notion I have superpowers?" Donald sighed. "I'm an accountant."

"Did you say mild mannered accountant?"

"Actually, I'm an easily irritated accountant."

"Aha! Do you fly into a rage and turn green?"

"Get to the point, please," Donald looked at his watch. "I have a goat yoga appointment at Miss Wheezy-Pop's Massage Parlour and leaf blower showroom in ten minutes."

"Donald," Bruce Payne said gravely. "I want to show you a very different side to my character."

"You did that at the office Christmas party."

"I'm going to finally reveal myself."

"Apparently, you did *that* at the office Christmas party too. I had to give the staff a raise and make them sign a non-disclosure agreement."

"Son." Bruce took up a heroic stance and clicked his teeth together. "I am the superhero they call... Ratman!"

"I know."

"I understand, it's hard to believe but..." Bruce blinked rapidly. "What do you mean, you *know*?"

"Little things gave it away. Like the Ratmobile always being parked outside our house. On a yellow line, too."

"Alfrick was supposed to hide it."

"Alfrick retired to run an ant farm in Burrumbuttock ten years ago."

"Did he?" Bruce scratched his cheek. "I better stop talking to him, then."

"There's also the fact that you're wearing a rodent costume in the middle of a heatwave."

"Bloody fashion expert," Bruce huffed. "Since you know my true identity, you must also realise I have an obligation to protect Gothum City from crime."

"And?"

"Times have changed, son. My knees are a bit stiff and people keep emailing my website to ask if I do pest control."

"Why don't you just retire?" Donald looked at his watch again. "Gothum City won't care."

"Why not?"

"We live in New Jersey."

"Beside the point," Bruce smiled winningly. "The world will always need a Ratman, even after I've gone to the great trashcan in the sky."

"Not a chance, father."

"Donny," Bruce said cajolingly. "Donny, Donny, Donny, Donny-DonnyDonnyDonnyDonnyDonny."

"Please don't call me Donny. Especially not that many times."

"You're the obvious person to assume my mantle. You don't know it yet, but in your genes there's a huge… thing trying to get out."

"*Excuse* me?"

"Your superpowers. Powers you inherited from me!" Bruce thought for a moment. "Now, if I can just remember who *I* am."

"Let's get a few things straight, shall we?" Donald sat down. "To begin with, I am not related to you in any way shape or form. I'm only your son-in-law. Furthermore, you do not *have* any superpowers. You've got a rodent suit, filled with inane gadgets like the rat bollock shaver."

He waved his tie at the elderly man.

"*Superman* has superpowers. And I'm not related to him either, be-fore you ask."

"Don't talk to me about that poncy, non-aging, do-gooding dobber in tights," Bruce sulked. "He looks like Elvis with his head on back-wards."

He limped round the desk and laid a furry glove on Donald's shoulder.

"Ye Gods," the man coughed. "When was the last time you had that outfit dry cleaned?"

"It's the only one I've got. Can't fight crime in my undies, can I?"

"It's probably against the Geneva convention but I'd still pay serious money to see it."

"Look, there's a reason Ratman must carry on a little longer," Bruce pleaded. "See, everyone thinks there are no super villains left in America. They believe Superman and I defeated them all."

"The way I heard it, Superman did that on his own."

"Oh, I must have been on *holiday* at the time!" Bruce exploded. "Then that smug git goes traipsing off into space, looking for his home planet, which the smarmy bumwomble never should have left in the first place. And I, who am obviously not a superhero by any *stretch* of the imagination, spend the next twenty years getting thrown off tall buildings - the kind Superman can leap in a single bloody bound - by psychopaths titting around like Marcel Marceau or dolled up circus freaks on happy pills."

"Take it easy, father." Donald held up a placating hand. "You'll have another stroke."

"Now I hear, through the rat-vine, the last group of supervillains in the world have gathered in New Jersey. But I'm no longer young enough to tackle them."

"And I'm not dumb enough."

"I suppose appearances can be deceptive," Bruce conceded. "In that case I have another idea."

"And I have another appointment. I missed the last one thanks to you jabbering on."

"It's a good idea," Bruce said slyly. "See this one through and I'll never ask you to become Ratman again."

"Really?"

"What's more, I'll retire and move to Florida with She-Gerbil." He blushed demurely. "We've got a bit of a thing going."

"I'm gonna regret this," Donald sighed. "But what's the plan?"

"You disguise yourself as a supervillain, infiltrate their group and find out what nefarious scheme they're planning. I'll take over from there."

"Hmmm. I can see why you didn't call yourself Mr Intelligence."

"But you'll agree, if it gets me off your back?"

"Oh, all right."

"I knew you were stupid enough!" Bruce crowed. "I've got your costume right here."

He dipped into the filing cabinet, pulled out a plastic carrier bag and handed it to his son-in-law.

"It's simple but functional. I feel it makes a real statement."

"Yeah," Donald peered inside. "It's saying, *hello sucker*."

"It doesn't talk, fool. Alfrick handled all that advanced gizmo stuff. I got this from K-Mart."

Donald sighed again.

"Stick it on and let's see what you look like." Bruce rummaged some more and retrieved a cigar from the cabinet. "I'll have a Rat-puff to celebrate."

"Stop smoking my Havanas." Donald put on the outfit. "They'll be the death you. Listen to your old lungs wheezing away."

"I'm not sure that's me."

Donald was now wearing flippers, swimming goggles and a snorkel, the noise of his laboured breathing drowning out all other sounds.

"Just which super villain am I supposed to be?"

"Frogman, of course."

"Great." He took a few waddling steps. "Now I can leap onto small pavements in a single bound."

"Here's where the villains will be gathered this afternoon." Bruce handed him a piece of paper with a map drawn in yellow crayon. "They'll most likely welcome another baddy to swell their ranks."

"Are these guys dangerous?"

"I defeated all the really serious ones," Bruce assured him. "Though they do have a leader you should watch out for. Doctor Baghead."

His voice dipped conspiratorially.

"Nobody knows his true identity because he's a genius. And because he has a bag on his head."

"Well, I'm off to the Frogmobile, otherwise known as my Volvo." Donald trudged out, making slapping sounds on the floor. "Please leave through the door or I'll have the fire escape removed."

"Don't need a fire escape," Bruce chuckled, pulling a can from his pocket. "I've got my Rat Ground Repellent. Or is it shaving foam?"

He squinted at it more closely.

"Can't be fake snow, can it?"

As Donald sped towards his destiny, his Volvo quickly converted to look like a pond, the villains were gathering.

Swedish Hairdresser and The Big Nipple carried a table into the middle of their meeting room, on the top floor of Madame Benbecula's House of Fluff.

"This hasn't been wiped down properly," Big Nipple squirted some milk onto the surface and polished it with his sleeve. "Last time I steal from *that* restaurant."

He plonked down his end.

"Did you bring a bottle? It was stipulated on Doctor Baghead's invite."

"Yah. Conditioner vit Henna."

In trooped The Rifter and Voiceover Man. They grabbed plastic chairs from the corner and sat.

"A gathering of villains," Voiceover Man rasped in a deep voice. "Each eying the other suspiciously. Waiting for their leader to arrive. What will be the outcome?"

"That's gonna get old, real fast," Big Nipple moaned.

"And one of them already marked for death." Voiceover man growled, glaring at him.

There was a knock on the door and Donald shuffled in. The others stared at him.

"Hi, fellow reprobates," he panted, hopping over to them. Before anyone could object, the opposite door opened and a suited man with a briefcase strode in. He placed his case on the table and opened it.

"I am Doctor Baghead's lawyer, Mr Kimkardashian." He took out a paper bag with eyeholes and put it over his hand. "Doctor Baghead regrets he cannot attend, for he has another important engagement."

"Someone vit his head is the shopping doing?" Swedish Hairdresser guffawed.

"Highly amusing." Kimkardashian appeared unruffled. "As I was saying, Doctor Baghead has instructed me to inform you why you are all gathered here.

"He wants an 'aircut, a pint o gold top an some swimmin lessons?" the Rifter cackled. He was a sweaty sort, who looked like a used car salesman from Albania.

"But that was not Baghead's plan," Voiceover man corrected. "Instead, he wanted his preposterous team to take over the world."

"Precisely. Doctor Baghead has a foolproof plan for global domination. Carry it out and you'll be rich beyond your wildest dreams."

"In me wildest dreams I'm floating down the Ganges on a giant avocado, being chased by the Ned Kelly Gang." The Rifter shrugged "I eat a lot o cheese."

"How do I know this lot won't cramp my style?" Big Nipple asked. "The personal grooming freak sounds like Muppet Yoda on acid."

"An I usually work alone," The Rifter added.

"That's cause you smell like a builder's jockstrap that's spent a week under a Bangkok tuk-tuk driver's armpit."

"Oh yeah? Well, check *this* out, mate."

The Rifter let loose an almighty parp that seemed to go on forever. Big Nipple was catapulted over the table by the sheer force and turned an alarming shade of blue. Donald clasped a hand over the top of his snorkel. Swedish Hairdresser pulled out a gigantic hair dryer and deflected the smell towards Voice Over Man.

"The stench was so overpowering, he could not help himself," Voice Over Man gasped, throwing up on Swedish Hairdresser.

"Projectile spew, his superpower is," the villain screamed, trying to scrape it off his face with a straight razor.

"Let me assist." Big Nipple squeezed the huge teat on his forehead and squirted milk into his companion's eye.

"Sorry. I've got a terrible sense of direction."

"Stone the bleedin crows," Rifter gagged. "That is truly disgustin!"

"Enough!" Kimkardashian shouted. "There will be plenty of time for fisticuffs later."

"Ere!" The Rifter goggled. "Ow come *you* weren't blown away by me epic pump?"

"I'm a lawyer. It's hard to move me." The suited man pointed at Donald. "What about you, newbie? Got a special talent?"

Donald sank down below the table. When he rose again, he had tousled his hair and wore a fake plastic nose and moustache.

"Not another damned shapeshifter," Big Nipple complained. "You guys are ten-a-penny."

"It works for me, yah? I'm tinking, perhaps, you would like a little tache wax?"

"All right." The lawyer clapped his hands. "Take a seat."

The villains did so.

"I mean, sit *down*." He shuffled some papers. "Turns out there is one obstacle in your path to world domination."

The villains looked at him expectantly

"Everyone else in the world."

"Say *what* now?"

"That was a joke," the lawyer sighed. "People just don't get my sense of humour. The obstacle, of course, is Ratman. He might be a bit long in his exceedingly buck teeth, but he's the last superhero left."

"Technically, he isn't *really* a superhero." Donald raised his hand, then glanced around at the hostile faces. "I'll shut up."

"So, Ratman we will be killing dead as last year's mullet. No problem."

"Yes, problem," the lawyer corrected. "You see, Doctor Baghead has heard a nasty rumour."

"That's just a rash I get from these tights." Big Nipple went red.

"No. Word on the street is that Ratman's son has superpowers too."

"Ratman hasn't got a son!" Donald tried again. "He has a daughter and a son-in-law. Both perfectly ordinary."

"Son, daughter... Whatever." Kimkardashian sniffed. "To be on the safe side, kill the whole family."

"The rest nodded in agreement," Voiceover man intoned. "It seemed like the perfect plan. Almost *too* perfect."

Donald rolled his eyes.

"Ratman lives near his daughter Lois and her husband, out in New Jersey." The lawyer continued. "Go to Lois' house and bump them off. Ratman too, if he's there."

"And if he's not?"

"He's always coming over to bug them. Just hang around. Order a takeaway. Watch Netflix." He stuffed the papers and bag into his briefcase. "Doctor Baghead will contact you with instructions, once the deed is done."

Donald sped ahead of the other villains, who had stopped to beat up a mime. He parked out of sight and rushed into his house.

"Lois? Lois!!!"

His wife entered, smoothing down her skirt and patting her hair into place.

"Hello honey," she stammered. "You're... eh... home early."

She gave a double take.

"Have you been swimming?"

"Pack your bags, right now!" Donald commanded. "We have to leave."

"I get it," Lois smiled. "We're going to the beach."

"No. We're going to die." Donald grabbed her arm. "There are four completely insane men on their way to murder us. I really think we should go."

"Oh, you!" Lois laughed "Don't you realise what's going on.

"I'm wearing a mask and snorkel. Do I look like I realise what's going on?"

"This is one of Daddy's tricks. He's trying to force out your hidden superpowers again."

"Of course!" Donald slapped his head. "He pretends to be Doctor Baghead and hires a bunch of no-hopers to spur me into action. That's why he didn't turn up at the meeting. Even with his head covered, I'd have recognised his voice."

"Dad's nothing if not persistent," Lois agreed.

"He's always pulling stuff like this. You know what I caught him doing last week? Putting gunpowder into my cigars. Said the shock would bring my abilities to the surface."

"So, it's all sorted, silly."

"It's not sorted," Donald groaned. "I don't *have* superpowers, as you well know. At school, even the kindergarten kids next door picked on me. When I went to the beach, I was so insignificant I had to kick sand in my own face."

"Point taken. I'll call daddy." Lois grabbed her mobile and dialled.

"Hi pops. Apparently, I'm about to be killed by a bunch of deluded villains in weird costumes, intent on taking over the world by nefarious means. Well, yes, they might be Trump supporters but that's not the point… Yes, I know you voted for him… Look, just get over here and save us, all right!"

She looked around.

"Darling? Where have you gone?"

Donald rushed back in, leading Big Nipple, Swedish Hairdresser, Voiceover Man and The Rifter. He pointed to his wife.

"That's Ratman's daughter, boys. Found her for you."

"Donny! What are you doing?"

"Frogman's the name, babe. Baddest of the bad." He shrugged. "You can shoot her now."

"Wait a minute!" Fats interrupted. "Are you sure this is what went down?"

"Think, Fats." Harlan said. "What happens if Ratman dies?"

"He goes to heaven?"

"Less literally. Lois inherits Bruce Payne's millions."

"Oh, yeah." Fats thought. "But if Lois dies too…"

"All the cash goes to her husband, Donald." Harlan patted Fats' head. "So, you see why he'd want her gone. Besides, she's really annoying."

"That's why Doctor Baghead couldn't be at the meeting. Doctor Baghead is really Donald!"

"Brilliant deduction, Fats." Harlan winked. "But totally wrong."

"Oh." Fats looked crestfallen. "Carry on then."

The villains halted in the middle of the living room, looking uncertain.

"Go on, kill her," Donald repeated. "What's got into you?"

"They won't do it, honey." Lois gave a sinister grin. "They work for me."

"I don't understand."

"I always suspected you married me to get your hands on daddy's money. So, I put together this little ruse." She pouted. "And you failed the test."

"I got it!" Fats' breathed. "Lois is Doctor Baghead! That's why she couldn't be at the meeting."

"Yeah. Wrong again."

"Huh?" Fats tugged at his hair. "I'm utterly bamplussed."

"That's not a word," Harlan sighed. "Will you let me finish?"

"I've been working with Doctor Baghead," Lois said. "He was the one who convinced me how dishonest you were."

"So Baghead *is* Bruce Payne! I knew he never liked me!" Donald tore off his mask. "Mind you, nobody does."

"Of course not, sweety. We're going to kill daddy too." Lois blew on her nails. "Then I can spend his money on buff gardeners and hair-dos."

"A wonderful beehive I can be giving you," Swedish Hairdresser offered.

"I accept. Dispatch my husband, please."

The villains circled Donald.

"You won't take me without a fight." He took up a boxing stance. "You bunch of dirty rats!"

His assailants stopped. Then they crouched, hands in front of them, making squeaking noises and bouncing up and down.

"What are they doing?" Donald gasped.

"They think they're rats." Lois wailed. "You told them they were rats and now they believe it!"

"I've got a superpower!" Donald looked at his hands in amazement. "OMFG."

"Great," Lois replied sarcastically. "Maybe you can open a pet store."

"I don't think a mere mortal like you should criticize." He turned to the villains. "You're all a bunch of..."

He glanced at Lois.

"What do you call those animals that destroy themselves in huge numbers?"

"Trump supporters?"

"Lemmings! That's it." He pointed. "You're all a bunch of lemmings."

The villains kept hopping around, staring at him vacantly.

"Not that different from rats. Lemmings," Donald observed. "Go on, then. Do what you do best."

The gang turned and scampered out of the front door. There was a sound of squealing tyres and several loud thumps.

Donald turned back to Lois, who backed slowly away.

"Now it's your turn, you snake in the grass."

Lois paused, tongue slipping from between her lips

"Ssssnkakes eat frogs," she hissed.

"Eh? Wait a minute."

"Come into the dining room, froggy." Lois shot out a hand and clamped it over her husband's mouth.

"And that," Harlan said. "Was the end of Donald and the supervillains."

"Lois ate him?" Fats wrinkled his nose. "Gross."

"All except the feet."

"So what happened next?"

Bruce Payne burst in through the window, clutching an egg whisk.

"I'm here to save you, baby," he cried. "Didn't even stop to put my rat suit on. I would have gotten here sooner but I forgot the address."

He glanced around.

"Don't muck about, Lois." He began searching the living room. "I've got a rat-souffle in the oven and I don't want it to go flat."

He was peering over the back of the couch when Lois ran in from the dining room.

"Ssssnkakes eat rats!" She launched herself at him and they disappeared over the couch

"Aaaaargh!" Bruce yelled, raising the egg whisk. "You've dislodged my contact lenses. Take that.. and that… and that."

Finally, he emerged, breathing heavily.

"I didn't know Lois had a python. Especially not one with arms and legs." He crawled into the centre of the room. "I'm getting to old for this."

His hand landed on Donald's cigar box, sitting on top of the coffee table. He grabbed one and lit it.

"Well done me, though," he puffed happily. "Still got what it takes. Now where the hell is everyone?"

He coughed violently and shook his head.

"Really must make this my last."

There was a loud boom.

"That's how it transpired, Fats," Harlan said. "Case solved."

"Not really, buddy. We still don't know who Doctor Baghead was."

"I do." Harlan looked smug. "I just pondered to myself, who would inherit the millions if *all* the Payne's died?"

"Who? Who?"

"Alfrick, of course."

"You mean, the butler did it?" Fats looked puzzled. "I thought he retired to Burrumbuttock?"

"Came back a few days ago, pal. Claimed he got an anonymous email asking him to attend a surprise birthday party."

"A likely story!" Fats scoffed.

"Of course. I tipped off the cops and they've just arrested him. End of story."

"What a tragic tale of greed and destruction." Fats shook his head. "What will happen to the money now?"

"It goes to Alfrick's only living relative, his long-lost nephew, Fats Norbett."

"What a coincidink. That's my name too."

"It *is* you, Fats. You're a rich man." Harlan looked sincere. "Sorry it ended with your only living relative getting locked away."

"It wasn't your fault, Harlan."

"I know. Go start the car."

Fats turned to leave, then stopped.

"If Alfrick was Doctor Baghead, why didn't he turn up at the meeting? Donald wouldn't have recognised his voice after all those years."

"Beats me. Maybe he had a dentist appointment this morning."

"Another coincidink! *You* had a dentist appointment this morning."

"Life is full of them, old friend."

"Poor uncle Alfrick," Fats sighed. "I guess you're my only family now. If *I* died, I'd leave everything to you."

"I was hoping you'd say that. Now let's proceed to the Sinister Clown Museum as planned. I booked you on the Pennywise Sewer Ride of Almost Certain Death."

"I can't *wait*!" Fats skipped towards the car.

"Me neither, buddy."

Harlan pulled a paper bag from his pocket and threw it behind the nearest bush.

About The S.W.G.

The Springfield Writers Group is a collection of writers from Springfield, Queensland and the surrounding area. Their aim is to encourage and support local talent and drink a lot of coffee.

https://www.facebook.com/groups/1720378808216956

The Authors

Aiki Flintheart was the founder of the SWG, the Aurealis shortlisted author of *Blackbirds Sing* and The *Kalima Chronicles* among others.
www.aikiflinthart.com

Pamela Jeffs is a winner of the Morrison Mentoring Short Story Award, Doug Murray Literary Award and Fraser Coast Writing Competition. She has been shortlisted for the Aurealis Awards, Elyne Mitchell Short Story Award and Toowoomba Literary Awards.
www.pamelajeffs.com

Monica Schultz is a high school mathematics teacher from Ipswich, Australia, with a passion for writing fantasy for young adults.
www.monicaschultzauthor.weebly.com @monicaschultzauthor

Dogs always appear as memorable characters in Sue's family dramas and romance stories. She is finishing her first novel, set in rural Australia, unravelling a three generational family drama.
https://www.facebook.com/Sue-Stubbs-Author

Sam Brown is the pen name of Robyn Evans. She is the founder of Iron Bridge Publishing.
sirenofbrixton.wordpress.com

Carrie Molachino is the pen name of Caroline Anne, author of the novel *Girl in the Gift Shop*.

Louisa Duval is the author of *Whisky and Sunshine*. To receive bonus material, alerts, new releases and the stories behind the stories, sign up for her newsletter at
www.louisaduval.com

Cassandra Kelly is the author of *The Green Wave*.
Check out her author page at
www.cassandrakellyauthor.com

Neen Cohen is the author of the novel *Cold As Hell*.
You can find her at
www.neencohen.com

Lynne Lumsden Green is a Steampunk and science blogger.
She specialises in short stories, many of which have been published.

Caitlyn McPherson is a Brisbane based writer, illustrator and wannabe ninja. If monsters, mayhem and magic are your jam,
you can check out more at
https://caitlynmcpherson.wixsite.com/author

Jem McCusker is the new head of the SWG and author of the novels
Stone Guardians, *Crossfire* and *The Last Druid*.
www.jemmccusker.com

Nicole Harvey is one of the most recent members of the SWG.
www.facebook.com/nicole.harveyauthor

Mandy Chandler is an author, copywriter, editor, marketer and word-wielding superhero. When not wearing her mask and cape, you'll find her wandering the hills of Springfield with her furry sidekick, Hunny.
www.facebook.com/mandychandlerauthor

A V (Aletia) Johnstone is a recent member of the SPG and *Cat Fight* is her first published story.

Jan-Andrew Henderson a freelance editor and author of 33 books. He has been shortlisted for 13 literary awards and is the winner of the Royal Mail Award and Doncaster Book Prize.

www.janandrewhenderson.com

www.greenlightliteraryrescueservice.com